PERFECT FOR YOU

She turned to go back inside when the front door opened and closed. She met Alex's penetrating gaze briefly before glancing away. One look was enough. She couldn't miss the desire in his eyes. He wanted her and she wanted him.

"How long do you intend to run from me? How long do you intend to run from your feelings?" he asked, blocking her escape back inside.

As long as I have to. One of us has to be strong.

"I don't know what you're talking about," said Samantha evasively, trying to walk past him. "I'm going back inside." His arm snaked out around her waist and he pulled her flush against him. Her body reacted instantly to his and she swayed into him.

"You know exactly what I'm talking about," said Alex softly. The hot air from his breath fanned her flushed cheek. She shivered at the contact. "There is something going on between us. It didn't happen overnight. You can't deny it or hide from it anymore, Samantha. Tell me you don't feel the same way I do when I take you in my arms. These feelings we have are not going to just go away because you want them to."

Perfect for You

Sylvia Lett

Kensington Publishing Corp.

http://www.kensingtonbooks.com

DAFINA BOOKS are published by

Kensington Publishing Corp.
850 Third Avenue
New York, NY 10022

All Kensington Titles, Imprints, and Distributed Lines are available at special quantity discounts for bulk purchases for sales promotions, premiums, fund-raising, and educational or institutional use. Special book excerpts or customized printings can also be created to fit specific needs. For details, write or phone the office of the Kensington special sales manager: Kensington Publishing Corp., 850 Third Avenue, New York, NY 10022, attn: Special Sales Department, Phone: 1-800-221-2647.

Dafina and the Dafina logo Reg. U.S. Pat. & TM Off.

ISBN-13: 978-0-7582-1979-4
ISBN-10: 0-7582-1979-2

First Dafina mass market printing: March 2007
10 9 8 7 6 5 4 3 2 1

Printed in the United States of America

Chapter One

"Gus, I need a favor," said Alex, twirling the phone cord around his finger. He stood up from his mahogany desk and paced the room. Opening the blinds, he looked out the window. "This one will take some time."

"Sure Dr. Carlisle," Gus answered, tapping the other security guard on the shoulder and gesturing to him to take over monitoring the parking garage. "What can I do for you?" He walked over to his desk and sat down. Picking up a pen, he was poised to take notes.

"I need you to find a security tape for me. It will be three years ago next Friday. I need you to check the footage of the nursery around 11 P.M. My guess is you will find two babies were switched in the nursery."

"Oh, my God! How soon do you need this done?" Gus dropped the pen for a moment. Picking the pen up again, he wrote down the date and time. "If this is true . . ."

"It is true and I need you to find the evidence. I need this ASAP. Gus, this is just between you and me," said Alex, pacing. He ran his hand over his head in frustration. "Thanks, Gus. I owe you one. I know this is asking a lot, but trust me for now." Alex replaced the receiver and sat down at his desk.

Alex had known Gus Sessions for over fifteen years. They met during his first year of residency at the hospital. Alex accidentally locked his keys in his car and Gus helped him get them out. As a thank-you, he took Gus out to dinner.

Gus was the head of security at Parkdale Hospital. He was promoted to chief security officer five years ago. Gus had a reputation for being thorough and always on top of everything at the hospital.

Alex knew if there was anything to find on the surveillance tapes, Gus would find it. He had a nagging suspicion the hospital nursery held the answers to his questions. It had to be the hospital. There was no other explanation for what happened.

Once I know the truth then I can decide what to do about it. Until then, I have to keep my mouth shut and go on with my life.

Oh, God, I can't believe this is happening. I can't believe this happened. Was this situation an accident, or was it deliberate? This is a no-win situation for everyone, especially Samantha. What am I going to say to Samantha? This is going to tear her apart. It's going to tear all of us apart.

He looked down at the thin gold wristwatch. It was 3:00 P.M. He'd seen his last patient thirty minutes ago. Alex was exhausted from another busy day. The office was now closed and he was ready for the weekend.

He took off his lab jacket and stethoscope. He carefully laid the stethoscope in the wooden holder on his desk. Getting to his feet, he hung the lab jacket on the coatrack behind the door. Taking his keys out, he locked his office door. He walked up front to let the nursing staff know he was gone.

"Trisha, I'm gone. Please let the answering service know Dr. Grayson is on call this weekend. I'll see you guys Monday morning. Have a great weekend," smiled Alex, rapping his knuckles on the counter.

"Have a good weekend Dr. Carlisle." Tina, the office nurse, smiled. She was young and fresh out of nursing school. Alex and his partner, Jeff, hired her as a favor to a friend. So far, they were not disappointed. Trisha made up with enthusiasm for her lack of experience. All the patients loved her and the other three women in the office also liked her.

Alex left his office the back way and exited the hospital with a smile on his face. It was Friday and he was leaving work early. He couldn't remember in the past year leaving work early on a Friday.

Instead of taking the elevator, he jogged down the stairs and left the building. Clicking the alarm, he unlocked the door to his black Porsche. He eased his six-foot frame into the gray leather seat and started the engine. The car purred as he shifted gears and peeled out of the parking lot.

Dr. Alexander Carlisle was a renowned and loved pediatric doctor at County General Hospital. He came to the hospital twelve years ago for his residency and stayed. He now ran a private pediatric practice inside the hospital. He and his partner, Jeff Grayson, recently celebrated their fifth anniversary at Carlisle & Grayson, M.D., this year. Their plush office was located on the second floor, overlooking the newly renovated Michael Carlisle Playground, named after his dead son.

It was an uphill battle with the hospital to convince them to let him pay for and have the memorial park constructed. The board of directors voted ten to one in favor of the memorial park. Alex used the life insurance money from his wife, Kirstin, and his son's death to pay for the renovations.

Alex and his younger brother, Keith, were raised in a

small East Texas town by their grandparents after both his parents were killed in a motor accident. Alex worked his way through high school and won an academic scholarship to college and to medical school. He made his grandparents proud, and they told him so every day. In his second year of medical school, he lost his grandmother to cancer. His grandfather died four months later, of what Alex believed to be a broken heart.

Alex was always the responsible brother. He was older than Keith by seven years. He put Keith through college and was proud when, at last, Keith received a BA in finance. Keith was now thirty years old and a vice president of a Fortune 500 technology company.

Alex's best friend was Greg Taylor. They met when Greg's family moved to Tyler the summer before eighth grade. What originally drew them together was that they were both avid sports-card collectors. They met at a sports-card convention and hit it off.

As kids, they always discussed what they wanted to be when they grew up. While Greg wanted to be president, Alex always knew he wanted to be a doctor. Alex played doctor with all the young kids in the neighborhood. Whenever anyone had a scratch or bruise, they would go to Alex. He chose pediatrics because of his love for children.

He married Kirstin Thomas Peterson once his residency was complete. They wed exactly six months after they met. It was love at first sight for him and Kirstin.

Kirstin was a single parent working as a real estate agent. Her two-year-old son, Derek, was from her first marriage. After her divorce, her ex-husband left town.

Derek was starved for a father figure, and when Alex entered the picture, they bonded instantly. Once they were married, Alex legally adopted Derek.

A year later, Alexandria was born. Derek began calling

her Lexi because he couldn't pronounce "Alexandria."
The name stuck, and they all started calling her Lexi.

A year later, Alex's sister-in-law, Kirstin's younger sister,
Samantha, married Greg. Kirstin and her parents were
strongly against the marriage because Greg was ten years
older than Sam and he had a child from a previous marriage whom he had sole custody of. At twenty, Sam was
not considered mature enough to handle marriage or
being a mother. She surprised everyone. She took to
both and she and Greg were happy for the brief three
years they had together.

Alex and Kirstin were married for a total of six years
before the car accident. Alex was receiving a Volunteer
of the Year award from the free clinic he worked at one
day a week. The ceremony was held at the Wyndham
Hotel. A patient came in to the office before closing
with an emergency and he ended up working later than
expected. He called Greg and asked him to drop Kirstin
at the hotel for him. They never made it. On the way to
the awards ceremony, a drunk driver hit Greg's Lexus
head-on. Greg never had a chance. He died on impact.
Kirstin, who was eight months pregnant, was rushed to
the hospital. Alex was leaving the hospital when he received the phone call. Turning around, he headed back
to the hospital. Kirstin never regained consciousness.
Alex was at her side when the doctors performed a
C-section that saved his son's life. An hour later, she
died.

Samantha was also about eight months pregnant. The
news of her husband's death sent her into premature
labor. She was also rushed to Parkdale hospital where
she also gave birth to a son the same night.

The babies were born less than two hours apart. Later
that night, one of the babies went into cardiac arrest

and died a few hours later. Alex buried both his wife
and son.

He slipped a Luther Vandross CD into the player and
sang along with "Here and Now." Luther always helped
him to relax.

At the red light, he eased into the left-turn lane. While
waiting for the light to change, he tapped his fingers
against the wheel. Another left put him on the express-
way headed north.

Traffic was bumper-to-bumper as he made his way
home. Alex pulled into the circular driveway of his two-
story red-brick home. He hit the garage-door opener and
pulled the car into the two-car garage. Hopping out of
the car, he unlocked the door and went inside the house.
He unbuttoned his shirt as he walked up the stairs to the
master bedroom. Stripping off his shirt, he threw it into
the white clothes hamper. He took off his slacks and
hung them back in the closet. He kicked off his shoes
and casually tossed them in the large walk-in closet
before turning on the shower. Slipping off his socks, he
dropped them in the hamper.

He sighed in bliss as the water washed over him. The
warm water helped to ease his tired, achy muscles. He
took a long, relaxing shower. He was exhausted from
being on call the past five days. He was called for an
emergency almost every night.

He dried off and stood naked in front of his closet door.
Deciding at last on a shirt and pair of jeans, he carried
them into his bedroom. Alex pulled the red polo shirt
over his head, smoothed the shirt down, tucked the ends
into his fitted black jeans, and snapped them.

Staring at his reflection in the mirror, he could not find
fault with his appearance. He ran his hand over his short,

wavy black hair. His skin was a flawless warm-cappuccino brown. Glassy black eyes peered back at him. Alex was athletic with a strong, solid chest and flat stomach. Muscular forearms flexed as he slipped his wallet in his back pocket. Slapping on his favorite aftershave, he grabbed his keys from the bureau, slipped his feet into a pair of loafers and left the room.

For the past three years, he had watched Samantha and yearned for her from afar. Today, that would all change. Today, he was determined to make her see she couldn't continue to live in the past. It was time she faced the future. Alex wanted to be a part of her future.

Alex practiced his speech as he drove the four blocks to his sister-in-law's house. *It's time to let go of the past, Samantha. Greg is gone. It's time to start living again.* He hit the steering wheel. *Surely I can do better than that. Samantha will laugh me out of the house. It's still too soon to tell her how I feel. She's not ready for a relationship. Am I ready for a relationship? I believe I am. What am I going to do?* His ringing cell phone cut into his thoughts. He plugged the earpiece into his ear.

"Hello," said Alex, stopping at the stop sign. He put on his right-turn signal and made a right. "Hello," he repeated.

"Dr. Carlisle, it's Chloe Bell," said the friendly voice on the other end. "I was wondering if you were free for dinner tonight?" His eyebrows shot up curiously. "You were kind enough to treat me to dinner a few weeks ago and I wanted to return the favor."

"Chloe, I'm sorry, but I already have plans," said Alex, pulling into Sam's driveway. He killed the engine and opened the door of the jeep. "Hang on a minute." He unplugged the earpiece and picked up the telephone. He got out of the car and walked to the front door. "Thanks for asking," replied Alex, not committing to any future plans with her. He disconnected the call before she could respond. It only took Alex one date to realize he wasn't interested in Chloe's blatant charms. He knew who he wanted, and it wasn't Chloe Bell.

When Greg died, Samantha Thomas Taylor was left a widow at the tender age of twenty-five. She was also left alone to raise two children, seven-year-old Hope and newborn Matthew. Greg's first wife died of breast cancer when Hope was two. Hope was four when Greg and Samantha were married.

Greg was a prudent businessman and a very successful financial advisor. When he died, he left Samantha and the kids well provided for. Sam never had to work another day in her life unless she chose to. Given that she now had two young children to take care of, she quit her job as a financial analyst and stayed home to take care of them. She also looked after Kirstin's and Alex's two children while Alex was working.

Samantha was setting the dinner table when the doorbell rang. Peering at her watch, she knew it was Alex. She looked down at her warm-ups and smiled.

She knew Alex hated to see her in her favorite pair of faded blue warm-up pants and T-shirt. Deliberately wiping her flour-coated hands on her gray T-shirt, she opened the door.

"Hello Alex," she smiled, taking a step back. "You're right on time, as usual. Come in and make yourself at home as you usually do." She hid a smile behind her sarcastic remark.

Alex surveyed her with distaste. It was obvious she had wiped her hands on her clothes. The flour prints stood out on her gray T-shirt. Her shoulder-length curly brown hair was carelessly pinned up with a much-too-small butterfly clip. Her beautiful face was clean of any makeup, and none was needed, because Samantha was a natural beauty. Her complexion was honey brown and devoid of any blemishes. Long black lashes covered clear gray eyes that turned to gray steel when she was angry. As she smiled up at him, her cheeks dimpled slightly. His eyes moved down her body to her loose-fitting, faded blue warm-up pants.

"Do you own an apron? If not, I know what I'm getting you for Christmas," said Alex, brushing past her. "What you're wearing is bad enough without flour added to the mix, no pun intended."

"Thanks. Hello to you too, sunshine," she replied sarcastically. Smiling in satisfaction, she followed him out to the kitchen. "Your approval of my wardrobe means the world to me."

Her eyes moved over him in appreciation. Alex looked yummy as usual in a pair of black jeans and a polo shirt. *What a pair of buns! Who am I kidding—what a total package!* Alex was not only handsome, but he had a great body. The goatee he now sported only added to his sex appeal.

"Where are the kids?" he inquired, looking around the empty room. He really didn't want an audience to their conversation.

"Derek is at Shawn's house, as usual. Hope is next door at Brittany's, and Lexi is upstairs with Matthew. All accounted for, Doc."

"Good, because we need to talk." He waved for Samantha to have a seat and sat across from her at the breakfast table. "It's time to let go, Samantha. You've mourned for three years. It's time to start living again." Her eyes met his briefly.

"I'm living," she said defensively, coming to her feet. She did not want to have this conversation with him. Her problem wasn't only letting go. It was moving on. She wanted to move on with him, but she knew it wasn't even a possibility. As much as she was attracted to him, she couldn't risk getting involved with him. Too much was at stake. She had to be strong and keep the wall between them.

"No, you're not," he argued, standing up and walking toward her. "You are only going through the motions. This is not what Greg would have wanted for you. You are a beautiful young woman who has cut herself off from the rest of the world. It's time to let the past go. You are hiding from the world and it's time you rejoined us. Take a good look in the mirror, Samantha. Tell me what you see. Look at yourself. Look at how you're dressed." His hand waved over her from head to toe in disgust.

Samantha glared at the man in her kitchen. Her eyes narrowed and she took several calming breaths to keep from lashing back at him. He had insulted everything from the top of her head down to her toes.

"What is wrong with the way I'm dressed?" she asked, defensively folding her hands over her chest. "I happen to like sweats. I do not dress to please you. I dress to please myself."

"That much is obvious," he shot back as his dark eyes raked over her clothing with distaste. Alex knew he was ticking her off, but he didn't care. This needed to be said. "You sure aren't dressing to impress anyone else. Not many men get turned on by fleece and cotton, but I'm sure there's a lush young body somewhere underneath all that loose-fitting, baggy, faded material."

Samantha turned another shade of red in anger. He had crossed the line again and she was furious. "No one asked you to look! Maybe I don't want to attract unwanted attention. This is ridiculous," she snapped, throwing up her hands in frustration. "My appearance has nothing to do with you. I'm not having this conversation with you again. Go home, Alex, now, before we both say things we will regret."

"Why do you want me to leave? Did I hit a nerve? I'm not about to let you continue to wallow in self-pity and misery. It's time to wake up. It's time to start living again. You are not going to meet anyone hiding behind this hideous outfit and locking yourself away inside this shrine to Greg. You need to get out and meet people. Get a life, Samantha. Have some fun. You do remember what fun is, don't you?"

She turned to walk away, but he caught her arm to stop her. Catching the clasp in her hair with his free hand, he unsnapped it and sent dark hair tumbling down her back in a cascade of unruly curls. Samantha seethed with anger as she glared up at him.

"Give that back!" She snatched the clasp out of his hand and their hands touched. Her eyes flew to his in alarm. They both felt the spark as their hands touched. It left them both momentarily stunned. Samantha was the first to recover. She took a step back from him. Catching her hair, she tried unsuccessfully to pin it up again. Exasperated, she finally let it fall to her shoulders. "Are you happy now?"

"Are you?" he shot back. Alex knew he was pushing her to the limit, but he didn't care. He had to get through her don't-care, touch-me-not facade. She bristled, but didn't bother to answer. "You didn't answer my question. Are you happy, Samantha? Let me answer for you. How can you be happy when you have no life? What little you do have revolves around the children. When was the last time you had a conversation that didn't include children? When was the last time you laughed?"

"Go home," she repeated, enunciating each word. His words hit a sore spot with her, and she lashed out in defense. She knew Alex hated the way she dressed. It was a defense mechanism for her. It was a way to hold him at bay. Keeping the wall between them was for both their protection. "What I do or don't do is none of your business."

"A little makeup and a new hairdo would do wonders for your self-esteem, not to mention your appearance. This look has gotten really boring. Where is the Samantha who was picture perfect and drop-dead gorgeous at all times? What happened to that woman? I know she's hiding somewhere deep inside you, and I would like to see her again. You have a great body. Or at least you did the last time I saw it." She flushed hotly under his heated gaze and turned away from him. She tried desperately to ignore the message his eyes were sending her, a message she didn't want to see or acknowledge. "Why not flaunt it once in a while? Stop hiding and get on with your life."

"If this is not the pot calling the kettle black. Get a life of your own, Alex, and stay out of mine," she shot back. "Maybe if you had a girlfriend, you wouldn't be so concerned about what I'm doing or not doing and who I'm not doing it with. I didn't ask for your opinion or your advice. Don't you dare try to tell me how to live my life!"

"I dare anything," he said, catching her hand and pulling her into his arms. Samantha trembled as their bodies touched. She felt the heat radiating from Alex and fought against her own rising desire. "You should know by now that I dare almost anything." Their eyes locked in silent combat. "I'd like to see you in something showing a little leg and a lot of cleavage. Hey, if you've got it, flaunt it, and you've definitely got it," he said, smiling down at her ample breast. She flushed again, but did not respond. "Something black, short and tight would be even better."

"Keep dreaming," she whispered breathlessly, trying to squirm out of his arms. Alex was unrelenting as he held her steadfast. His nearness was getting to her and she felt her resolve slipping. She refused to deal with it or him. Samantha could not and would not let this happen. She had to be strong for both their sakes. This would be a terrible mistake.

"Believe me, I do, but you are wearing much less in my dreams." His hypnotic dark eyes held her spellbound. She followed the dissent of his mouth. As his head lowered to hers, Samantha turned her face away at the last possible moment. His lips landed on her cheek and Samantha sucked in her breath at the contact.

The heat from his mouth seared her clear down to her toes. Samantha trembled and tried to squirm her way out of his arms again. He pulled her closer and her breast flattened against his massive chest. Her nipples hardened and her breathing was shallow. Taking slow, deep breaths, she fought her inner feelings for this man as she trembled in his arms.

"Let go of me," fumed Samantha, fighting not only him, but also the feelings he was arousing in her. She renewed her struggle in his arms. "Alex, don't do this, please." Her voice begged him to stop even as her body urged him on. "We can't do this."

"Are you fighting me or yourself?" he asked knowingly. "Give in to what you are feeling. You want me. I can see it in your eyes and feel it in your body. You are just too afraid to admit it." Samantha stopped struggling as his head lowered again. This time, she didn't turn away. His lips touched hers tentatively. They brushed hers again and again. Samantha didn't respond, but she didn't pull away either as her resolve slowly melted. At last, her lips parted of their own free will.

Alex knew the moment she weakened and he moved in for the kill. He pulled her closer and deepened the kiss as his mouth plundered hers. His tongue slipped between her parted lips. She moaned softly as her arms went around his neck and she returned his kiss eagerly. His rough tongue explored the honeyed recesses of her mouth. Her tongue mated with his and she pressed her body closer to his. Alex groaned in pleasure and his mouth feasted on hers like a starving man.

All thoughts of right and wrong fled from her mind and her body responded to his. She was starving, and Alex offered her a feast. Samantha held him tightly and moaned in pleasure when his hand slid up her waist. Cautiously his hand covered her hardened nipple.

He lifted her up and sat her on the counter. He moved to stand between her thighs, never breaking contact with her mouth. His hands moved under her T-shirt to cup her lace-covered breast. He unsnapped and pushed the offensive material aside.

"Alex, we can't," whispered the breathless voice fighting for control. His lips trailed the line of her jaw and moved on to tease her earlobe with his teeth. Licking the wounded lobe, he planted hot kisses on her throat. He caught her face between his hands. Their eyes locked in a battle of wills. Samantha's smoky gray eyes saw the raw passion in his eyes and it scared her.

"Yes we can. You have no idea how much I want you," he whispered hoarsely before his mouth covered hers again in a hungry kiss. His tongue plunged into her mouth and Samantha gladly accepted it and everything else he had to offer. She was beyond saying no as she surrendered to Alex and to the feelings he was arousing inside her.

His mouth left hers to take a quick breath and then returned. Samantha's arms went around him, and this time her tongue was the aggressor, and it slipped between his lips. He caught it and sucked gently on it.

"Kissing Mommy," laughed the childish voice behind

them. It took them both a few seconds to realize they were not alone.

Samantha froze in Alex's arms. Opening her eyes, she met the silent laughter in Alex's sparkling brown eyes. Her arms dropped from around his neck in embarrassment. Her eyes moved past him and came to rest on her son, looking up at them with questioning eyes.

Alex released her with much regret. Samantha's body was blocked from Matthew's view. Good thing it was, because Alex's hands were still under her shirt. Getting his emotions under control, he snapped the closure on her bra and set Samantha on her feet.

She moved nervously away from him. She smoothed down her T-shirt and took several deep breaths to get her emotions under control.

"Alex, you didn't answer his question," said Samantha, avoiding eye contact with him. "I can't wait to hear this one."

"Mommy was sad, so I was trying to cheer her up," Alex lied for a lack of a better answer. "I think it worked. I think I started a fire inside her."

"Fires can be dangerous," she said, turning to her son and picking him up. "Uncle Alex was just leaving." She met his smiling gaze.

"Down." Matt squirmed to be put down. "Daddy." He reached for Alex to take him. Sam held her son in front of her like a shield.

"Oh, look at the time," she said, glancing down quickly at her watch. "Uncle Alex has overstayed his welcome once again. That makes what, the third time this week? Have a nice night, Alex."

"I can take a hint," he smiled, brushing a strand of hair away from her flushed face. Samantha took a step back to break the contact.

"Apparently not," she retorted, moving a safe distance

from him. Matt kept squirming and she put him down. "Good-bye, Alex." Matt ran to Alex and lifted his arms to be picked up. Alex lifted him.

"Where's Uncle Alex going?" asked Hope, coming into the kitchen. She embraced her favorite uncle, and he returned her hug. "I thought you were staying for dinner." She looked from her mother to Alex in confusion. Before Samantha could answer, the front door opened and closed.

"Where is everyone?" Derek yelled. "I'm starving. Aunt Sam, what's for dinner?" She heard him run up the stairs and then come back down.

"We're in the kitchen!" Hope yelled, walking over to the double doors and pushing them open. Samantha flinched at her daughter's shrill voice.

"Is it time for dinner?" Lexi asked glancing around the room. "Hi, Dad." She went to her father and hugged him.

"Hi, sweetheart." Smiling, he returned her hug. "Yes, it is time for dinner. Your aunt was just putting the finishing touches on dinner and on her clothes."

Derek walked into the kitchen and smiled when he saw his father. "Hey, Dad," said Derek, walking over to his father and giving him a quick hug. "I'm starved, Aunt Sam. What's for dinner?"

"Gang, why don't you all go wash up while Samantha and I finish our conversation?" Samantha was about to protest when Alex shot her a warning look. The kids filed out of the room.

"Am I still invited to dinner?" asked Alex, closing the distance between them. "I've already had my dessert." She flushed hotly and turned away from the twinkle in his eyes.

"Talk like that could get you thrown out of my house without dinner." Samantha frowned, retreating.

"Can I stay for dinner, Aunt Sam? I'll be a good boy. Scout's honor," said Alex holding up two fingers.

Sam crossed her arms over her chest, clearly not believing him. "I find it hard to believe you were a Scout. I can't even imagine you as a child. I bet you were a handful even then."

"Believe it, sweetheart. I made it all the way to Eagle Scout. I know how to start a fire without matches also. Just rub two hot bodies together and watch the fireworks."

"What fireworks?" Derek asked, taking the plates from the counter. He didn't bother to wait for an answer.

"We were talking about July Fourth," said Alex quickly, turning to wink at Samantha. "We are trying to plan ahead."

She glared at him. "Are you ever at a loss for words?" Samantha asked, taking the salad out of the refrigerator and following him out to the formal dining room.

The rest of the kids came back, and the conversation ended. They all sat down to a nice family dinner. Samantha and Alex had dinner with the kids at least once a week.

During dinner, the kids kept the conversation going, talking about their day, sports, and everything that happened to them during the week.

Each time Samantha looked up, Alex was watching her intently. She looked away quickly. She didn't want him to see the fear and longing in her eyes.

She wanted him, but she was very afraid. Samantha knew she had to be strong enough for both of them. The situation earlier had gotten quickly out of hand. She had to make sure it didn't happen again. She had to make sure she wasn't left alone again with Alex.

Samantha was relieved as she stood at the door watching Alex and the kids get into the green Jeep Wrangler.

The car backed out and then stopped. Sam frowned as Alex pulled back in and put the car in park. He got out of the Jeep and walked to the door.

"Derek forgot his backpack in the den," he explained, brushing past her. She caught his arm to stop him. They both froze at the contact, and she immediately released her hold.

"I'll get it," said Sam, fleeing. *Please don't follow me. Please don't follow me.* She found the backpack on the couch. Picking it up, she turned and stopped when she saw Alex leaning casually against the door. Her heartbeat accelerated.

Walking toward him, she held out the backpack. Hefting the backpack on his shoulder, he reached out and pulled her into his arms. Her eyes flew to his in alarm. His mouth swooped down and covered hers in a hard, possessive kiss before she could protest. She was breathless and trembling when he raised his head.

"Don't forget—short, tight, and black," he whispered against the side of her neck. As his lips touched her neck, she shivered in anticipation. "See you tomorrow night."

Samantha watched him go with her hand to her mouth. *Oh, God, that felt so right. So what happens, Doc, if I call your bluff?*

Chapter Two

Samantha called her stepmother early the next morning to see if she could drop the kids off with her early. She made an appointment at Chez Juliard to get a full-body massage, a facial, and a complete makeover.

She left the shop feeling like a million bucks. Her unruly hair was now hanging down her back in soft waves. Her makeup was picture perfect. She even treated herself to a manicure and pedicure, replacing her clear gloss for a ruby-red polish.

Samantha's next stop was the mall. She tried on several outfits that were totally out of character for her, but the salesgirl convinced her to get them. She had to admit, miniskirts and short dresses did look great on her. She also bought several different styles of pantsuit.

Alexander Carlisle, eat your heart out! She twirled in front of the mirror, smiling. *He won't know what hit him.*

Samantha arrived at her best friend Dana's early for their once-a-month adult's night out get-together. Dana was shocked and speechless when she opened the door. Her husband, Tomas, did a double take.

"Sam, you look gorgeous," said Dana, hugging her. "Should I even ask what or who happened to you?"

"Dana's right, you look fantastic," smiled Tomas. "You could almost make me forget I'm a married man," he teased.

"Knock it off," laughed Dana, elbowing her husband in the ribs. She led Samantha into the living room and away from Tomas. "Spill it, Sam. Why the dramatic change? Don't get me wrong—it's about time you came out of your shell—but why now? You go from house-mother to sexy diva in a day?"

"Okay, Alex and I had a discussion," she hedged. Dana's eyebrows rose knowingly. "All right, it wasn't a discussion exactly. It was more like an argument. He knows how to push all my buttons. He is driving me nuts."

"I think the feeling is mutual. Sam, the man is crazy about you. You go out of your way to avoid him. It's time to stop running from your feelings."

"Why should I?" The doorbell rang, and Samantha stared at her friend. "Aren't you going to get that?"

"No," Dana said, shaking her head. "You aren't getting off that light. Tomas can answer the door. Okay, so you got all dolled up to prove a point to Alex. What happens next?"

"That's a million-dollar question." Alicia smiled, walking into the room. "Samantha, you look absolutely gorgeous."

"I second that," smiled her cousin Jeremy, walking in behind his wife. "You look hot. What's the occasion?"

"For the last time, everyone," said Samantha, getting to her feet. "There is no occasion. I bought a new outfit, big deal. Can we drop this interrogation?"

They all suspiciously watched Samantha pace the room nervously. She waited impatiently for Alex to get there. For once, she was early and he was running late.

When the doorbell rang, no one moved. They all sat back and waited expectantly for Alex's reaction.

Taking a deep breath, she went to answer the door.

Wiping her sweating palms on her hips, she slowly opened it.

As their eyes met, she watched Alex do a double take. He blinked several times to make sure he wasn't imagining the seductress before him. His brown eyes darkened as they slid down her body in a soft caress.

She blushed to the roots of her newly highlighted hair under his heated gaze. She was clad in a short black minidress. It hugged every curve of her body. The bodice was snug and low cut. His eyes devoured as they moved down her shapely legs encased in a pair of sheer coffee pantyhose. On her feet she wore a pair of black high heels.

His eyes devoured her from head to toe and then back up again. Against her will, her body responded to his. She felt her nipples harden at the hungry leer in his eyes.

"Wow. How much?" he asked with raised eyebrows. "Gold card or platinum?"

Samantha tried to slam the door in his smiling face, but he anticipated her move and stuck his foot in the door. "I'm just kidding. Where's your sense of humor? It sure can't be hidden anywhere in that outfit. Not much can be hidden in that dress." Her eyes narrowed at him. "Hey, if you didn't want me to look, you wouldn't have worn the dress. You now have my undivided attention. It's up to you whether you keep it. Has anyone told you how beautiful and sexy you are?" He smiled as she blushed. "I thought not. See what a difference a new outfit and hairdo can make? I wonder what a little sex would do." He winked. Leaning over, he kissed her cheek and then walked past her and into the room, leaving her fuming by the door.

Samantha was tempted to run out the front door, jump in her car, and head home. Her confidence was waning. Straightening her shoulders, she took a deep breath and exhaled. She was determined not to run away this time. She would stand her ground, at least for now.

Alex stared at Samantha over the rim of his glass. Samantha Taylor was constantly in his thoughts. As if sensing someone watching her, she looked up and smiled seductively at Alex. Alex groaned as she crossed her long legs again. He watched the material of her dress ride high up her shapely thigh. He wondered if she knew how much she was actually revealing. His guess would be no.

He hadn't realized the torture he would have to endure when she called his bluff and showed up at the party in a sexy black dress. His mouth had dropped open in surprise when she opened the door. He was more than pleasantly shocked and amazed at the transformation. He also hoped his little chat with her had something to do with her appearance tonight.

She was sitting on the couch talking to Dana and Alicia. They followed her line of vision and turned to look at Alex. Dana waved him over, but he shook his head, declining the offer.

"Samantha, do us all a favor and put the poor man out of his misery," said Dana, leaning back against the cushion of the plush white leather sofa.

"What man?" she asked, still watching Alex. Her eyes followed the glass to his lips as he took a sip of his drink. He raised the glass in salute to her.

"The one you can't seem to take your eyes off of. You've been undressing him with your eyes all night," said Alicia, smiling. "You are teasing him unmercifully."

"I'm not," she denied, hiding a smile. She turned to face Alicia and Dana. "So, do you think he likes the outfit?"

"He more than likes the outfit. I'm sure he'd like it off

you even more. He can't take his eyes off you. Okay, so you called his bluff. Now what?" Alicia asked, not willing to drop the subject.

"Now nothing," Samantha said, crossing her long legs. "Alex and I are just friends. It's just harmless flirting. Nothing will come of it."

"There is nothing harmless about Alex Carlisle. It's your choice you are just friends, not his," said Dana. "Something could definitely come of it, if you would stop being so stubborn."

"Anyone can see he wants a whole lot more than your friendship," added Alicia. "The way he is looking at you is positively indecent. It's the same way Jeremy looks at me." They all laughed at her comment. "Hey, can I help it if my husband finds me irresistible? It's when he stops looking that I will worry and wonder."

"I can't give Alex any more than friendship. It's too risky," said Samantha, toying with the glass in her hand. "Alex and I are friends. I don't want to lose what we have. It's taken us a long time to get where we are. I don't want sex to change it."

"Coward," teased Dana. "Look at him. He's gorgeous. Most women would kill to have someone like him panting after them."

"Sam's a masochist. You can't tell me that in the twelve years you've known Alex, you and he haven't made love once," concluded Alicia, rising to her feet.

Samantha's face turned red, but she didn't admit or deny it. How could she tell them the truth? While they had come close several times, nothing had come of it.

"Don't bother trying to deny it! It's written all over your beautiful face. With as much chemistry as you guys have, it was inevitable. I bet it was fantastic." Alicia smiled and left them staring after her.

"How about it, Samantha? Are you and Alex secret

lovers?" Dana asked, setting her half-full bottled water on the table.

"No, we've never made it that far," Samantha admitted. "We've come close a couple of times, but each time we were interrupted."

"Tonight could be your lucky night. Aren't the kids at Uncle Nathan's?" Dana winked at Samantha. "Go for it, Sam. I'm pretty sure you won't be disappointed."

"I can't," she sighed in resignation. "As much as I want to, I can't take the chance." She looked up, and her eyes locked with Alex's. Samantha was mesmerized and couldn't look away. His heated gaze left her breathless. "I have to be strong enough for both of us."

One of his favorite ballads by KC & JoJo filled the room. He watched Samantha from across the room. He swayed to the music and hummed softly.

"She looks great, doesn't she? She called your bluff, Doc. Check and checkmate. The next move is yours. I dare you to ask her to dance," said Jeremy, walking up beside him. "You know you want to."

Hesitating only for a moment, Alex handed him the glass and came to his feet.

"It's about time you made a move. You're not getting any younger," Jeremy said.

"Thanks, Jeremy," said Alex sarcastically. "You are always good to have around whenever I need a reality check." He walked away.

When Samantha looked up to see Alex standing in front of her, she almost forgot to breathe. Their eyes held as she stared up at him. Her heart did a little flip-flop at the smoldering desire in his eyes. He extended his hand to her. Samantha felt a ripple of pleasure run down her spine.

Placing her hand in his, she shivered in fear and need as she let him pull her to her feet. Everyone else was forgotten as he led her over to the small, makeshift dancing area.

He took her in his arms, and they both trembled as they began to move with the music. The smell of him, the essence of him was intoxicating. They were both lost the minute his arms went around her. Samantha shuddered when his hand began to caress her back.

The heat from his touch began to radiate through her body. The feel of his hard frame pressed against hers caused all sorts of sensations she'd thought she would never feel again. She closed her eyes and relished the moment. This felt so right.

Alex was in his own private heaven and hell holding her this close. She fit perfectly in his embrace. His arms tightened around her and he closed his eyes in pleasure. One dance was not enough. He wanted more. His body craved more.

When the song ended, they stopped moving and stared longingly at each other. Alex's head lowered to hers slowly. She was mesmerized as she anticipated his kiss. Her eyes were closing when a movement out of the corner of her eye shattered the moment. Realizing what was about to happen, Samantha took a step back and rushed from the room. She didn't stop in the hallway. She continued out the front door.

Samantha shivered when the cool night air hit her hot skin. She took several deep breaths; it cleared her head and helped to cool off her hot body. The dance with Alex had affected her more than she cared to admit.

Why did I even dance with him? Why did I let him touch me? I knew better. I have to be more careful. It can't happen again.

I have to keep him at a distance because if I don't, I know what will happen. This chemistry is there. It's always been there. I can't let my guard down.

Her body tingled with desire, and she closed her eyes and counted to ten. She breathed in and out slowly.

Okay, so ten is not high enough. Count to twenty. Damn it it's not working. I still remember what it feels like to be held in his arms. I still want to be in his arms. Maybe it's not Alex. Maybe it's the fact that I've been celibate for three and a half years. Maybe I'm crazy for talking to myself. Maybe I should just sleep with him and get it over with. Sure, Samantha—out of the frying pan and into the fire.

She turned to go back inside when the front door opened and closed. She met Alex's penetrating gaze briefly before looking away. One look was enough. She couldn't miss desire in his eyes. He wanted her and she wanted him.

"How long do you intend to run from me? How long do you intend to run from your feelings?" he asked, blocking her escape back inside.

As long as I have to. One of us has to be strong.

"I don't know what you're talking about," said Samantha evasively, trying to walk past him. "I'm going back inside." His arm snaked out around her waist and he pulled her flush against him. Her body reacted instantly to his and she swayed into him.

"You know exactly what I'm talking about," said Alex softly. The hot air from his breath fanned her flushed cheek. She shivered at the contact. "There is something going on between us. It didn't happen overnight. You can't deny it or hide from it anymore, Samantha. Tell me you don't feel the same way I do when I take you in my arms. These feelings we have are not going to just go away because you want them to."

"Alex, leave it alone," she begged softly, trying to pull

out of his arms. "I don't think it's a good idea for us to become involved. I think we should just leave things the way they are. We're friends, sort of. Let's leave it that way. It's safer for both of us." Her tortured eyes met his, and he could see the fear in her etched there. The hunger in his smoldering eyes was as frightening as it was arousing. She was so tempted to throw caution to the wind.

"Safer be damned. I want you." He caught her face between his hands and his mouth swooped down and covered hers in a hungry kiss. At the first touch of his mouth on hers, she froze then tried desperately to push him away. Alex's arms tightened around her. As the heat from his mouth spread through her body, she relaxed in his arms and pulled him closer. Her resistance melted away. Moaning in surrender, her lips parted beneath his and she returned his hungry kiss. Her tongue met his in an erotic dance. Samantha moaned in protest when his mouth left hers. Hungry for more, she pulled his head back down to hers and kissed him feverishly, not holding anything back.

Alex ended the kiss. "You can't tell me you don't feel anything." His mouth was inches from hers. "I want you and I know you want me. I can feel it in your body and I can feel it in your kiss. Your body is hungry for my touch." As if to emphasize his point, his hand covered her breast. Her nipple hardened instantly beneath his skilled hands. Samantha closed her eyes against the truth. "Stop fighting your feelings, Sam. Let me take you home right now. Let me make love to you."

Samantha knew everything he said was true. She did want him. Her body craved his touch as she pressed it closer to his. Her body and her head were waging a war. A war she knew her head had to win, for both their sakes. She had to stop before it was too late, before things went any further than they already had.

"This is wrong, Alex," said Samantha, trying to pull away from him. He silenced her protest with another kiss that left her trembling and breathless in his arms. This time when she returned his kiss, he pulled back. Her smoky passion-glazed eyes fluttered open and she stared at him in confusion.

"You can't tell me this is wrong," he said brushing his lips across hers. "This is right. It's what we both want. I've dreamed for months about you being in my arms like this. I know it's a little complicated because of the kids, but we can deal with it."

Samantha closed her eyes and took a deep breath. She had to try and gain control of her emotions. "I don't want to deal with it." Slipping her arms between their bodies, she gained her release. Alex let her go and took a step back. "This is not what I want." His eyes dared her to lie. "Okay, so maybe I do want it, but it still has to stop. I don't want to lose your friendship. It has taken us years to get to this point and I don't want to mess it up. You need to get on with your life Alex, but not with me. With someone else." Her words were like a knife through his heart as he met her tear-filled gray eyes.

"Why not with you? Why can't it be you, Samantha?" he persisted. "Make me understand why it can't be you. You and I have fire. We have passion."

"But it's not right. You are my sister's husband." Samantha tried unsuccessfully to blink back the tears. "My husband was your best friend. To me you will always be Kirstin's husband and Greg's best friend. Nothing you say or do will change that."

"And they are both dead," he argued. "We are alive. Kirstin and Greg are gone. There is nothing standing between us, but you."

"Because they are gone doesn't make it right," she reasoned, losing the battle with her tears as they spilled down her cheeks. "I can't deal with this. I can't deal with you on a personal level. I can't become involved with you. I feel guilty for wanting you. I don't want to feel that way. We are not right for each other. We are not meant to be together. Why can't we leave things the way they are, simple and uncomplicated?"

"Because life isn't simple or uncomplicated. Things have changed between us. You proved that when you kissed me. Do you know how hard it is for me to keep my hands off you? Do you know how hard it is for me to see you every day and keep my distance? Every time I see you I want to take you in my arms and make love to you." She trembled at the intensity of his stare. "You just proved to me that you want the same thing. You want me, but you are afraid to admit it. Honey, there is nothing to feel guilty about. We are not doing anything wrong. Samantha, sometimes you have to take a chance. I realize we are dealing with a somewhat difficult situation, but that doesn't mean it wouldn't work. We could make it work. Sam, we could be so good together. We *are* good together. You can't respond the way you do and tell me you don't feel anything. I know better. You want me as much as I want you. You can lie to yourself all you want, but don't lie to me."

Samantha turned away from the yearning in his eyes. She had the same yearning. She wanted him, but she was afraid to let him into her life any further than he already was. She was even more afraid to let him into her heart, but was she too late to stop him.

She couldn't face him right now. "I'm sorry, Alex. I care about you, but I'm not the one for you. Please, if you care anything about me, just leave it alone. Leave me alone. You deserve so much more than I can give you. I can't be what you want me to be. I can't love you the way you deserve to be loved. Don't ruin our friendship over an impossibility that is doomed from the start," pleaded Samantha. "Face facts, Alex. We will never be together. Kirstin and Greg will always be there between us. Maybe it's not you I want, Alex." She knew she was lying as the words passed her lips. "It's been a long time for me, and yes, I find you very attractive, but maybe it's because you are the only man I am in constant contact with. I don't want sex to ruin our friendship and for me that's all it would be. Your friendship means more to me than one night of passion."

"I don't believe you. I think it's more than sex. If sex was all you wanted we would have been in bed together a long time ago. You are afraid, Samantha. Afraid to take a chance on life and afraid to take a chance on me. One night would not be enough for either of us."

"You're right. I am afraid. The kids depend on you. I depend on you. I am afraid of losing you. Your friendship means everything to me. I need you in my life, not in my bed. Please try and understand that."

"Why can't I be in both places? We are inevitable. Us going to bed is inevitable. Delaying it is only frustrating both of us."

"No, Alex. We are not inevitable. It can't happen," she said with very little conviction. "I won't let it happen, not now, not ever." Turning on her heel, she sadly walked back inside.

Alex stood there staring into space. He had given it his best shot and failed. He had waited patiently for three long years to be with her. Apparently the wait was for nothing. Samantha didn't want anything to do with him. Her body said one thing, but her heart and soul still belonged to Greg. They would probably always belong to Greg.

I gave it my best shot and it failed. It is time to get on with my life, or at least pretend to until I get all the information I need.

*It's only a matter of time before I have everything I want.
Samantha, you are mine already and you don't even know it.*

When he entered the house, Samantha was putting on her coat. Their eyes met briefly. She looked away quickly. Saying good-bye to everyone, she all but ran from the room.

"So what happened?" asked Jeremy pouncing on him the minute Samantha was out the door. "Samantha was pretty rattled."

"What can I say?" said Alex opening the closet door and taking out his coat. "I have that effect on people. She told me she's not interested." He shrugged into his coat.

"Of course she's interested. Are you giving up on her? Anyone with eyes can see she's interested. She wants you," said Jeremy, following him out the door.

"Not according to Samantha. She doesn't want to become involved with me. Samantha looks at me as a complication she does not need in her life. She made that pretty clear." Jeremy eyed him warily. "Have you ever known me to give up on something I want? I'm just waiting for some answers before I make my next move."

Chapter Three

A few days later, Samantha was surprised when Alex told her he would respect whatever decision she made about them. Samantha knew Alex well enough to be leery. She had never known him to give up on anything. So he had to be up to something.

He floored her again when he proceeded to set her up on a blind date. Samantha, of course, tried to wiggle out of it, but Alex wouldn't let her. He told her it was time to start living again and that she could take the first step by meeting Philip for dinner. He volunteered to stay at her place and sit with the kids. After Alex shot down all her excuses, she reluctantly agreed.

At the same time, she did the same to him. She set him up with an old acquaintance of hers whom now owned her own real estate company.

Linda Randolf sold Samantha her house a few years ago, and they'd kept in touch. Samantha thought Linda would be perfect for Alex—maybe a little too perfect.

Unlike her, Alex was more than willing to meet Linda for drinks. Samantha was not at all surprised when they hit it off. Samantha was kicking herself for introducing them.

Samantha glared at the phone in her hand. She knew she only had herself to blame for this situation. She'd put Alex and Linda together.

"So, you and Linda hit it off," she said dropping down to the sofa. "Did you meet for drinks or what? Spill it, Doc."

"No, we actually had a real date. I picked her up from her house and took her to dinner. She's an extraordinary lady." Samantha rolled her eyes. Jealousy ate at her. She didn't want to hear him sing praises about Linda.

"I'm glad it worked out," came her terse reply as she picked up the pillow and punched it. "Sorry to cut this short, but I've got to go." Despite what she said, she didn't want to hear the details of their date.

"Are you okay?" asked Alex, smiling. "You sound funny. You are not getting a cold are you? Have you been taking your vitamins?" If he read the signs correctly, she was jealous and he was enjoying her discomfort.

"I'm fine," she snapped, sending the pillow flying across the room. "Something went down the wrong way. Listen, I've got to run. I'll talk to you tomorrow."

"Can you drop the kids off around two o'clock? Linda and I are meeting for lunch, and I should be back by then."

"You're seeing her again tomorrow. Two dates in two days. Sure, no problem," Samantha said through her teeth. She walked over and picked up the pillow. Dropping it, she kicked it across the room. She cringed as it knocked the candy bowl off the table. The bowl crashed and shattered on the hardwood floor.

"Are you sure?" he persisted, ignoring the sound of shattering glass. "If it's a problem, I can make other arrangements. We can take the kids with us."

"I said it wasn't a problem. I'll drop them around two. Have a good lunch." Not able to hold her emotions in check any longer, Samantha slammed down the phone. *First dinner, now lunch, next I suppose they will be picking out china patterns!*

Alex was laughing when he hung up the phone. He knew anger and jealousy when he heard it. Samantha was jealous.

Samantha, sweetheart, make up your mind. You either want me or you don't, but until you decide, I'm not sitting around waiting. Linda is extremely stimulating company.

He picked up the phone and dialed. He knew the perfect guy to further his plans. Philip would drive Samantha nuts. Philip was the beginning of Phase One. Alex had a few other tricks up his sleeve to win her over.

Philip Morgan was a former pro football player whom Alex went to college with. He and Philip used to hang out together occasionally. Any woman was Philip's type. By far, he was probably the most self-centered, egotistical person Alex knew. He changed women like some people changed underwear. Philip was an attractive guy, but he knew it. He played on his good looks and took advantage of every possible situation.

Alex ordered a pizza as he waited for Philip. Samantha was still upstairs getting dressed. Alex prayed Philip would get there before she came downstairs. He wanted to have a little chat with his college buddy about Samantha.

He shot to his feet when the doorbell rang. Alex rushed to answer it before Samantha came down. Smiling, he opened the door.

"Philip, come in," said Alex, opening the door and stepping back for him to enter. They shook hands and then embraced.

"It's good to see you, Alex." He looked around the room for Samantha. "This is a nice crib. What are you doing here?"

"I'm baby-sitting for Samantha." Alex surveyed Philip's outfit with raised eyebrows. He smothered a laugh. Samantha was going to flip out when she saw him. He was willing to bet money on it.

Philip was clad in black leather pants, black shirt, and black leather jacket. On his shaved head, he wore a black leather cap. He looked like he just stepped out of a rap video or a Hell's Angels rally. The sentiment you can take the boy out of the 'hood, but not the 'hood out of the boy definitely applied here.

"Is she a honey?" asked the deep baritone voice looking down at his Rolex. He looked around the house. "Looks like she's done pretty well for herself."

"That's putting it mildly," he said smiling. "Samantha is beautiful inside and out. She's an incredible woman." *If you touch her, I'll rip you apart.*

"So why aren't you hitting it?" he asked winking. "If she's such a knockout. Why are you hooking me up with her?"

"Samantha is my sister-in-law. We have a special relationship. Her deceased husband was my best friend. I was married to her sister."

"I don't see a problem. There are no blood ties between you. Oh well, your loss is my gain." He rubbed his hands together in anticipation. "So she's a widow. They usually make easy pickings."

Alex rolled his eyes. He was torn between laughing and slugging his friend. "If that's what you are thinking, you are in for a rude awakening. Samantha is nothing like that," he defended.

"All women are like that," argued Philip. "Rub them

the right way and they are putty in your hands. I'll have her in my bed tonight."

Again, it took all Alex's self-control not to slug him. His breathing was labored as he fought to control his emotions. His fists were clinched at his side. Exhaling, he unclenched his hands. "Not a chance. Philip if you hurt her, you will answer to me. I want you to treat her with the utmost respect. Samantha is a lady."

"They all are at first," Philip remarked snidely, "but when the lights go out, the real fun begins. Are you telling me you haven't hit it even once?"

Alex shook his head in denial. He gave up trying to reason with Philip. Alex realized he had made a terrible mistake by putting Samantha and Philip together. He doubted once he made the introductions Samantha would even leave the house.

He looked up when he heard her come down the stairs. His breath caught in his throat at how beautiful she was. She wore a form-fitting, royal blue dress and matching heels. The dress stopped just above her knees. He stared at her, mesmerized, as she stopped in front of him. They only had eyes for each other. They both forgot the other man in the room.

"You look great," said Alex, eying her body in appreciation. Her eyes twinkled at the admiration she saw in his. Samantha returned his warm smile.

"You must be Samantha," said Philip, moving forward and taking her hand.

Samantha and Alex broke eye contact and her eyes moved to the man now standing at her side. Her eyes scanned his appearance. The handsome man dressed all in black leather gave her a moment of pause. He was definitely not her type. She knew it right away. "Beautiful name for an even more beautiful woman. Alex's description didn't do you justice." Alex rolled his eyes at the line he'd heard thousands of times from Philip.

"It's nice to meet you, Philip," she smiled, shaking away her misgivings. Her eyes moved to Alex and narrowed. "Any friend of Alex's is a friend of mine. Shall we go?" She tore her eyes from Alex and they returned to Philip.

Alex smiled as he watched them leave the house. Alex knew from that spark in her eyes he would catch hell later. Looking down at his watch, he figured the date would probably be over within an hour or so.

The ride to the restaurant in Philip's red Corvette was the longest thirty minutes of her life. Philip talked nonstop about his glory days in the NFL and how great he was. She was tempted to tell him to take her back home, but she didn't want to see the smirk on Alex's face.

Samantha looked around the expensive, five-star restaurant, annoyed. This was obviously a hangout for Philip since all the waiters knew him by name. Several women and men came up to Philip during dinner to ask for his autograph. Philip loved the attention.

Samantha was glad for the interruption. She didn't have the stomach or inclination to listen to another football story. She realized on the ride to the restaurant that Philip lived and breathed football. He had no other interests, except one. This dawned on her as she removed his hand from her leg.

"Have you known Alex a long time?" asked Samantha, sipping her wine. She didn't really care, she simply wanted to take charge of the conversation and steer it away from him and football.

"Does twenty years count? We grew up together and ended up going to the same college for about a year.

He's one of the few good guys left that I've kept in touch with over the years. How long have you known him?"

"Ten years. He was actually the best man at my wedding. He and my late husband were best friends. He was also married to my sister."

"So there's nothing going on with the two of you." Samantha shook her head. "How long has it been since your husband's death?" he asked with raised brows.

"Three years." She mistakenly assumed he was simply referring to how long she'd been a widow. "Alex is helping me get back into the dating world. You are my first date."

"So, you want to go back to my place and have sex? Three years is a long time to do without."

Samantha choked on her wine. Setting the glass down, she put the napkin to her mouth and continued to cough.

"You won't be disappointed." He winked, covering her hand with his. Samantha pulled her hand away.

"Thank you for the kind offer, but I think I'll pass. Thank you for dinner and for showing me what I'm not missing by not dating. I think I'll just take a cab home." She smiled, getting to her feet. He started to come to his feet. "Please don't get up on my account. It's a little late to become a gentleman in this late stage of the game."

"Your loss," he said, sitting back down. "I would have rocked your world." He couldn't believe she was turning him down.

"I'm sure it is my loss. I'm also sure you won't have any problem replacing me tonight. Have a nice night."

"If you change your mind, give me a call. There is enough of me to go around." He held out a business card to her. Samantha looked at it and then at him, refusing to take the card.

"No thank you. If I get an itch that needs scratching,

you would not be an option. Good night." She left him sitting at the table in stunned silence.

Samantha stood in the foyer of the restaurant and called a cab. She looked back inside to see a woman sit down at the table with Philip. Samantha shook her head.

What a jerk. I can't believe you did this to me, Alex. I owe you one for this. Oh well. At least I got a lobster dinner out of it. But a great dinner is a high price to pay to be stuck with Philip Morgan for the evening.

Alex was exhausted after finally getting the kids to bed. They were rowdier than usual tonight. He sat down for a quiet night of beer and pizza. He finished the pizza and two beers during an action movie. He was at the end of the movie when he heard the front door open and close.

Smiling, he looked down at his watch. It registered ten o'clock. She'd stayed half an hour longer than he expected her to.

Samantha stormed into the house. Resisting the urge to slam the door, she closed it softly behind her and went looking for Alex. She didn't have to go far to find him lounging on the couch in the den.

"Did you have a nice evening?" he asked, hiding a smile. He took a sip of his beer and set the bottle back on the coffee table.

Tossing her purse on the couch, she picked up the flowered throw pillow and threw it at his smiling face. Alex caught it and put it behind his head. "As opposed to what, Alex, oral surgery without the Novocain, childbirth without the epidural? Thanks for nothing," she snapped. "Next time just slit my wrists. It would be less painful than an evening with Philip."

"What happened?" he asked, swinging his legs off the

couch and coming to a sitting position. "I expected you back an hour ago."

"What?" She glared down at him. "This was a test. You set me up with Attila the Hands as a test. I know more about Philip Morgan after one evening than I would want to know in a lifetime. Why, Alex? What have I ever done to deserve this type of punishment?" she asked hotly. "That jerk couldn't wait to get his hands on the desperate widow. He thought I would just jump right into his bed." Catching her hand, he gave it a yank, which brought her tumbling down on top of him. Samantha looked down at him in surprise. "What are you doing?"

"Shutting you up. You talk too much." He pulled her head down to his. Heat suffused her body as her breasts pressed against his solid chest. His lips had barely touched hers, when she scrambled off him. "Still running from the truth, I see."

"Don't," she pleaded turning away from him and fanning her hot face. She closed her eyes and counted silently.

"Don't what? Don't want you? Don't make you want me?" Alex got to his feet and moved closer to her. He pulled her body flush against him, and she felt his arousal pressed against her backside. His hands gently caressed her stomach and moved up to cup her breasts. Samantha moaned aloud at the pleasure. Her body tingled clear down to her toes. "Stop fighting me, Sam. We both want the same thing." His lips trailed a fiery path down her throat.

Oh, God. I have to stop him. I can't let this happen. As much as I want this man, I can't let it happen.

"Alex, please stop." She moved from the circle of his arms. Samantha felt cold and alone without his body heat to keep her warm. She couldn't even turn around and face him. "I think you should go, now." She hugged her arms protectively around her middle. "Thanks for watching the kids for me. I'll drop Derek and Lexi off with you tomorrow."

"Good night Samantha. Sweet dreams," said Alex, throwing up his hands in frustration. "You get your wish."

She turned around when the door closed behind him and let out the breath she was holding. Samantha collapsed on the sofa.

I can't keep doing this. He's wearing me down. I have to be stronger.

Alex called about an hour later. He promised her he would back off. He sweet-talked her into giving him a second chance in the matchmaking department. Alex said he had another friend he wanted her to meet. Samantha was skeptical, but she agreed to get him off her case. His friend Roger was a CPA who owned an accounting firm.

Chapter Four

"Gus, I got your message," said Alex, closing the door to the surveillance room behind him. "Don't keep me in suspense. What did you find?"

"Have a seat." Alex sat down in the black rolling chair next to him. "I think this is what you are looking for," said the older man, putting a tape in.

His eyes were glued to the monitor as he watched the nursery scene unfold before him. One nurse was in the nursery when a baby being monitored went into cardiac arrest. She tried to revive the baby, with no luck. She then ran from the room to get help. A man in the hallway came into the room. He looked at the baby and then moved to the next chamber to look at another baby. He did something Alex couldn't quite make out.

"Back it up and zoom in on the babies." He couldn't read the names on the incubators clearly. "Back it up a little and zoom in more." He read the names with a heavy heart: Baby Taylor and Baby Carlisle. "Now zoom in on the man," said the emotion-filled voice. He watched the camera zoom in on the man and he frowned. "Closer." There was something vaguely familiar about the man. "Can you zoom in closer without distorting the picture?"

The clear picture of Jason Thomas came into focus. "Oh, God," said Alex putting his head in his hands. Everything just got a little more complicated. The man responsible for switching the babies was Samantha's half brother. "Print the picture." Alex got up from his seat and paced the room.

"Watch what he does." Alex watched as Jason Thomas switched the names and beds of the babies. Closing his eyes, he sat down again. He now knew how it happened and who was responsible. Matthew Taylor was in fact Michael Carlisle, his son. "That bastard switched the babies. We could be in big trouble for this. This hospital could face a major lawsuit."

"That's not going to happen, Gus," said Alex sadly, shaking his head. Now he had some of the answers he was searching for. Matthew had died of cardiac arrest only a few hours after he was born. The babies' name tags were switched to make it look like Michael had died instead.

Poor Samantha. He had no idea how he was going to tell her about this. Not only had she lost her husband and sister that night, but she had also lost her baby.

"We have to let the families know what happened. The poor woman whose baby died has been raising someone else's child the past three years. That poor woman who thinks her baby died. They all have to be told the truth. This is going to destroy a lot of lives, but we have to get those two babies back where they belong. I need to inform the chief of staff about this."

"Gus, it doesn't have to leave this room. Let me handle this situation." Gus looked at Alex, puzzled. "I know whose baby lived and whose baby died." Alex took a deep breath and wiped the tears from his face. "My son lived and my nephew died. The man who switched those babies is my brother-in-law. He gave my wife's sister our baby, and I buried hers with my wife."

"I'm totally confused," said Gus, printing out the picture. "This was your son." Alex nodded sadly and took the printout. Folding it, he put it in his pocket.

"My wife and her sister both gave birth the night my wife and best friend died in a car accident. Greg was pronounced dead on arrival. Kirstin lived long enough to give birth to our son. The shock sent my sister-in-law into labor also. She and Kirstin both delivered within minutes of each other. My nephew died instead of my son. My brother-in-law switched babies to give my sister-in-law a reason to live. It worked," said Alex sadly. "He gave her my son. Don't do anything with this information, Gus. Let me handle this my way."

Alex wasn't sure how long he stood outside the security room with tears streaming down his face. His gut instincts told him Matt was his son. He had hoped and prayed it was true, but now it was reality. His son was alive. Samantha had his son and he had no idea what to do about it.

The Porsche's tires squealed as Alex pulled out of the parking lot. He called to make sure Jeremy was home and sped the short distance to get there.

Alex strode into the house, holding the tape in front of him. Closing the door, a puzzled Jeremy followed him into the den. Jeremy watched Alex turn on the television and put the tape in the VCR. Alex held up his hand to silence him.

"Just watch. I have the proof I've been looking for, Jeremy. You are not going to believe who is responsible for this mess."

"What mess?" he asked, confused. He sat down on the sofa. "Alex, what are you talking about? What am I watching?"

"I'm talking about Matt being my son. I have proof, Jeremy. I did a blood test months ago. I didn't tell you because I didn't want to hear a lecture. Now I have the answers I need. Watch the tape." Unable to watch the tape again, Alex paced the room while Jeremy watched.

"Oh my God," whispered Jeremy, staring at the television screen. "Someone purposely switched the babies. Michael didn't die. It was Matthew. Samantha and Greg's baby died. Who was the guy? How can we get a close-up of him?"

"I already did. Brace yourself for a shocker." Alex took the photo out of his pocket and handed it to Jeremy.

"Jason switched the babies! Samantha's brother did something this unthinkable. He gave Samantha your son," said Jeremy in disbelief, dropping down to the couch. "Why would he do something like this? This is low even for Jason."

"Tell me where he is, and I will go ask him the same question, personally." Jeremy wrote down the address on a piece of paper and handed it to Alex.

"What are you going to do now? You have to tell Samantha. She needs to hear this from you, Alex." Alex shook his head. "What do you mean, no? You have all the facts now. What are you going to do with them?"

"I can't be the one to tell her this. It needs to come from the source. After your cousin explains his reasons to me, then he can explain to his sister. I'm leaving town right now to confront Jason. If Samantha asks you where I am, tell her I had to go out of town unexpectedly and I'll be back tomorrow in time for Matt's birthday party."

Alex took the first available flight out to Oregon. His thoughts were jumbled as he tried to figure out what he would do and say once he saw Jason. Jason was Sam's younger brother.

Leaning his head against the window, he tried to get some sleep. Closing his eyes became a nightmare. He kept seeing Sam's smiling face. He had no idea how he was going to break the news to her.

When the plane landed, he took a cab to Jason's house. Standing outside the door, he had to take control of his emotions.

Smiling, Jason opened the door. In the space of a heartbeat, Alex slammed him against the wall with a force that knocked several hanging photos to the floor. He pressed his elbow against Jason's throat.

"You jerk, give me one good reason why I shouldn't end your miserable life right here and now. Give me a reason," repeated the cold, deadly voice.

"I don't know what you're talking about," said Jason gasping for breath and struggling to break Alex's hold. "Take your hands off me or I will have you arrested for assault."

"Good idea, Jason. Why don't you call the police? Maybe you can explain this to all of us," said Alex, shoving the photo of him in the hospital nursery. "Remember this? Remember what you did three years ago in the nursery? You stole my son. You took my son and gave him to Samantha. You made me and everyone else believe my son died." Jason sagged against him. "Now are you starting to remember? You'd better remember, because you have about five seconds to give me one good reason why I shouldn't end your miserable life here and now."

"Daddy!" yelled Charlie from the kitchen. Alex released Jason and took a step back from him. He did not want Charlie to witness what he wanted to do to her father.

As she entered the room, Jason swept her into his arms. Alex wasn't sure if it was to calm her or for his protection. He hugged his daughter protectively.

"Where's Mom?" he asked calmly while meeting Alex's furious gaze. The little girl pointed towards the double doors. "Debbie," called Jason, walking toward the door. Alex paced the floor furiously as a very pregnant Debbie Thomas appeared in the doorway. Her appearance took some of the anger out of him, but not all. "Deb, can you take Charlie upstairs?"

"Sure. Is everything all right?" she asked. Jason nodded. "Alex, how are you?" She embraced him, and he returned her hug. A little more of his anger disappeared at her warm greeting.

He didn't want to hurt Debbie or Charlie, but he knew he couldn't hurt Jason without hurting them. It was a trade-off. One he wasn't sure he was willing to make at this moment.

"It's good to see you, Debbie," responded Alex. "I really need to talk to Jason right now." Her eyes moved from Alex back to her husband, and she left the room with Charlie in tow.

"How did such a nice woman end up with a piece of garbage like you? I should go right up those stairs and tell her what you did." The fear in Jason's eyes spurred Alex on. "There is no explanation or excuse for what you did. Ever heard of the Infant Protection and Baby Switching Prevention Act? Let me recite if for you. 'Sec. 1205. Baby switching: Whoever being in interstate commerce knowingly alters or destroys an identification record of a newborn patient with the intention that the newborn patient be misidentified by any person shall be fined not more than $250,000 in the case of an individual and not more than $500,000 in the case of an organization, or imprisoned not more than ten years, or both.' So give me one good reason why I shouldn't send you to prison?"

"I did it for Samantha! She lost Greg and her sister, and then she lost her child. She wouldn't have been able to bear it. I did it for her. I knew if she lost her baby on top of losing her husband and her sister, she would probably have a nervous breakdown. I couldn't let that happen. I did the only thing I could think of to help her get through their deaths."

"So you gave her my son! After the pain I went through of losing my wife, you let me think my son died also. What about my pain? What about the hell I went through? Do you have any idea of the pain I felt when they told me my son died? You robbed me of the first three years of his life!"

"Not really. You've had free access to him. Samantha would never keep you from him. You are a part of his life and you always have been. She even made you his godfather. You're a doctor; you deal with life and death every day. Samantha doesn't. You and I both know she would not have made it without that little boy. She needed him and he needed her. He needed a mother. I gave him one."

"That doesn't excuse what you did. He is my son! He should have been with me! You robbed me of that! I needed him!"

"Samantha needed him more! She loves that little boy. He was her last link to Greg. He was her link between reality and insanity. I did what I had to do to protect my sister. I know it was wrong, and I'm not asking for your forgiveness. I know there's nothing I can ever do to right the wrong I did to you."

"You're right about that, but there is something you are going to do. You are going to tell Samantha the truth."

"I can't do that. It will destroy her. She loves that little boy. She will never give him up. To her, he is her child. What about Matthew? He loves her. She is the only mother he has ever known. You are not so unfeeling that you would take him out of his mother's arms."

"You should have thought about that. Your time is running out, Jason. You have until Thanksgiving to tell her the truth, or so help me I will have you arrested. That will only be the beginning of the pain you will feel. I will destroy you publicly and financially. I'm not giving you an easy way out. You are going to own up to what you did. You are going to tell your sister what you did, and when you do, you'd better duck. Samantha has forgiven your miserable hide for a lot of things in the past, but I don't think you can weasel your way out of this one. She'll write you off this time, permanently, and I will say good riddance to bad rubbish."

"How did you figure this all out?" asked his brother-in-law, grasping at straws. "It's been almost three years."

"You obviously haven't taken a close look at your nephew. He looks more like me every day. I took a good look at my baby pictures and at Matt's. Imagine my surprise at how much alike they were. We even have matching birthmarks. That was something I couldn't explain away.

"As to how I pulled it all together, I had the hospital security tapes of the nursery pulled from the day of the accident. Can you guess what I saw? I saw you switching the nametags on those babies. You can't deny it! The evidence speaks for itself. I saw you with my own eyes."

"And I would do it again to save my sister. I lost one sister that night. I was not about to lose the other one. I did what I had to do to save Samantha."

"Is that what you call love? How can you say you love anyone after what you've done to Samantha, to me? How can you look your own wife and child in the eye knowing you've deprived another father of his child? You don't know the first thing about love."

"What are you going to do, Alex, suggest marriage to her so the two of you can share Matthew? I'm sure she'll jump at the chance to stay with him. Just don't fool yourself and think she's marrying you for any other reason than to keep her son. She loved your worthless cheating friend. He wasn't good enough for her and neither are you. In her eyes, you will never measure up to Greg Taylor. Isn't that ironic? He cheated on her repeatedly and she will never know because you were his best friend. You wouldn't betray the trust of a friend, not even a dead one. To her, he will always be her knight in shining armor. Where does that leave you?"

Alex shoved him away in anger. "What about your wife, Jason? How much do you love her? That is, if I can assume you love someone other than yourself."

"I love my wife and my daughter with all my heart." He wiped the tears from his face with the back of his hand. "I would do anything for them."

"You don't have a heart! Does your wife love you?" Alex asked, turning away. A plan formed in his mind, one he knew would hurt Debbie, but it needed to be done. It was time she knew the truth about her husband. "Let's find out how much, shall we? Call her downstairs."

"What are you going to do?" Jason panicked, pacing the room like a caged animal. "You can't tell Debbie. She's pregnant."

"I'm not going to do anything, you are." Alex smiled, turning back around to face him. Alex wanted Jason to feel half the pain he left in losing both is wife and son. "Because of Samantha, I won't have you prosecuted, but I can make sure you get what's coming to you. Your punishment begins right now. You are going to call your wife downstairs and tell her what you did."

Jason shook his head. Alex saw the fear in his eyes. "No," he pleaded. "Please don't make me tell Debbie about this. This will kill her. It will kill my marriage. We are expecting a baby any day. This will destroy my family."

"What's wrong, Jason? Are you afraid she doesn't love you enough to forgive you? You're probably right. She's a mother. Nothing you say or do will make her understand and forgive you for what you did to me and to Samantha. From where I'm standing, you are getting off lightly. If you didn't have a child and one on the way, I'd send you to either hell or prison. It's still an option."

"I'll tell Samantha, but please don't make me tell Debbie. She'll leave me. I love her, Alex. I know what I did was wrong, and I'm sorry. I had no right to play God with your lives. Ruining my life will not make up for what I did."

"It's a start. I feel no sympathy for you. It's Debbie and your little girl I pity. They have no idea what you are capable of. I think it's time they found out about the real Jason Thomas, the monster behind the mask. Don't you think your wife has the right to know what kind of man she married?"

"I know what kind of man I married," said Debbie, coming slowly down the stairs. "He's changed, Alex. He's not the same person you knew." She walked over to her husband and caught his hand. "People can change. You and Jason are both living proof. I've heard all about your past. You overcame it; so has Jason."

"Maybe, but the past has a way of rearing its ugly head when you least expect it. Some things can't be forgiven or forgotten. He did something I can never forget or forgive. He took something from me I can never get back: time. When you hear what he did, you will understand why I feel justified. I'm not going to tell you what he did. It's part of his punishment to tell you the ugly truth. Jason has something to tell you. You may want to have a seat."

"Jason, what's wrong?" asked Debbie, sitting down on the sofa. "What did you do to Alex to make him wish you were dead?"

"Debbie, I'm so sorry," said the tearful voice. "Please don't hate me too. I did something three years ago that was beyond belief. I took something from Alex and gave it to Samantha." Alex was forgotten as Jason sat down next to his wife on the sofa. He stood by quietly while Jason confessed the truth. "I took his son. I switched the name tags in the nursery to make it look like Alex's child died. It wasn't his child. It was Samantha's. I was there when the baby went into cardiac arrest and I switched the babies. I stole his son and gave him to my sister."

Alex would never forget the look on Debbie's face as long as he lived. She was horrified by what her husband had done.

Alex slipped unnoticed from the room. If it weren't for Debbie and the kids, he would let Jason rot in prison for what he had done. He deserved nothing less.

Chapter Five

Samantha and Dana sat at the breakfast table getting the food ready for Matt's birthday party. Samantha's mind was million miles away.

"Samantha, you are crazy if you let Alex slip through your fingers," said Dana earnestly. "He is crazy about you. You're crazy about him or you're just plain crazy if you let him get away. What more could you ask for in a man? He's handsome, successful, a great father, and a good friend to you; not to mention he is sexier than hell with that goatee thing going. You were a fool to set him up with Linda. She's too gorgeous and too perfect. He seems to really like her."

"Linda is what he needs," she replied between clenched teeth. "She's great with the kids. She's crazy about Alex, and she would make him a good wife," said Samantha past the lump in her throat. She closed her eyes, trying unsuccessfully to block out the picture of Alex with another woman. "Alex and I are friends. I don't want to lose that friendship. He's a big part of my life and there's nothing I can do about that because of the kids. He's been a wonderful substitute father to them. They love him. He loves them."

"How long did it take you to rehearse this little speech? I'm not buying it. What about you? Do you love him too?" Samantha turned away from her friend's probing stare. "Cut the bull, Samantha. This is me you're talking to. You and Alex generate enough heat to thaw out Alaska. The two of you have been dancing around each other for years. Why do you keep pushing him away? You two have so much in common. He's perfect for you. You can hand him over to a thousand Lindas on a silver platter and the bottom line will be the same—he will still want you. How do you feel knowing he's making love to another woman and probably fantasizing it's you?"

"Dana, stop. I don't want to hear this." She tried unsuccessfully to block out the mental picture of Alex with Linda. It hurt too much to think about it.

"We can't call it making love because he loves you. You put him in her arms and you put him in her bed. Don't you care?"

Samantha yanked open the bag of chips with more force than necessary and potato chips flew all over the table and floor. Dana smiled at her frown and gave her a smug *I told you so* look.

"See what you made me do?" she accused, going to the closet to get a broom and dustpan. She swept up the mess and put the broom back in the closet.

"No, jealousy made you do it. You can't stand to think of Alex with another woman. Well, you are to blame for it. You served him up to her. If she gets hurt because you can't make up your mind, then that's your fault too. You know you have feelings for Alex. He knows you have feelings for him. If you want him, all you have to do is tell him and Linda is history. Take a chance, Samantha. Don't you believe in second chances? This could be a new beginning for you and Alex. Why are you so afraid to take a chance?"

"Alex was my sister's husband. He was Greg's best friend. That's how I see him. I wouldn't feel right about making it more than that."

"No, that's how you choose to see him to protect yourself. You want him. You know it and I know it. You know what else? Alex knows it. He knows you want him physically. Stop hiding behind Kirstin and Greg. They have been dead for three years. It's time to stop mourning for your husband and start over. There is nothing and no one standing between you and Alex now, but you. If you don't go for it you're a fool."

"I can't," said Samantha, pacing. "Dana, you don't understand. I want Alex. I admit that, but I am not willing to take the risk. I have everything to lose."

"And everything to gain," Dana argued, getting to her feet and facing Samantha. "How much longer do you think he is going to wait for you? He's a man, Samantha, with a man's needs. If you can't give him what he needs, then he is bound to go elsewhere. Linda is elsewhere. When he dumps her—and he will—it will be on your conscience. What if he doesn't dump her? What if he falls in love with her and marries her? Then you've lost any chance you two might have had. Is that what you really want? How can you stand on the sidelines and watch while he and Linda grow closer? Do you want Alex to marry someone else? Do you want him to spend the rest of his life in the arms of another woman, while you try and decide what it is you want? Samantha, don't want until it's too late to see what's staring you right in the face."

"I'm scared. This could get so complicated if we started seeing each other and things didn't work out. The girls have been trying to push us together for months. Even Derek has mentioned to me on several occasions how nice it would be if we all lived together. Believe it or not, Dad has even tried his hand at matchmaking. I'm not sure what his reasons are, but we know with my father, he has one." She hit her forehead in remembrance. "Silly me, I already know his reason. He thinks Matthew is Alex's son. Don't get me started on that subject. Dad and Alex are still like oil and water. They still can't stand to be in the same room together for more than five minutes at a time. No. It's way too complicated. I'm tired of playing referee between my father and Alex."

"Let them have it out once and for all. You're only making excuses for why you shouldn't be together. Think of all the reasons you should. You two are so good together. You have fun together. He makes you laugh. Samantha, you are a different person around Alex. He brings out a side of you that is so full of life and carefree. He makes you happy. If you let Alex get away, you'll regret it. You'll always wonder what could have been. Men like him are rare. I think you are starting to realize this. You made a mistake when you set him up with Linda. You'd better think long and hard before you let him walk away."

"I'm thinking long and hard. That's the problem," said Samantha, closing her eyes and picturing Alex naked for the twentieth time today.

"Why do I get the feeling we are not talking about the same thing?" Dana laughed. "I guess in a way, we are. You want to sleep with the man, but you're afraid of making a commitment to him. If you could have one night of passion with him and then walk away, would you?"

"I don't know that I would be able to walk away," she confessed softly. "I don't know that I would want to walk away from him. Alex scares me. The way I feel about him scares me." Samantha threw her hands in the air. "I thought you were here to help me put the finishing touches on Matthew's birthday party, not preach to me about Alex. Can we talk about something else? I don't want to talk or think about Alex Carlisle today."

"Why not? Am I hitting to close to home? How can you not think about him? He's going to be here in the flesh in a couple of hours. Stop running and let him catch you. I guarantee you will enjoy it."

"I have no doubts about that," she mumbled. "I've fantasized about what it would be like," she admitted reluctantly. "In my dreams it was wonderful. It was magical, but the dream always ends badly."

"I'll say this one last time. He is crazy about you and I think you are crazy about him. Or just plain crazy if you let him get away from you." Samantha was not sure what to say, but was saved from answering by the doorbell.

"We're early," said Alicia walking into the kitchen. "We thought you might need some extra hands."

"Three hands are better than two any day. Hi, Nicholas. Hi, Gabriella." She smiled, hugging each of them.

"Hi, Aunt Samantha," they chorused, returning her warm embrace. They were both wearing red turtlenecks and blue slacks. Their hair was coal black and straight like their mother's. They took everything after Alicia.

"Why don't you both go into the den and see what's in the toy box?" They watched the children leave the room. "Where's Jeremy?"

"He was on an overseas call when we left. He said he'd be here before the party starts," said Alicia. "So, have you slept with Alex yet?"

"I give up," laughed Samantha, throwing her hands into the air in defeat. She walked out to the kitchen followed by Alicia.

"Should I call Dr. Carlisle and tell him you surrender?" Alicia laughed, taking a seat at the kitchen table.

"Can we talk about something else?" Samantha smiled. "Alicia," Samantha handed her a platter, "can you please take this out to the living room?"

Samantha, Dana, and Alicia were finished with the

decorations when Nathan and Laura arrived with the kids. Minutes later, the guests started to arrive. The house was brimming with people, but no Alex. Samantha pulled Jeremy into the kitchen.

"Have you seen Alex today?" she asked worriedly. "He should have been here by now. Do you know where he is? He's not answering his cell phone."

"I talked to him yesterday. He had to run out of town on an emergency," said Jeremy. "He did say he would be back in time for the party. Come on, Samantha. Don't you trust me?" Her brows rose and her eyes clearly told him she didn't. "Forget I said that. Don't worry. I'm sure he'll make it. Alex wouldn't miss Matt's birthday party. Nothing could keep him away. Have a little faith in the man."

"Okay. I get your point. I should trust him. Why is everyone trying to shove me into Alex's bed? Don't you people have something better to do than to worry about my non-sex life?"

"Hey, you're the one talking about sex and being in Alex's bed," he threw back at her. "No one can put you there but you."

Her face flamed and she crossed her arms across her chest and took a deep breath. She knew what Jeremy said was true. This was her choice.

"Jeremy, I don't want to get into this discussion right now. Today is my son's birthday party. That's all I want to think about. I don't need a recap of my relationship with Alex."

"Fine," he said holding up his hands. "I give up anyway. Alex will be here. Has he ever let you down?"

"Uncle Al!" squealed Matt excitedly from the other room. Samantha felt queasy at the deep voice in the next room. Like her son, she wanted to run out and throw herself into its owner's arms too, but she knew she couldn't do that.

"I told you he'd be here," said Jeremy. "Aren't you coming?" he asked, holding open the door for her.

When Samantha entered the room, she stopped cold at what she saw. Matthew was in Alex's arms and Alex had his arm around Linda introducing her to everyone.

Samantha felt more than a twinge of envy at seeing Alex with his arm around Linda. She was downright jealous. They looked good together; too good. She could have died a thousand times at the picture of happiness and bliss they made.

"A picture is worth a thousand words," whispered Dana, noting the jealous glint in her eyes. "I think they make a great couple. When they get married, you can baby-sit their kids, Aunt Samantha." Dana's words barely penetrated the haze she was in.

Even though she had gotten them together, she had not seen them together until now. The reality of the situation slapped her in the face. Pasting on a smile, she made her way over to them.

"Hi, Linda. I'm glad you could make it," she said cordially, taking in the other woman's natural elegance in a gray pantsuit. Her short, chic haircut framed her small, heart-shaped face.

"Thank you for inviting me," said Linda, returning her smile. She looked from Alex to Samantha, noticing the tension.

"Alex, can I talk to you for a moment in the kitchen?" asked Samantha, turning on her heel and walking away. She didn't give him a chance to refuse. He set Matt on his feet.

"I'll be right back," he whispered to Linda, kissing her cheek before following Samantha into the kitchen.

Alex knew from her expression she was either pissed off at him for being late or for being with Linda. He couldn't tell which. Either way, he was about to find out. When Samantha was ticked off, she became cold and reserved.

"Where have you been?" asked Samantha, furious at Alex. "You knew what time the party was starting. You were supposed to be here early to help me decorate. Instead, you and your girlfriend stroll in late."

"You're beginning to sound more and more like a wife every day," he mumbled. He watched her gray eyes narrow at his comment. "I'm sorry to hold things up. Didn't Jeremy tell you I had to run out of town?"

"Like I'd believe Jeremy any more than I believe you," she shot back.

"What's the problem? I'm here now. Lighten up. Boy, do you ever need a man," he said under his breath.

"I do not need a man," she snapped. "A man is not the answer to my problem. A man is my problem. You are my problem." His eyebrows shot up, and he smiled smugly. "Is sex all you ever think about? Is that the only thing men ever think about?"

"Pardon me. You need batteries." Samantha's face turned beet red at his insinuation, and she threw a kitchen towel at him. He caught it and tossed it on the counter.

"I happen to keep a ready supply of C batteries," she shot back, meeting the laughter in his eyes. She would call his bluff.

"Where do you keep them?" He challenged. "In the nightstand by your bed? Show me. I don't believe you."

"Show you what?" she asked in exasperation. "I'm not following you. What, pray tell, are you babbling about now?"

"Where do you keep your batteries?" She blushed furiously, and he laughed. "I called your bluff again. Sex is not the only thing men think about. Money comes in at a close second—okay, so maybe not that close. Let's go get this party started," said Alex, walking away.

Samantha was determined to start a fight. Alex was equally determined not to let her. He had hoped her seeing him and Linda together would make her jealous.

"Knowing you, that's probably why you're late. Were you and Linda having a little party of your own?" Samantha regretted the words as soon as they were out.

Alex's eyes sparkled with merriment. She was jealous. He turned around to face her with a big smile on his face. *Bingo!* "What a lovely shade of green you're wearing today. You are not mad because I'm late. You are just mad because you thought Linda and I may have been having a quickie to tide us over until tonight." Alex smiled wickedly, advancing on her. Her face turned red and she took a step back with each one he took forward. "Jealousy becomes you."

"I am not jealous. I could care less about your thriving sexcapades," she lied, taking another step back.

"At least I *have* a sex life, thanks to you," he lied, brushing a strand of hair from her flushed cheeks. She swatted his hand away. He was not about to let her know he and Linda were not sleeping together. Linda was definitely giving him all the right signals, but Linda wasn't the woman he wanted in his bed. "Samantha, I never do anything quick," said Alex caressing her flushed cheek. She slapped his hand away from her face and turned another shade of red—if that was possible—and took another step back. Alex kept coming until he had her where he wanted her. He placed both hands on the bar, trapping her between it and his body. His mouth was mere inches from hers. "I can see you weakening, Samantha. The brick wall surrounding your heart is starting to crumble. I can see it in your eyes." He watched the rise and fall of her chest at her labored breathing. He knew his nearness was affecting her as much as it was affecting him. "How long do you think I'm going to wait? I'm a man, Samantha, and it's been a long time since I've been with a woman. If I can't be with the woman I want, I guess I'll have to love the one I'm with."

Her eyes widened as his meaning became clear. She searched his eyes for the truth. Samantha was shocked to discover she actually believed him.

Could it be he hadn't slept with Linda or any other woman since Kirstin's death. Was it possible?

She placed both hands on his chest to shove him away, but lost her train of thought as her hands made contact with his muscular chest. His heartbeat quickened at the sensation of her hands on him, and their eyes locked in silent communication. Samantha felt his accelerated heartbeat beneath her palm. Her hands slid up his chest in a caressing motion.

Catching her hands in his, he brought them to his lips. Samantha was mesmerized as she watched him. Slowly his head lowered to hers. Her eyes closed as she anticipated the feel of his lips on hers. She could feel his breath on her face right before his lips touched hers lightly. His touch was light and questioning.

Samantha almost thought she imagined it. His lips brushed across hers again. Questioning. Teasing. Tempting. Samantha could no longer resist temptation. Her lips parted beneath his, and she took a step closer to him. His arms went around her and he deepened the kiss.

Alex wasn't disappointed by her response. She held him close as her mouth eagerly met his. His hands moved from her waist down to her bottom before gliding up to cup her breasts. Her nipples hardened instantly under his exploring hands.

"How long are we going to play this game?" he asked breathlessly. "I'm not a yo-yo. You can't keep pushing me away and pulling back. Make up your mind, sweetheart." His lips moved down her throat in a soft caress. "Tell me what you want." His hands moved back up to caress her breast. A soft moan escaped her lips at his tender seduction. "Admit it, Samantha. You want me." His tongue glided down her neck and up to her ear. He nibbled her lobe and she swayed against him.

"I want . . ." the interruption stopped her confession. It was on the tip of her tongue to tell him she wanted him.

"Oops!" The swinging doors opening brought them both to the present. Alex raised his head and his arms dropped to his side. Samantha looked up guiltily at the uninvited intruder. "Sorry." Dana smiled, staring from Samantha's red face to Alex's smiling one. Alex took a step back from her. She watched him pick up a napkin and wipe her lipstick from his mouth. "You missed a spot," smirked Dana, taking the napkin from him and wiping the rest of the lipstick off. "That was some liplock. Somehow I don't think Linda would find this situation as interesting or as amusing as I do."

"I think you're right," said Alex kissing her cheek. "Thanks. Samantha and I were just fooling around." He winked at Samantha and dropped the napkin in the trash. Turning on his heel, he left her to explain the situation as best she could to her best friend.

Samantha looked for something to throw at his retreating back, but then thought better of it. She wasn't going to give him the satisfaction of knowing he had gotten to her again.

"Don't say a word," warned Samantha to her smiling friend. Dana picked up a napkin and handed it to her. "It was only a moment of temporary insanity. I'm sure it will pass, soon."

"Fooling around is good. I like to fool around. What if your insanity doesn't pass? You might want to fix your lipstick before you go back out there." She smiled, following Alex out of the room.

Refreshing her lipstick and taking a deep calming breath, Samantha rejoined the party. The remainder of the afternoon went by without any incidents.

Chapter Six

Alex started the second movie and sat down with a big bowl of popcorn. This was becoming a ritual with him. When Linda hinted she would come help him watch the kids, he declined. He didn't want company tonight. He was finding it hard to keep things light and uninvolved with Linda when she wanted to move things full speed ahead.

Because of his feelings for Samantha, he couldn't do that to Linda. She was a nice lady and he didn't want to lead her on. He enjoyed her friendship, but his heart belonged to one woman.

Plopping down on the couch, he put his feet up on the coffee table. The kids were finally in bed and he had the rest of the night—what was left of it—to himself.

When Alex heard the doorbell, he bounded off the couch. He didn't want anything to wake Matt. He had a hard enough time getting him to go to bed without Mommy there to tuck him in and read him a story. He read three bedtime stories, drank water, and then had to potty twice. After that, Alex had to lie down with him until he drifted off to sleep.

Opening the door, he was not surprised to see Samantha

standing there. He looked down at his watch and noted it wasn't even ten o'clock yet.

Putting his finger to his lips, he waved her inside and closed the door quietly behind her. He tried in vain to hide the smile on his face.

"I guess accountants aren't your thing either," said Alex, smiling knowingly. She rolled her eyes and walked past him. He followed a silent Samantha into the den, where she sat down and picked up the bowl of popcorn. "Did he divide up the tab evenly?"

"To the last penny. He even had a 'buy one, get one free' coupon, and he still made me pay half the bill. Maybe you should tell your friend it's not in good taste to use a coupon on first dates. That's the last blind date I will let you sucker me into. Don't do me any more favors, Alex. I can be just as miserable alone. At this rate, I'd rather be alone."

"You don't have to be alone," Alex said, sitting down next to her on the sofa. Her eyes met his briefly, and she looked away. His eyes spoke volumes. They held a message she was afraid to acknowledge.

"Do you mind if I hang out here for a while?" she asked, changing the subject. "It's the least you can do for setting me up with two of America's Most Unwanted bachelors. What did I ever do to you? Why do you keep torturing me like this?"

"I figure turnabout is fair play. You've been torturing me for months." He brushed a strand of hair from her face. She saw the seriousness in his eyes and looked away uncomfortably. "So have you come to finally put me out of my misery?" Samantha couldn't say anything. She didn't know what to say. She was miserable as well. "I take your silence as a no. Oh well, you can't blame a guy for trying. Take your jacket off and relax. I'll go get two glasses and a bottle of wine."

"Wine and popcorn, sounds interesting," said Samantha, crossing her legs uncomfortably. She shifted nervously under Alex's gaze.

"You haven't seen nothing yet," winked Alex. "Get comfortable and I will get the wine." She watched him leave the room.

God that man is sexier than anyone has a right to be. Samantha, what are you doing here? This is crazy. Alex is off-limits. This could get very complicated. Why did you come here? You should have gone straight home. What brought you here? The same thing that always brings you to Alex. You can't seem to stay away from him.

It has taken almost ten years for you and Alex to get this kind of rapport. You don't want to destroy that with sex, or do you?

I guess that all depends on how great the sex is. What am I saying? I know the sex will be great. There's too much fire for it not to be great!

You can't stay here, Samantha! You are asking for trouble! Get out while you still can!

She came to her feet ready to make a quick exit and ran right into Alex. The breath left her as she collided with his solid frame. Her eyes met his guiltily.

Walking past her, he sat down the wine and glasses on the coffee table. "Running away?" he asked, sitting down on the sofa. She stood in the doorway and watched him pour two glasses of wine. "You're becoming quite the sprinter. Did you ever run track?" A smile broke out on Samantha's face. "I promise to keep my hands and lips to myself unless invited." She noted the laughter in his eyes. "I dare you to stay."

With that, he turned on the movie and picked up a glass of wine. Leaning back on the sofa, he waited for her to make the next move.

Alex knew Samantha couldn't resist a challenge. He

hid a smile behind his glass as she sat down beside him and picked up the glass of wine.

During the movie, he watched her fill her glass twice. He'd never seen her drink more than one glass of anything alcoholic. Alex knew she had one too many glasses of wine when she took the remote and stopped the movie.

Going to the stereo, she turned it on. As a soft ballad filled the room, she crooked her finger at him. Alex came easily to his feet and walked towards her. She went easily into his arms.

Samantha was in heaven in his arms. She had so missed the feel of a man's arms around her. Alex breathed in the fragrance of Samantha as they swayed softly to the music. Her hands caressed his back and he tensed. When her hands dropped to his buttocks and squeezed, he stopped dancing.

"I think that's enough." Alex dropped his arms from around her and took a step back. He held up his hands in defense to ward her off. She was getting to him. *Remember your promise. Remember your promise.* As long as she wears Greg's ring, you can't make a play for her. She has to take off the ring. He knew Samantha would probably not remember any of this in the morning. He went back to the sofa and sat down. Samantha followed him to the sofa. She lay down on the sofa, putting her head in his lap.

"Let's play a game," she giggled. "Truth or dare. You like games, don't you, Doc C? I bet you're good at games."

"I'm a little out of practice myself, but okay, Samantha, I'll play your game," he agreed against his better judgment. "Explain the rules to me and then you go first."

"It's simple really. I ask you a question. You have two choices. You can either tell the truth or take a dare. Telling the truth is much simpler. I can be quite inventive. Okay, I'm first. Truth or dare—do you want to make love to me?" she asked, pointedly staring up at him with sultry gray eyes.

Alex was in the process of taking a sip of his wine when she asked her question. The wine went down the wrong way and he choked. He coughed several times trying to clear his throat. "Samantha, you're drunk," said Alex returning her to a sitting position. "You are not going to remember any of this tomorrow, and if you do, you are going to be embarrassed and blame it all on the alcohol."

"No, I won't. I promise. You know what they say about alcohol. It only makes us do the things we want to do but wouldn't normally without the little push. Now stop avoiding my question and answer it." She leaned over and blew in his ear. When he shifted uncomfortably, she caught his earlobe between her teeth and nibbled gently. Her hand moved caressingly over his muscular thigh, and he caught it.

"Yes, Samantha, I want you." His free hand caressed her soft cheek. "You already know I do. I've made no secret of the fact I want to make love to you. Now I've answered your question, you can answer mine. Why do you need alcohol to make a pass at me? Are you afraid of me or just afraid of the way I make you feel? If you want me, just say so. Don't play games with me. Do you want to make love to me?"

"That's more than one question," she giggled. "You didn't say 'truth or dare,'" she whispered, running her fingers down his chest. "You have to play by the rules."

He caught her hand and brought it to his lips. "Forgive me," said Alex rolling his eyes and getting fed up with her games. "Truth or dare. Do you want to make love to me?"

"More than you know," she confessed, rising to her knees. She stared intently into his eyes. "I've dreamed about you for years. You make me feel things I never felt before. I think you've cast a spell on me. I want no other man," she laughed caressing his face. "I want you to make love to me. I want more than the dream to keep me warm tonight. I want you."

Alex was speechless. Her confession floored him completely. He knew the wine must have gone straight to her head or she would not have said what she just said. Even if it were true, she would never have admitted it to him, he was sure of that much.

Alex was surprised when she leaned over and brushed her lips across his lightly. Her arms slid around his neck and she deepened the kiss. Her tongue slipped between his lips and searched the warmth of his mouth. All thoughts of pushing her away left him as she pressed her body to his and pushed him backwards onto the sofa.

His arms went around her and he held her close. Her lips parted eagerly above his and her tongue teased his. Alex returned her hungry kiss with a passion that matched hers.

His mouth left hers long enough for him to pull the black sweater over her head. He tossed it carelessly to the floor. Warm hands cupped her lace-covered breasts. Samantha shivered when his tongue snaked out and licked the tops of her breasts.

Her head was spinning as he unsnapped her bra and pushed it from her shoulders. Samantha gasped in pleasure when he sucked first one and then the other nipple into his mouth. She held his head to her throbbing breast as he feasted.

"Don't stop," pleaded the soft voice. "Don't ever stop." Her body slid down his, and her mouth covered his in another steamy kiss. "Make love to me, Alex." She pulled his shirt over his head and tossed it aside. Her hands splayed over his hair-roughened chest slowly, as if to memorize each plane and contour. The hairs on his chest scraped her sensitive breast as she leaned over him and kissed him again. "I've dreamed about you, about us."

"Samantha, we have to stop," said Alex, fighting for control of his emotions. His hands trembled as he set her away from him. He knew she would regret this in the morning. As much as he wanted her, he had to stop for both their sakes. He knew it was the alcohol making her lose her inhibitions. He could not and would not take advantage of her. He wanted her, but not like this. He wanted her to be fully aware of what was happening.

"No we don't. I can't stop. I want you too much. I can't fight it anymore. I need you Alex. Please don't turn me away," she whispered, trailing kisses down his neck. "I know you want me as much as I want you. Put us both out of our misery. Make love to me."

"You have no idea how much I want you." Alex was fighting to control his runaway emotions. "I have dreams about you that would make you blush if I told you."

She put her finger to his lips. "I'm not a dream. I'm here and I'm real. Don't tell me your dreams," she whispered breathlessly against his lips, "show me, again and again."

Coming to her feet, she reached behind her and unzipped her skirt. Alex almost forgot to breathe as he watched the soft material slide down her long, shapely legs. The pantyhose followed just as gracefully. His mouth watered at the vision before him. Samantha stood in front of him in only a skimpy pair of black lace panties.

She caught Alex's hands and placed them on her bare breast. Moving to the edge of the sofa, he pulled her to him. His mouth planted hot kisses on her breasts and moved downwards. Samantha closed her eyes at the sensation of his warm mouth on her hot body. His hand cupped her through the lace panties. Samantha closed her eyes and moaned in pleasure.

Catching the material of her panties between his

teeth, he slowly lowered them. Samantha shivered as his mouth brushed the nest of curls between her legs as he slid the panties down her legs. Strong, firm hands moved up her calves, to her thighs.

"You are so beautiful." His hands outlined every inch of her body. Samantha trembled in anticipation of what was to come as he pulled her closer. She could feel his warm breath on her stomach.

"Uncle Al!" Alex and Samantha both froze. Matthew. Something was wrong. Alex came quickly to his feet.

"Stay here. I'll be right back. Don't move a muscle. Here's your chance to run, Samantha. You have ten minutes or less."

"I'm not going anywhere," she promised. "Hurry back." Alex leaned over and gave her a quick kiss before leaving the room.

Samantha yawned and lay back onto the sofa. I'll only rest my eyes for a few minutes. Pulling the throw blanket over her, she drifted off to sleep.

Alex jogged up the stairs to his son. Opening the safety gate, he lifted the sleepy-eyed little boy into his arms. He carried his son to the bathroom and back to bed. Alex turned on the sleepy-time tape and quietly slipped from the room. Opening and then closing the child-safety door, he went downstairs.

The sight that greeted him was not what he had expected. He walked further into the room and kneeled down beside a sleeping Samantha.

"Samantha." Alex softly stroked her cheek. She moaned softly and turned towards the sound of his voice. "Samantha."

"Alex," she whispered without bothering to open her eyes. "I was having the most wonderful dream about you. We were making love." Coming to his feet, he lifted her blanket and all into his arms. She nestled against him. "Where are you taking me?"

"To bed, where you belong." He carried her up the stairs to his bedroom where he laid her on the bed. He went to his bureau and took out a T-shirt for her to wear. Unwrapping her from the throw blanket, he slipped the T-shirt over her head. Pulling the comforter up and over the sleeping beauty in his bed was one of the hardest things he ever did.

He went into the bathroom, took a couple of aspirin out of a bottle, and filled a glass half full of water. Going back to the bed, he forced the tablets and the water down her throat.

"Alex, stay with me," she whispered, clutching his arm. "I don't want to be alone. I need you. Don't ever leave me." He stretched out beside her on the bed and pulled her into his arms.

I'll never leave you, my love.

When he heard her even breathing, he eased out of bed and pulled the comforter up to cover her. Grabbing sheets and a blanket from the linen closet, he quietly left the room.

Alex took the cushions off the sofa sleeper and made up his bed for the night. He lay down and stared up at the ceiling. Images of Samantha naked in his bed kept him from sleeping. He got up, grabbed his jacket and keys and left the house.

He didn't go far. He drove the couple of blocks to Samantha's house and let himself in. Going up to her bedroom, he found the overnight bag he was searching for.

He packed a toothbrush, underwear, and a pair of navy blue warm-ups. Leaving the house, he went back home. Alex took the case up to his room and sat it at the foot of the bed.

Soon, Samantha. It is inevitable. I love you and I know you love me. We will be together. Before leaving the room, he grabbed a pillow from the bed and a sheet from the closet. *The sofa sleeper it is.* He made his way downstairs to make his bed.

Samantha woke up the next morning with a splitting headache. She sat up and looked around the room, frowning. As the reality of where she was hit her, she bolted from the bed with her hands to her head.

She was in Alex's bed. Samantha blushed furiously when she realized she was naked beneath Alex's T-shirt.

Alex's T-shirt! Oh my God! I'm naked. Please tell me we didn't make love. I wouldn't have been that stupid. Would I? I would.

Samantha paced nervously around the room, almost tripping over her overnight case. Frowning, she kneeled down and picked up the case.

How did this get here? Alex. He thinks of everything. What would I do without him? What am I saying? I must be losing my mind. Alex is off-limits. I've got to get out of here. I don't want the kids to see me here and get the wrong idea. Or the right one.

She carried the case into the bathroom. After taking a long, relaxing shower, she sat down on the foot of the bed. Samantha still could not get up the courage to leave the room.

How am I going to face him? Remember, damn it! I can't remember what happened! Did we or didn't we make love? Surely I would know if we had. Maybe we didn't.

Lying back on the bed, she had flashes of herself and Alex dancing. Then they were on the sofa kissing. He removed her sweater. She was standing in front of him taking off her clothes, then blackness. She had no memory of what happened next.

Just great. I probably had the best sex of my entire life and I can't remember it. Serves me right for drinking so much. Why do I keep letting him get to me? I have to get out of here. This is insane. This is a no-win situation.

Gathering all her courage, she left the room. The house was still dark and quiet. She tipped quietly down the stairs in search of Alex.

When she opened the door to the den, her fears were put to rest. Alex was sound asleep on the sofa sleeper. His torso was naked, but he wore a pair of paisley pajama bottoms. A black sheet was draped carelessly over him. He was on his stomach with his head facing the door.

He stirred, but didn't wake as she picked up her purse from the coffee table. She searched the room until she found her shoes. Slipping them on her bare feet, she quietly left the room.

Alex sat up when he heard the front door close. He knew Samantha would take the easy way out. She didn't want to face him after last night.

She would either pretend nothing ever happened or be too embarrassed to face him. He also knew what she was thinking and he would let her until she got up the courage to ask him.

"Well how did it go last night? That must have been some blind date, since you didn't come home last night," said the bright, cheery voice on the telephone.

Samantha lay back on the sofa and closed her eyes. She twirled the telephone cord around her finger. Dana waited expectantly for her to tell her about her date last night.

You don't know the half of it," she said, letting out the breath she was holding. "My date was over around 9:30. It's where I went next which created a problem." Dana's eyebrows rose in question. "I went to Alex's house."

Dana smiled knowingly. "So you had a lousy date and

you went running to Alex as a consolation prize. Why doesn't that surprise me?"

"You can wipe that smirk off your face," remarked Samantha, shifting from her back to her side. "I don't consider him a consolation prize."

"So let me get this straight. You spent the night at Alex's or with Alex? There's a big difference in the phrasing."

"How about almost with Alex, at Alex's house." Samantha got to her feet and paced the room.

"Uh-oh. Why 'almost' with Alex? Why not with Alex? What stopped you this time? Tell me you didn't get cold feet?"

"What happened is I made an absolute fool out of myself. I had one too many glasses of wine and tried to seduce him. For all I know, I did seduce him. I don't remember anything after a few kisses and me doing a strip tease act. This morning I woke up in his bed, in his T-shirt and nothing else."

"So, what did Alex have to say for himself?" Dana asked with a sense of dread. "You did talk to him about this, didn't you?"

"And say what, exactly? I did what any coward would do. I ran away. I left before he got up this morning. Dana, what am I going to do? How can I face him now? For months I've been telling him I don't want to be anything but friends and he gives me a little alcohol and I come on to him like a sex-starved widow."

"Samantha, I hate to break it to you sweetheart, but you are a sex-starved widow. You want Alex Carlisle."

"I am not sex starved. Okay, so maybe I am a little," she admitted reluctantly. "That man is driving me crazy."

"With desire maybe. Just sleep with him and get it over with. Put us all out of our misery. I've got to run. I'll talk to you tomorrow," said Dana, hanging up.

Samantha replaced the receiver and stared at the telephone. She was tempted to call Alex, but she didn't. As much as she wanted to, common sense prevailed and she backed away from the phone.

Chapter Seven

Samantha stirred the frozen piña colada with the straw. She scanned the room for the mysterious date Dana and Jeremy set her up with. All Dana would say was "He's tall, dark, and gorgeous from head to toe." Samantha looked down at her red dress and frowned.

I feel like I'm at a bullfight. Well at least he can't miss me. Not many people can miss me dressed like this.

She was waiting for a distinguished-looking man wearing all black. Talk about finding a needle in a haystack. Most of the men in the bar area were wearing black. Well, he would have no trouble finding her. She stood out like a red flag at a bullfight.

What am I doing here? I must be crazy. No, I'm not crazy. I'm getting out of here.

She hopped down from the stool and ran right into a brick wall. Strong arms came out to steady her and to prevent her from having a nasty fall.

"I'm sorry." Her eyes moved slowly from his chest up to his face. She stared in surprise and took an involuntary step back. Surely this was just pure coincidence.

"I'm not. You are the woman I wanted in my arms tonight," said the familiar sexy voice. If she had to guess, the expression on his face told her he was completely serious. "But the question is, would she still be there in the morning?" She flushed hotly under his appreciative perusal. His hands on her waist burned through her flaming red dress to her bare skin.

Alex was just as surprised to see her as she was to see him. It had taken Jeremy all of three days to talk him into a blind date. If he had known it was Samantha, he wouldn't have put up a fight. So Jeremy and Dana were now in the matchmaking business.

Samantha looked stunning in a form-fitting red knit dress. Her shoulder-length, curly hair was pinned on top of her head.

"I think we were set up," she said, turning to leave. "Alex, I don't think this is a good idea. I think I should go."

"Don't go." Alex's hand tightened on her waist. "Jeremy and Dana went to a lot of trouble to get us together. Why not stay and have dinner with me? We both have to eat."

"Don't they ever give up?" Samantha let him lead her over to the hostess. "Why can't they leave well enough alone?"

"We'd like a table for two in nonsmoking," said Alex, smiling at the young waitress. They followed her to a table. Alex pulled out the chair for Samantha before sitting down. "Maybe they don't give up as easily as we do. Maybe they see something we don't or maybe they see something you don't want to see. I think we have some unfinished business to discuss regarding the other night."

"I guess we do," said Samantha, blushing. "So how big of a fool did I make out of myself?" Her eyes met his briefly before they lowered in embarrassment.

"You came on pretty strong," admitted Alex, studying her closely. She flushed hotly under his close scrutiny. "You floored me with some of the things you said to me.

I'm still not sure if it was you or the alcohol talking. Which was it, Samantha?"

"I guess to answer that question truthfully, I would have to remember what I said," she confessed, looking down at her folded hands. "I only remember bits and pieces of the evening."

"So what pieces do you remember?" He placed his hand on top of hers. She flushed again and nervously moved her hand from beneath his. Then she picked up her glass and took a sip of water.

"I remember us dancing and kissing." She took another sip of water. "I don't remember much after that."

"Selective memory. To make a long and very steamy story short, we were making out pretty hot and heavy when Matthew woke up. I went upstairs to put him back to bed. When I came back to finish what you started, you were asleep on the couch. I carried you upstairs and put you to bed. End of story."

"That's it?" She sighed in relief. She wanted to ask more questions, but thought better of it. "We didn't . . ."

"No we didn't make love," he finished. "If you want all the hot and heavy details that led up to you falling asleep, I will be more than happy to give them to you. Would you like for me to start before or after you stripped for me?" Her face flamed at his bluntness. "Are you sure you never danced for extra money during college?" he teased, embarrassing her even more. "You were damn good at it." Samantha couldn't meet his gaze. She could feel his eyes on her hot skin.

"Okay. You can stop right there. You don't have to tell me any more. I can imagine the rest." Samantha picked up her menu to hide behind. *I stripped for him! What did I say to him? I'm sure I don't want to know.* "So what's good?" she asked changing the subject. "I'm starving."

"So am I," responded Alex, not talking about food.

She got his meaning all too clearly as his eyes devoured her. She blushed to the roots of her hair.

Samantha barely tasted the steak and lobster. The way Alex was looking at her was indecent. She blushed to the roots of her hair when their hands touched. Samantha pulled back as if burned. Alex smiled at her discomfort.

Halfway through the meal, she realized Alex was playing a game with her. He was deliberately trying to make her uncomfortable. Alex waited patiently for the waiter to clear the plates away.

"I think it's time we laid all our cards the table. I'll go first. I keep getting mixed signals from you. I don't think I've made any secret of the way I feel about you. I want you, Samantha. I want to be with you." Samantha's eyes met his and she sucked in her breath at the need she saw reflected in his heated gaze. "I need to know how you feel. Sometimes you are flirty and sometimes you are distant. I don't know how to read you anymore. You go through the trouble of finding me a girlfriend, but when I start showing interest in her, you get jealous." Samantha opened her mouth to speak. He held up his hand to silence her. "No, let me finish. You told me to back off. When I do, you try and seduce me. I don't know what you want, Sam, or what you expect from me, but I'm not made of stone. The next time you get drunk and throw yourself at me, Matthew may not be around to save you."

Samantha hesitated before saying anything.

"I'm sorry," said the soft voice. "It should never have happened."

He threw his arms up in frustration. "Why?" he asked pointedly. "Why shouldn't it have happened? Make me understand, Sam. It's what we both want."

"That's the problem, Alex. I don't know how I feel or what I want. I should have gone straight home. I'm not going to blame my actions on the alcohol, because we both know it would be a lie. I introduced you to Linda to take your mind off me, but you're right, I did get a little jealous when you clicked with her. I'm not playing games with you. I swear I'm not. Everything is a little confusing to me right now."

"You are attracted to me and it's got you running scared? Why is it so hard for you to admit you want me? You had no trouble admitting it under the influence of alcohol. You admitted it to me and much more."

"Okay, I'm physically attracted to you," she admitted grudgingly. "What else did I say the other night?"

"Believe me when I say you don't want to know. It'll only embarrass you more. Don't worry," he said, smiling. "You didn't declare your undying love for me or anything mushy like that. Do I scare you that much?" he asked, reaching across the table and catching her hand. The sparkle of the diamond ring blinded him momentarily. Both of their gazes locked on her wedding ring. Samantha self-consciously tried to pull her hand away, but Alex wouldn't let her. He held her hand up so they could both see the ring. "This is what's holding us back. I made myself a promise that I would stay away from you as long as you wear Greg's ring. This is a symbol of what the two of you meant to each other. I almost broke that promise the other night when I had you in my arms. It won't happen again. As long as you wear this ring, there is no place in your life for me. You have to let go of the past, Samantha, and let go of Greg. I can't compete with a dead man. Greg was my best friend. He was like a brother to me. I loved him, but he is gone, and so is Kirstin. We have to get on with our lives. The time has come to move on. Whether we are together or apart, the choice is yours, but you have to put the past to rest. To do that, you have to let go of Greg. Until you take off his ring, we can't take another step. Maybe that's what you want. If that's the case, then just tell me. I'm through waiting, Samantha. Your time is up. Either you want me or you don't. No more head games. No more late-night visits. If all you want is sex, then tell me that too. At least I will know where you stand. If and when you are ready to take our relationship to the next level, let me know, but don't expect me to be sitting by the phone waiting for your call. I have a social life thanks to you." Alex rose to his feet.

"I never asked you to wait for me," she said, softly, biting her trembling lip. "I never asked you for anything."

"My mistake," he snapped, throwing his hands in the air. "I won't make it again. Have a nice, safe, uncomplicated, and lonely life. I won't do the same. I'll try not to think about you while I have another woman in my arms and bed. You win, Sam. I'm done."

Samantha was speechless as she watched him drop money for the bill onto the table and leave. She blinked back the tears that threatened to fall. When that didn't work, she wiped them away. Gathering what little strength she had left, she got up and left the restaurant.

Samantha was in a daze as she walked to her car. She failed to hear the car coming towards her or someone yelling to her. Seconds later she was grabbed from behind and pulled out of the way of a speeding car. All the air left her as she realized what almost happened. Her knees buckled and the guy who saved her held her up.

"Lady, are you okay?" asked the man holding her up. "That lunatic almost ran you over. Do you want me to call the police?"

"No. I'm fine," Samantha replied shakily. "Thank you. It was a stupid accident. I should have been paying attention. Anyway, they are long gone now. I'm okay now." On trembling legs, she walked to her car.

Sitting in her car, she twirled the wedding rings around on her finger. She stared at them as tears spilled down her cheeks, but she couldn't bear to take them off. Drying her eyes, she headed for home.

I could have been killed tonight, and Alex would never know how I feel about him. I've been given a second chance with Alex. Can I afford not to take it?

Alex's words kept ringing in her ears. *As long as you wear this ring, there is no place in your life for me. You have to let go of the past. You have to let Greg go. Until you take off his ring, we can't take another step.*

When she got home, she went straight up to her bedroom. The message light on the answering machine was blinking, but she ignored it. It was probably Dana or Jeremy wondering how the evening went. Samantha showered and got ready for bed.

Plopping down in the middle of the bed, she stared at her wedding rings. Taking a deep breath, she slid the rings from her finger. Clutching them in her fist, she hopped up from the bed and placed them in her jewelry box.

Am I ready to take that step? Do I want to take it with Alex? If I don't give it a shot, I will always wonder. I don't know when or how it happened, but I think I love him. I'm sorry, Linda, for bringing you into the middle of this mess, but he's mine. I thought I could hand him over to you and walk away, but I can't do that. I can't let him go. I owe it to both of us to take the chance.

In the days that followed, Samantha didn't mention her brush with death to anyone. It was an accident, and she wanted to forget it and get on with her life. Taking the next step with Alex was foremost in her thoughts.

Tonight she was going to make her move. She watched him with hooded eyes as he brought the kids inside. He helped them carry their things upstairs and then came back downstairs.

True to his word, Alex had steered clear of Samantha since the night of their dinner date. It took all his willpower to just walk away from her when he wanted nothing more than to take her in his arms, but he made a promise and he was bound and determined to keep it.

Her eyes moved over him in appreciation. He was dressed in a pair of black slacks, a black button-down shirt and black leather loafers.

You look great in black, but there are other colors, Doctor Carlisle.

"Earth to Samantha." He smiled, catching her staring at him. "The girls are upstairs getting ready for bed, and I'm taking off. I'll see you tomorrow." Samantha watched him walk to the door and open it.

"Alex." Samantha hesitantly followed him to the door. It was now or never to make her move. He stopped, but didn't turn around. "Are you busy tomorrow night?"

He closed the door in surprise and turned to face her. He watched her play with her hands. He knew this was a nervous gesture.

"I don't know yet," he said. "I do have a hot date tonight." The hurt look in her eyes didn't go unnoticed by him. *She's jealous. She can't stand the thought of me with anyone else, but she's not going to do anything about it.* "Can I let you know tomorrow, when I get home?"

Samantha's heart fell. He was seeing Linda again tonight. He was spending the night with her. The pain was almost more than she could stand.

"If you've got a date, Linda and I can rent a movie and watch the kids," Alex said. "I'm sure it's okay with her. She'll have me all to herself tonight."

"I don't need a sitter." Her heart sank. She was trying to build up her courage and took a step closer to him. "Dad and Laura are keeping the kids tomorrow night."

As the light went on in his head, he looked at her warily.

Samantha shifted nervously from one foot to the other. "I'm asking you out on a date?" Her words came out in a rush. There, she'd said it. She watched Alex closely for his reaction.

His eyebrows shot up in surprise and he did a double take, and then laughed. "Why would you go out with me now?" Alex asked, folding his arms across his chest.

She stared blankly at him. He was not going to make this easy for her.

"Did I miss something? I thought you couldn't stand to be in the same room with me, and now you're doing an about-face, again. Why are you asking me out on a date? Our situation hasn't changed. I'm still your dead husband's best friend. Remember, I'm the guy who was married to your sister. Those factors haven't changed."

"Why?" Samantha repeated in surprise. This was not the response she was hoping for. "Greg is dead, and so is Kirsten. We're alive. I would like for us to spend an evening alone together."

"Samantha, with you nothing is obvious. You've been pissed off at me for the past couple of days, and now you are asking me out on a date. What gives? Why do you want to spend an evening alone with me? Have you been tippling at the wine again?" He moved closer to smell her breath. Samantha pushed him away, half in anger and half in disbelief. "I know alcohol makes you amorous and makes you lose your inhibitions."

She blushed furiously. "I'm not drunk, nor have I been drinking, if that's what you're implying." Samantha seethed, folding her arms over her chest. "If you're not interested, just say so." Her angry gray eyes met his confused stare.

"That's not what I said," he hedged, still trying to make heads or tails of what was going on in her mind. "I didn't say I wasn't interested. I'm just a little confused.

Correct me if I'm wrong, but about two weeks ago, didn't you tell me to go take a flying leap off a short pier? A week later, you strip down to your teeny-weenie sexy black panties and try and seduce me." He watched her face flame with embarrassment. "Then you want to pretend it never happened. Now you want to go on a date with me. Am I missing something? I have reason to be cautious where you are concerned. Your feelings change like the wind. So why the change of heart this time? Is celibacy not agreeing with you?" he asked, catching her hand and pulling her closer to him. Alex was testing her to see if she would back down. Samantha had no intentions of backing down. She was right where she wanted to be. Their eyes locked in a silent battle.

As their hands met, sparks flew. Something was different about her. Alex's eyes went to her left hand. Her wedding ring was gone. Samantha's eyes followed his to her now-bare finger as he held up her hand with raised eyebrows.

"Someone told me I should let go of the past and look to the future. I took his advice. I'm ready to get on with my life." She saw the surprise in his eyes and smiled. Her heartbeat quickened as he kissed her hand and then entwined his fingers with hers. "So what do you say to dinner and a movie tomorrow night?" she asked again.

"I say," smiled Alex staring into her sparkling eyes, "what time are you picking me up?" They both laughed. "Are you for real this time? Are you sure this is what you want?"

"It's a real date, Doc. You're picking me up. Seven is good for me. Try to find something in your closet that isn't black." They both laughed again. "I'm dropping the kids off at Dad's around four." As they stared at each other, his head lowered. Her eyes closed in anticipation of his kiss. His lips touched hers tentatively. Alex half expected her to back off like she always did when he tried to get to close to her.

Their attraction was something they had both been fighting for years. Each time their hands or bodies touched, Samantha would move quickly away from him.

Samantha avoided being alone with him. She'd been on edge since the night they almost made love. Even though her memory was fuzzy, she could still remember bits and pieces of the evening. Her memories were enough to make her blush. Now, she wanted more than memories of what could have been. She wanted Alex.

"I'm through running, Alex. I want to be with you." Her words took him by complete surprise. For once in his life, he was left speechless.

Throwing caution to the wind, Samantha moved closer. Liquid fire spread through her as their bodies touched. She trembled as his arms closed around her. Her arms went around his neck and she pulled his head down to hers.

Alex needed no further encouragement. His mouth met hers with a hunger that matched her own. She kissed him with all the pent-up passion inside her. Her tongue slid smoothly into his mouth and teased his. Her tongue played a cat and mouse game until he captured it. When he raised his head, they were both breathless and dazed. Her lips brushed his again and he kissed her again until her toes tingled and her body turned to liquid fire.

She moaned in protest when he raised his head. Pulling his head back down to hers, she kissed him again and again, making up for lost time.

"I'll see you tomorrow night at seven." He released her and backed away regretfully. Alex stopped at the door and then rushed back to her and pulled her back into his arms. Samantha shivered at the intensity of his masterful kiss, but returned it eagerly, putting her arms around his neck and pulling him closer still. He molded her body to his and she reveled in his touch. "As much I hate to, I'd better go," said the husky voice.

"Yes, you'd better," she agreed. "Linda's waiting for you." Her words brought both them both back to reality. Samantha didn't mean to sound so catty, but she was jealous of his relationship with the other woman.

"Samantha, don't even go there," he warned. "Linda was your idea. You are the one who set me up with her."

"Not exactly one of the smartest moves I've made thus far." She tried to move away from him, but he wouldn't release her. Instead, he caught her hand and kissed her palm, which sent a new wave of shivers down her spine.

"Sam, I want you to be sure this is what you want. Be sure I am what you want." Their eyes met and held. His held questions and doubt. Her eyes assured him she knew what she was doing and saying.

"I am sure, Alex. This is not a passing fancy for me. I want to be with you and you alone. I hope you want the same."

"It's what I've always wanted," he said resting his forehead against hers. "You are the only woman I want. I'd better go. I need to talk to Linda."

"What are you going to tell her?" Samantha was feeling more than a little guilty about the situation she created. She hated seeing Linda get hurt.

"I don't know yet," he said tiredly. "I think we owe her the truth. You did serve me up to her on a silver platter."

"Tell her I'm sorry. I know it won't mean much, but I am sorry for hurting her. She really cares about you." His mouth silenced her with a tender kiss. "You'd better get going before I decide to keep you here."

"Don't tempt me," he said as his mouth touched hers again. "I'd better go before I decide to stay. I'll see you tomorrow night. Good night."

Neither one of them saw Derek and Hope sitting at the top of the stairs quietly giving each other a high five. They tipped quietly away before Samantha started up the stairs.

* * *

Alex had no idea what he was going to say to Linda when he got to her place. Samantha was ready to give them a chance and he was ecstatic. He also felt very guilty about Linda.

When he got to Linda's house, he rang the doorbell. Pacing back and forth, he waited for her to answer the door. The wind left him when the door opened. He stared in surprise and embarrassment at the beautiful woman in the purple negligee.

"Come in," Linda said with a smile, moving back for him to enter the house. Alex was not only speechless but hesitant as he walked into the house.

"You look great," said Alex, not knowing what else to say. Instead of responding, she pulled him close and kissed him. Alex was taken off guard, and he momentarily responded to her kiss. Half a second later, he pulled back from her.

"What's wrong?" she asked, watching him closely. "Did I misread the signals you were giving me? Isn't this the next logical step for us?"

"No, you didn't misread the signs. Linda, I'm sorry," said Alex moving away from her. "I should have been honest with you from the beginning. I have to cancel for tomorrow night. Something has come up. I can't stay tonight either."

"Some*thing* has come up, or some*one*?" She tied the sash of her wrapper. "I've tried every seduction I know and you've gently refused. I'm ready to take our relationship to the next level, but apparently you're not. What's really going on here? Who is she? Who is the one who has a hold on your heart, Alex? I envy her. She's a very lucky lady. Am I getting the brush-off? You've been distant since you got here. If nothing else, Alex, I thought we were honest with each other."

"I should have been honest with you about Samantha. I have a date with her tomorrow night," he admitted, watching her expression change several times as she walked away from him. Turning back to face him, her questioning eyes met his.

"Let me see if I've got this straight. You have a date with the same Samantha who introduced us." Alex nodded, and Linda shook her head and rolled her eyes. "You and Samantha both went overboard to convince me there was nothing going on between you. Now you two are dating? Did I miss something?"

"There was nothing going on between us. This is our first date. Samantha made it pretty clear to both of us she wasn't interested in me. I simply followed her lead."

"But you were interested in her? My gut feeling told me there was more to you and Samantha than met the eye. I see my instincts were right."

"I never said I wasn't interested in her," he said softly, not wanting to hurt her further. "I said she wasn't interested in me."

"But now she is and all is right with the world. Are you in love with her?" Linda sat down on the sofa when Alex made no reply. He didn't need to answer; she saw the truth in his eyes. "You are in love with her. Never mind," she said quickly. "I don't want to know." She ran her hands through her hair. "What have I gotten myself in the middle of? Don't you think you should tell her how you feel?"

"Someday I will," he said evasively, "but only if our relationship progresses. I don't know where this date will lead."

"I guess if she really cares about you, then seeing us together couldn't have been easy for her. If I remember correctly, she didn't look too pleased to see me at Matt's birthday party. Samantha was jealous, wasn't she? Did seeing us together change her mind? So you asked her out and she accepted."

"Not exactly," he hedged. "She asked me out, tonight. It's just a date, Linda. Don't read more into it."

"If it was just a date, you wouldn't be saying good-bye. If it were just a date you would have been in my bed by now. Don't lie to me and don't lie to yourself. You told me you haven't been with a woman since your wife died. You told me you wanted more from a relationship than sex. It wasn't a lie, was it? Samantha is the woman you are saving yourself for." She walked gracefully over to the door and opened it. "I hope she appreciates the man she's getting. You are a very special man, Alexander Carlisle. No, it's not just a date, Alex." He tried to interrupt her and she held up her hand to silence him. "Let me finish. You love her and she has feelings for you. You and Samantha getting together would be the ideal solution for everyone. She's practically raising your kids. You are a father to her children. Be honest with me—if things go well tonight, it would be a new beginning for you and Samantha. There would be no place in your life for me. She is the woman you want to spend the rest of your life with. I hope things work out the way you want them to with Samantha. You both deserve some happiness. If they don't, give me a call. Maybe we could do lunch or something."

"Good-bye, Linda," said Alex, kissing her cheek. "I'm sorry. Samantha and I never meant to hurt you."

"I know," she smiled through her tears. "You're a nice guy. Take care of yourself." She sadly closed the door behind him.

Chapter Eight

Samantha paced back and forth in the den, peering down at her watch every five minutes. When the doorbell chimed, she rushed to the door.

Looking in the hall mirror, she pushed her hair behind her ear. She wiped her sweaty palms on her skirt. Taking a deep breath, she opened the door.

Alex let out a whistle of appreciation at the vision before him. His brown eyes moved from the top of her curly head to her feet and back up again.

Her hair was pinned up with a few loose tendrils around her face to soften her features. Samantha wore a simple red silk minidress. Her legs were encased in red sheer pantyhose, and she wore medium-heel red pumps.

"Hello, beautiful," said Alex, whistling in appreciation. "You look phenomenal. These are for you." He handed her a bouquet of flowers.

"Thank you, sir. You don't look too shabby yourself," she responded, taking the flowers. "Come on in."

Alex was clad in a black Italian suit. He had decided against wearing a tie and left the top two buttons of his shirt open. Coarse black hairs peeked from his shirt. Around his throat he wore a gold chain.

He followed her into the kitchen, where she put the flowers in a vase and added water. She turned around to find Alex watching her. She moved nervously away from him. "Out of curiosity, is there anything in your wardrobe other than basic black?" she asked, smiling. "We'll work on that. I'm ready if you are."

"Promises, promises," he teased, caressing her soft cheek. He felt her tremble beneath his touch. "Relax, I don't bite much." Samantha smiled back at him.

"It's been a while since I've been on a real date," she explained. "The two you set up for me don't really count. Those were not dates. Those were cruel and unusual punishment for some crime I must have committed in a past life. No, come to think of it, they were more like revenge. You found two guys you knew I wouldn't like and you set me up with them. Why?"

"I wanted you to get a taste of the single life. Dating is not all it's cracked up to be. I hate the single scene, don't you?"

"Alex, I know what you were trying to do. I can see right through you. You wanted to make yourself more appealing to me."

"It worked, didn't it," laughed Alex, holding out his hand to her. Samantha took it without any hesitation.

"No," she replied honestly, "You have always been appealing to me. I was just too afraid to go after what I wanted. I'm still a little nervous. Shall we go?"

They ate dinner at one of Alex's favorite seafood restaurants. They shared a crab platter of fried crab claws, stuffed crab, curried blueshell crabs, and steamed king-crab legs.

They laughed about different things the kids had done and said during the week. By the time they finished with dinner, their movie had already started.

Alex was hesitant when Samantha suggested they just

go home. They both had mixed feelings about being home alone together.

I want you to take me home and make love to me.

Don't look at me like that. I don't want to rush things. I can go as slow as you need me to, sweetheart. It's killing me, but I've waited this long.

When they pulled up in front of Samantha's house, Alex didn't turn off the engine. Instead, he put the car in park and turned to face her. Her eyes met his in a question.

"Aren't you coming in?" she asked softly, wetting her dry lips. His eyes darkened as they watched her lips. Her words held an invitation.

"If I come in, we both know what's going to happen."

Samantha lowered her eyes shyly.

"If that's not what you want, then I won't come in," Alex said. "I'll walk you to the door and say good night." He raised her chin and caressed her cheek with the back of his hand. "Tell me what you want, Sam." She wet her dry lips nervously.

"I want you," she replied, catching his hand and bringing it to her lips. "I want you to stay, Alex." Her eyes held his.

"Are you sure you're ready? Honey, this a big step. There is no pressure involved here. I've waited this long, I can wait a little longer if that's what you want. It's killing me, but I can wait. Sam, once we take this step, you realize there is no turning back. I want the timing to be right for both of us."

She put her finger to his lips. "The time is right. At least it is for me," she amended. "I don't want to wait anymore. I want you to stay with me tonight. I want to make love with you. I am tired of wondering what it would be like."

Her words sent him into action. He'd waited what seemed like forever to hear her say those magic words. Alex leaned over, popped open the glove compartment,

and took out the spare garage-door opener Samantha
had given him. He pulled into the garage.

Hopping out of the car, he came around to her side
and opened the car door. He held out his hand to her.
Taking his outstretched hand, Samantha let him help
her out. He unlocked the door to the house and immediately turned off the alarm system.

Alex followed her up the stairs to her bedroom. He
watched her set the small purse on the dresser. He could
sense her nervousness.

Her bedroom was a mixture of burgundy and hunter
green. The bold colors surprised him. He had expected
frilly pink with flowers.

The king-size bed seemed to fill the room and beckon
them. Samantha kicked off her shoes and walked towards him. Alex met her halfway. He felt her tremble as
he took her in his arms.

"It's okay to be nervous. I know it's been a while. It's
been a while for both of us. Three years is a long time for
a man." She looked up at him in surprise. "I waited for
you, Sam. I saved all the desire and pent-up passion just
for you."

Her look told him she clearly did not believe his confession. "Are you trying to scare me away?" she asked
nervously. "I thought you and Linda were lovers." He
shook his head in denial. "You waited for me." At his
nod, her heart caught in her throat. "That's a lot of pressure to put on someone. I hope I'm worth the wait. I
don't want to disappoint you."

"You couldn't." Alex shrugged off his suit jacket and
draped it over the Queen Anne chair. "Tell me what I
can do to put your mind at ease."

She began to pace, wringing her hands nervously.

He caught both of her arms and turned her to face
him. "Sam, talk to me."

"I don't have a great deal of experience in this area," she confessed. "I've only been with one man, and that man was Greg."

"I know," he said, softly caressing her cheek with the back of his hand. "There's nothing to be afraid of. I would never hurt you. Do you believe that?" She nodded, not trusting her voice to speak. In her heart, she did believe him. "I've dreamed about you a thousand times, you lying naked beneath me. You fill my dreams, Samantha Taylor." His lips brushed hers.

"I've dreamed about you too." She pulled his head down to hers for another kiss. "I want you so much. No more interruptions. No more waiting. Make the dream a reality. Make me whole again."

He kissed her cheek and then her neck. Samantha was melting in his arms. "I told myself I was going to be the perfect gentleman tonight. I was supposed to kiss you good night at the door and then leave. I was kidding myself. I knew we would not be able to stop with a few kisses. I was certain that once I held you in my arms, we would both want more."

"You were a perfect gentleman. Outside that door you can be the perfect gentleman. Inside my bedroom I want you just as wild and untamed as I know you are. I don't want the perfect gentleman in my bed. I want you, Alex."

"Rrrrrr," he growled right before his mouth covered hers in a hungry kiss. He buried his hands in her thick hair. Samantha moaned softly as she returned his kiss.

He removed the clip from her hair, and it fell in a dark cloud to her shoulders. He turned her around and slowly lowered the zipper down her back. The soft material parted effortlessly under the guidance of strong, capable hands. Samantha shivered as warm hands made contact with her heated flesh. His lips moved softly down her neck to her trembling shoulders. Turning her around to face him, he pushed the dress down her hips and watched it drop to the floor.

His eyes darkened with passion at the vision before him. Samantha stood nervously before him in a pair of red panties and matching lace bra. He traced the outline of her bra with his finger.

"You are so beautiful." Each word was enunciated with a hot steamy kiss. "Reality is even better than the fantasy. You are a dream come true."

She shook her head. "No, Alex. I'm not a dream. I'm very real. Touch me." Her plea moved him. He cupped her breast and squeezed slightly.

With trembling hands, Samantha unbuttoned his shirt. Her breath quickened with each button that came undone. Pulling the shirt from his pants, she pushed it from broad brown shoulders.

Her hands glided over his chest and down his flat stomach to the top of his pants. She quickly unbuttoned and unzipped them. Pushing them from his strong hips, she stared at the magnificent male specimen before her.

Her eyes moved from his handsome face down to a pair of the broadest shoulders, to bulging biceps, perfectly sculptured chest, and a stomach flat as a washboard. She slid the black briefs down strong, muscular thighs. She watched his member spring free and stand proud. Her breath was shallow as she reached out and touched him tentatively.

Alex jerked beneath her caressing touch. Catching her hand, he pulled her to him. His mouth covered hers in a hungry kiss. He ravenously sucked her tongue into his mouth as his hands roamed over her body. Her tongue teased and taunted his. Breathless, they pulled back slightly.

His eyes never left hers as he unsnapped her bra and

let drop to the floor. He leaned over and flicked one nipple with his tongue, sending shockwaves of pleasure coursing through her.

She sucked in her breath as he slid the panties down her long, shapely legs. His hands slid up her calves to her legs and thighs. They settled on her hips, but evaded the place she wanted most for him to touch. His eyes darkened further as he stared at the naked beauty standing proudly before him.

Her passion-glazed eyes beckoned him closer. His hands covered her breasts and he felt her nipples harden instantly beneath his touch. Strong sure hands moved down her flat stomach and stopped before reaching their ultimate goal. Her legs parted for him as her eyes pleaded with him to continue. His hand slid lower and cupped her.

Samantha bit her lip to keep from crying out in pleasure when one finger slipped inside her. She was wet and ready for him. He gently lowered her backwards onto the bed without breaking contact. His exploring hand was driving her wild.

"Alex, I can't wait," she whispered breathlessly, thrashing under his tender ministrations. "Come to me now."

"You don't have to wait. We have all night," said the husky voice. He watched her expressive face as she climaxed beneath him. "That's only the beginning, sweetheart," he promised before his mouth covered hers. His mouth moved down the side of her neck, planting little kisses before he reached her heaving breast. He sucked first one and then the other nipple into his hot mouth. Samantha's body came to life again beneath him. Her hand went to his head to hold him in place. His mouth followed the planes of her flat stomach. At the first flick of his tongue between her thighs, she lurched and let out a loud gasp.

Closing her eyes in pure bliss, she let him transport her to the stars and then beyond. His mouth did things to her that had her panting, screaming, and begging for more.

Just watching Samantha's reaction was enough to almost send Alex over the edge. She heard the distinct rustle of plastic before he slid back up her body. She was glad he thought of protection, because it was the furthest thing from her mind. She was beyond all rational thought as her body moved seductively beneath his, seeking what she desired most.

His mouth covered hers and his tongue thrust into her mouth as he thrust into her writhing body in one smooth stroke. His mouth covered her gasp of pleasure as her body welcomed his.

She clasped him tightly to her and held on for the ride of her life. Alex took her higher and higher. Her body was on fire. She matched his movements, thrust for thrust. This time, when she reached out to grasp a piece of heaven, she wasn't alone. She felt Alex tense above her and let out a guttural groan as his body convulsed above her.

Alex collapsed on top of her in utter exhaustion. His breathing was heavy and labored as was hers. Rolling to his side, he pulled her with him. Sated and depleted of energy, they lay silently in each other's arms.

Samantha's head rested on his chest. She kissed his chest and she ran her fingers through the short, coarse hairs on his chest. The hairs tickled her cheek, but she didn't mind. There was no other place she would rather be than here with Alex. They lay like that for several minutes, both trying to catch their breath and too exhausted to move.

"Are you alive?" Samantha kissed his sweaty chest again. She looked up at him with all the love she felt for him shining in her eyes. She finally came to grips with the fact she loved this man. A peaceful calm settled over her at the realization. She wasn't ready to tell him, but she knew she loved him.

"Barely," said Alex, caressing her back and bare thigh. Burying his fingers in her hair, he gently pulled her head back so he could see her face.

Samantha leaned over and brushed her lips across his. "Am I dreaming or is this the real thing?" She took his hand and placed it on her breast. Her nipple hardened again in his hand.

"Sure feels real to me." He smiled, stroking her breast. "I suppose I'd better check out the rest of you." His hand slid down her stomach. Her legs parted for him to continue his exploration. "Real accommodating, aren't you?" She moaned softly when he slid two fingers inside her.

"I hope you've been taking your Vitamin E," she said, "because you are going to need it. We have quite a bit of lost time to make up for." Alex groaned. "You know, they say that's the first thing that goes."

Alex rolled over on top of her. His body was primed and ready for her. "I am not old," he laughed, smiling down at her. "Obviously whoever 'they' are, they have never met me. The older I get, the better I get."

"Prove it," challenged Samantha pulling his head down to hers. Alex couldn't resist a challenge. Grabbing a condom off the nightstand, he quickly put it on. "Gladly. I hope you took *your* vitamins. I have three years to make up for."

He proved to Samantha that he was up to the challenge time and time again that night. They slept in the next morning.

Samantha woke first. She watched Alex sleeping. He was lying on his stomach facing her. His handsome face was relaxed and unguarded. Long, thick black lashes covered his dark penetrating eyes. His cheekbones were high and he had a small nose. His lips were average size, but oh so kissable. The thin mustache and goatee added to his rugged good looks.

I could easily get used to waking up like this. Oh God. Where did that thought come from? Samantha, pull yourself together. Just because you and Alex had a night of incredible sex does not a relationship make. What if sex is all he wanted? What if he doesn't want a relationship? Okay, stop it Sam. Take a deep breath and relax. We have to take it slow and easy.

She stretched her sore aching muscles before easing out of bed. Samantha was careful not to wake him. Slipping open the double doors to the bathroom, she quietly closed them behind her.

Turning on the shower tap, she went into the closet to get her robe. She laid the robe on the chair at the bureau and stepped into the shower. The warm water soothed her aching body as she stood while the water splashed her, helping to ease the soreness between her thighs.

Remembering last night and the wee hours of the morning brought a flood of color to her face. She would gladly suffer the aftereffects of soreness for the pleasure she and Alex shared. Alex was a skilled and considerate lover. He made sure she received as much or more pleasure than he did.

Samantha brushed her teeth and then brushed out her hair. Her face was flushed and her skin glowed. She dried off and slipped into the robe. She laid a spare toothbrush and towel on the vanity for Alex. Tiptoeing out of the bedroom, she went downstairs to fix a late breakfast.

Samantha was famished as she prepared a meal fit for a king; waffles, scrambled eggs, ham, bacon, sausage, orange juice, and hot chocolate. Placing her bounty on the wicker serving tray, she carried her feast upstairs to her waiting king. Using her hip to open the door, she smiled when she heard the shower.

How am I supposed to act the morning after? What do I say? What should I do? Should I get back into bed? Should I get dressed? I'm no good at this. She fished in the nightstand for a coin. *Okay, heads I get back into bed and tails I get dressed. Here goes nothing.* She tossed the coin in the air and caught it. The shower stopped and she nervously dropped the coin. The coin landed on heads. *I guess I get back into bed. I hope I'm doing the right thing.*

Slipping out of the robe, she eased back into bed. Placing the tray over her lap, she waited for Alex. When he came out of the bathroom, the sight of him took her breath away. He was naked except for the towel wrapped carelessly around his waist.

"Good morning," said Samantha, shyly pulling the sheet up to cover her nakedness. "I made breakfast. I thought you might be hungry."

"I'm starving," said Alex, leaning over, kissing her parted lips. If Samantha had any doubts, they went out the window the minute his lips touched hers. "You taste like strawberry jam." He walked around to the other side of the bed and dropped the towel. Her heartbeat quickened as he climbed into bed and eased over next to her, careful not to upset the tray. "Everything looks delicious."

His words warmed her. "Are you referring to me or to the breakfast?" she teased and then blushed to the roots of her hair.

"Both," he replied, kissing her bare shoulder. Samantha closed her eyes and trembled as his lips moved over her bare skin. Warmth spread through her body at his practiced seduction. "I know you are delicious. Breakfast I haven't tasted yet," he winked suggestively. "Any regrets?" he asked staring into her sparkling eyes. Her hand caressed his stubbly cheek.

"Only that I waited so long," she replied, brushing his lips with hers again and again. "What was I thinking?"

"I've been wondering the same thing. Eat up," smiled Alex, placing a piece of bacon to her lips. "After this appetizer, I'll be ready for the main course."

They ate breakfast in bed and then picked up where they'd left off. It was hours later when they finally left the bed. After showering for the second time, Samantha had to drag Alex out of the bedroom.

She prepared them a late lunch while Alex went home to change clothes. She had everything ready by the time he returned.

Over lunch, they agreed to keep their relationship just between them for the time being. They both knew how much the kids wanted them together, but they agreed to go slowly.

Samantha and Alex spent the whole day together lounging around talking and watching old Westerns on television. Their peaceful world was shattered when the front door banged against the wall.

"Mom! Dad! We're home!" shouted the kids, running into the house. Alex and Samantha looked at each other as their blissful evening came to a close.

Alex gave her a quick kiss before moving away from her. Samantha came to her feet and waited for the kids to enter the den.

"Mommy!" Matthew yelled, running to her. Samantha picked him up and gave him a hug and kiss. "I missed you." He planted a noisy kiss on her cheek.

"I missed you too," she smiled kissing him again. "Did you have a good time with Grandma and Grandpa?" He nodded enthusiastically.

Alex smiled as he watched them. He knew he was doing the right thing for everyone. They would all be a real family soon.

"Uncle Al!" He lunged and Alex caught him. Alex didn't even realize he had his arm around both Samantha and Matt, but Nathan did. Nathan watched Samantha and Alex with open curiosity.

"Hope, why don't you take your things upstairs?" suggested Samantha, still smiling. She elbowed Alex and his arm dropped from her waist.

"Derek, catch." Alex tossed him the car keys. "You and Lexi go put your things in the car. We'll leave in a few minutes."

He and Samantha stared at each other in longing as she walked him to the door. Alex wanted desperately to take her in his arms and kiss her, but he couldn't with the kids in the car and Nathan standing in the living room, eyeing them suspiciously.

"I'll call you," he mouthed, closing the door behind him. Samantha leaned against the door smiling dreamily.

"So you and Alex are finally together," guessed Nathan, carefully watching his daughter for a reaction. Samantha looked squarely at her father, but made no reply. "You're glowing." Blushing, she turned away from his close scrutiny. "It's about time. I'm not going to give you a hard time if you and Alex are together," he assured her. "I'm all for it. You could do a lot worse."

"Gee, thanks," said Samantha crossing her arms over her chest. "I'm neither admitting nor denying anything. I do have to admit this is a lot better than the 'Alex Carlisle is a scum' lecture you gave Kirstin when they started dating. I guess times have changed. So what has changed your mind, Dad? Why is Alex suddenly acceptable?"

"Honey, that was a lifetime ago. He's not the same man. Your sister changed him. I'm not sure how she did it, but she did. Do you know that when you look at him your eyes shine and your face lights up?"

Samantha shook her head in denial and turned away

from his perusal. "I think it's your overactive imagination. You are seeing what you want to see."

"No. It's true. This didn't just happen overnight. You have been looking at him that way for a while now. Don't be embarrassed. He looks at you the same way. He's in love with you, and you love him. Honey, I don't have a problem with this. It's the perfect solution for everyone."

"Can we talk about something else?" Samantha asked nervously. "I'm not discussing Alex with you."

"You and Alex should give Matt the mother and father he deserves. He needs a mother and a father."

"That's rushing things a bit, don't you think? He has a mother, and Alex is a good substitute father."

"'Substitute father'," he charged, throwing his hands in the air. "That's a bunch of crap. Alex is his father and you and I both know it."

"Dad I'm not going to get in to this with you again. Matt is not Alex's son. He is Greg's son. How you could think I would do something like that to Kirstin is beyond me. I was faithful to my husband. Why am I explaining this to you, again? You obviously don't believe me. There is nothing I can say to convince you otherwise, so I am through trying. You have it in your mind that Alex and I have been screwing around for years. You're wrong, Dad."

"Then explain the resemblance between Matt and Alex. He's a miniature Alex Carlisle. You know it and I know it."

"I don't have to explain anything. I can't explain it. I'm not going to even try. Believe whatever it is you want to believe. Thank you for keeping the kids," said Samantha, walking over to the door, opening it. "It's always a pleasure chatting with you. Have a nice evening."

Chapter Nine

The kids were upstairs in their rooms and Alex was downstairs watching television when the doorbell rang. Looking out the peephole, he debated opening the door. When he did open it, his uninvited guest strode into the living room.

"We need to talk," said Nathan looking around the room to make sure they were alone. "Where are the kids?"

"Upstairs," answered Alex closing the door and facing his father-in-law. "As far as I'm concerned, we have nothing to talk about. What do you want, Nathan?"

"I want to know when you and Samantha are going to stop this farce about you being Matt's godfather?" Alex met the older man's accusatory stare. "Matthew is your son and I dare you to stand there and deny it. You and Samantha are making a huge mistake."

"Leave it alone, Nathan," he warned. "Stay out of it. This is none of your business. This is between Samantha and I."

"Like hell it's not. He is still my grandson. He deserves better than this. Are you and Samantha going to lie to him his entire life? Do you want Matt to grow up thinking you are ashamed of him? Aren't you tired of living this lie?"

More than you know, Nathan, but the time is not right yet. Soon the world will know I'm Matt's father, but not the way you think. I hope you can handle the truth. I'm not sure Sam can.

"Stay out of it. Samantha and I are together now, so give us a chance to make this work for everyone's sake."

Nathan looked at him strangely. "This is the first time you haven't denied Matt is your son," said Nathan watching him closely. Alex turned away from Nathan's piercing stare. "Your silence tells me everything that you and Samantha are afraid to admit. How does that make you feel, Alex, to know your wife and her sister were both pregnant by you at the same time? Does it make you feel like a big man?"

Alex furiously turned back to face him. "You don't know anything, Nathan," said Alex between clenched teeth. "The child Samantha carried was Greg's. If you think Matt is my son, then do you know what that means? It means he can't be Samantha's child. It would mean he was Kirstin's and my son. Do you understand what the implications are if what you are saying is true? Leave it alone. Let me handle this my way."

"What are you saying?" Nathan asked angrily. "Is Matt your son? Answer the damn question, Alex, and stop sidestepping."

Alex glared at his father-in-law. "You're so smart, Nathan. You figure it out. Think about it. What you think you know is only the tip of the iceberg. If you keep interrogating Sam about this, you are going to push her away. Is that what you want? You've lost one daughter. Do you want to lose another one? When the time is right, I will tell you everything you need to know, but for now, I'm asking you to let me handle this my way. You and I want the same thing. Give me a little more time and we will both have what we want. Back off and leave Samantha alone or you will push her away."

"Fine," snapped Nathan, glaring at Alex. "Handle it your way, Alex. I hope this doesn't blow up in your face."

You and me both! It's getting harder to keep the truth from Sam. I'm lying to the woman I love. I hope she can forgive me when I tell her I'm the one who discovered the truth. Please God, help me to do the right thing for all of us. I don't want to lose my family. We've come too far to turn back now. Please help me get through this. Help us all.

Alex was beyond frustrated when he locked the door behind Nathan. He was tired of withholding the truth from Sam and from everyone. He was proud of Matt and wanted everyone to know he was his son. He grabbed the phone. Dialing Jason's number, he paced the room.

"Hi, we're not in right now. Please leave a message at the beep."

Alex slammed down the phone. He ran his hands over his head in frustration.

"Where are you, Jason? You are running out of time, and so am I. I can't keep this up much longer. The pretense is killing me. Either you tell her or I will," he vowed to the empty room.

On Monday morning, Alex shocked everyone by clearing his schedule for the next two weeks. He was taking some much-needed time off from work. His partner and Darla, the physician's assistant, divided up his patients.

He was smiling and on top of the world when he left the hospital. A giant weight was lifted from his shoulders. He now had time to spend with the kids and with Samantha.

When Alex picked Samantha up for their date, she greeted him by throwing herself into his arms and kissing him passionately. He was pleasantly surprised and pleased by her response. He lifted her and she wrapped her legs around his waist.

"I missed you," she whispered against his lips, kissing him again. Alex twirled her around and carried her inside.

"I missed you too." His hands moved over her bottom, and he gave her a kiss that curled her toes. She clung to him and returned his kiss. He let her slide down his body until her feet touched the carpeted floor. She kissed him again and again. "If you don't stop, we will never get out of here. Are you ready?"

Guilt ate at him as he stared back into her sultry gray eyes. She loved him and she trusted him. She didn't need to say the words. He could see it in her eyes. Alex knew Sam well enough to know she wouldn't have made love to him if she didn't love him. He was about to destroy her world and it was killing him. He loved Samantha and would do anything for her, but the truth had to come out. She needed to know the truth about Matthew.

Alex drove them to Dana's house for their monthly Saturday-night get-together. Samantha made him promise he wouldn't tell anyone they were involved. She wasn't ready for the world to know yet. She wanted to keep the secret a while longer.

Alex hated the idea of keeping his hands to himself all evening, but in the end he agreed to go along with her. Samantha promised to make it up to him later. Her father and stepmother were keeping the kids overnight. She told him she had a full bottle of whipped cream and a sweet tooth. Of course after that confession, she had to drag Alex out of the house.

"Good thing this place is well insured," said Tomas, sipping his beer and watching Alex watch Samantha. "Yep, my policy is all paid up for the year."

"And why is that?" asked Alex taking his eyes off Samantha momentarily and taking a sip of his rum and coke.

"Because with all the heated looks you and Samantha are sending each other, it could burn the place down if you're not careful."

"Very funny." Alex laughed and turned his attention to the man sitting next to him at the bar. "Now you're a comedian."

"It certainly explains the glow on her face. She seems happy. I'm glad." Alex opened his mouth to respond when Tomas waved his hand to cut him off. "Don't even bother denying it my friend. I'm not blind. You and Samantha are lovers. All I can say is it's about time."

"Yes," he admitted, "Sam and I are lovers. She's not ready to share the news with the world yet. So don't make an announcement just yet. What gave us away?"

"Well two things. Number one, you came in together. That's a first in itself. Number two, Samantha didn't do a good job of wiping her lipstick off your mouth," he laughed. "Nice shade on you, by the way."

"You should have been a detective Tomas, but don't give up your day job." Alex looked around the room. "Does anyone else know or suspect?"

"I haven't said anything, but we've all known it was only a matter of time before the two of you got together. You can only fight chemistry for so long."

"So, Samantha, how are things with you and Alex?" asked Dana, smiling. "Are you two still playing touch-me-not? You haven't taken your eyes off him since you got here, nothing new there."

"What can I say," she said sipping her soda. Her eyes devoured the man she loved. "He's a handsome man."

"You admit that he is handsome. That's a start. And you're just now realizing this? Are you blind or something? Alex is hot. Do you remember Tomas' cousin Tia? You know the one with the hair down to here," said Dana, touching her bottom, "and legs up to here," she concluded, placing her hand under her chin.

"The model," replied Samantha, frowning. "Yes, I remember her. The one who couldn't keep her hands and the rest of her anatomy off Alex? How is dear sweet Tia these days?"

"Well, she was here about a month ago, and Tomas set her up with Alex." Samantha choked on her soda. "She's quite smitten with him. Let's see—he picked her up on Friday night and we didn't see her again until Sunday. I think maybe you kept his kids that weekend." Samantha glared across the room at Alex. He lied to her when he said he waited for her. Sam fumed. She would give him a piece of her mind on the way home. That was the only thing he was getting tonight. "Well anyway, she's coming back next weekend. She asked Tomas to see if Alex was free for the whole weekend. One guess as to what she has in mind. Who could blame her? Look at him. Hey, maybe you could keep the kids that weekend. You probably don't have plans. You aren't seeing anyone, are you?" Sam didn't see the smug look on her friend's face.

Samantha wasn't listening any more. The thought of Alex with Tia or any other woman sent her into a fit of jealousy. She watched Alex and Tomas laughing.

Without giving it any thought, she came to her feet and walked over to them. She tapped Alex on the shoulder. When he spun around on the barstool, she stepped between his parted legs.

Taking the drink from his hand, she set in on the bar behind him. Leaning over she kissed him in front of everyone. Alex was caught off-guard, but genuinely surprised and returned her kiss. His arms pulled her closer and he deepened the kiss. His mouth plundered the sweetness of hers as she clung to him.

"I guess this means the cat is out of the bag," he whispered against her lips. "What was that for?" He kissed her again.

"Tia is off-limits, and so is Linda," warned Samantha, brushing her lips across his. "Tia will have to find someone else to entertain her on her next visit here. There are a few things I don't mind sharing, but you aren't one of them."

"Tia?" he asked frowning. "I haven't seen her in about six months. She's not exactly my type. We didn't click. We went out once. I don't want Tia or Linda, I want you." He brought her mouth back down to his and assured her in no uncertain terms she was the only woman for him.

When they finally remembered where they were, they looked up to see everyone watching them and smiling. Dana walked over to them with a smug look on her face.

"I knew mentioning Tia would send you over the edge," laughed Dana. "You should have seen your face. You were ready to kill Alex. He didn't spend the weekend with Tia. I made it all up to make you jealous. I'm real good." Tomas gave her a high five.

"This is great," chimed in Alicia. "We were all hoping you guys would quit playing games with each other and admit how you feel."

"I told you they were sleeping together," said Jeremy smugly. "Alex was way too relaxed and Samantha hasn't stopped beaming since they walked through that door. Alicia, you owe me fifty dollars, babe."

"You bet on us," Samantha asked, facing her cousin. "What exactly was the bet, or do I want to know?"

"Trust me, cuz; you don't want to know." Jeremy

winked, moving a safe distance away from her. "Just go with the flow and enjoy your newfound relationship. You both deserve all the happiness in the world."

Sunday after church, they sat the kids down to tell them they were dating. Samantha and Alex were not sure what to expect when they shared the news with the group. What they got was quiet acceptance. They didn't even seem surprised by the confession.

"We already know, Mom," said Lexi crossing her arms in boredom. "This is old news. Can we go now?"

"How can it be old news?" Samantha was puzzled by her response. "We are just now telling you. Alex and I want to know what you guys think about us dating each other?"

"We're cool with it." Derek's response was much too quick. "Can I go now? Halftime is almost over. The Dolphins are up by 14."

"Derek, sit down." He did as his father instructed. "We are trying to have a family meeting here. The game can wait. This discussion can't."

"Lexi and I saw you and Dad kissing. We were hiding on the stairs the night you asked Dad out on a date. I saw you kissing the other night, when you thought no one was looking." Derek seemed bored by the entire discussion and was anxious to get back to the game. "Aunt Sam, it's all right. We all want you and Dad to be together. We think it's great. Can we go now?"

"Okay." Samantha was blushing like a teenager at Derek's comment. "I think I'm done. Alex, do you have anything to add?"

"Do you guys have a problem with us dating each other?" Alex asked, making eye contact with each of their children.

"No," they chorused. She looked each child in the eye

to make sure they were being honest and not trying to weasel out of the meeting. Satisfied with what she saw, she gave Alex the thumbs up signal.

"Meeting adjourned." They all ran from the room. "I think we handled that pretty poorly." Alex dropped down to the sofa. He pulled Samantha down onto his lap and kissed her.

"I know something that will take your mind off the kids," she whispered seductively against his lips. Her tongue snaked out and outlined his lips with the tip.

"Call a sitter and meet me at my house in half an hour," he whispered against her lips. "I have a pressing problem that needs taking care of."

"You're kidding." He took her hand and placed it on a part of his anatomy, which assured her he was not. "You're not kidding." Her hand moved over him in a gentle caress.

"Keep that up and I'll lock the door and have you on your back in two minutes flat," he promised. His mouth covered hers in a hungry kiss. Pulling his mouth from hers, he set her on her feet. "Make the call, babe. I'll see you in half an hour at my place. Don't bother showering. We'll shower together when you get there."

She was giddy as she watched him leave the room. She didn't hesitate as she called Karen from down the street to come sit with the kids for a couple of hours.

Samantha was pacing the room waiting for Karen's arrival. When the doorbell rang, she ran to get it.

"Hi, Karen." Sam smiled, stepping back for her to enter the house. The teenager was wearing jeans and a sweatshirt. Her short hair was blonde this week. Last week it had been jet black; the week before, it was red.

"Hi, Mrs. T." She smiled, coming inside with her books. "I've got some studying to do, so I'll go into the den. How long do you need me?"

"About an hour and a half. I should be back by 9:30 P.M. Is that okay? I'll leave my cell on just in case you need me."

"That's fine. Are the kids in bed?" Samantha nodded. "Good. I've got a lot of work to do. I'll see you around nine."

"Thanks, Karen." Grabbing her purse and keys, Sam left the house. She felt like a naughty teenager as she drove the short distance to Alex's house.

He greeted her at the front door with a steamy kiss. Locking the door behind her, he led her upstairs to his bedroom. He turned on the shower before turning to face Samantha.

Without a word, he pulled her shirt out of her jeans and pulled it over her head. He tossed it aside. Samantha extended him the same courtesy as she removed his shirt. Her hands splayed over his chest and moved down to unsnap and unzip his jeans. Her hand caressed him and she felt him jerk beneath her touch.

Reaching behind her, he unhooked her bra and removed it. His hand moved down her stomach to unhook her jeans. He pushed them down her thighs.

They both wiggled out of their jeans. Naked, he stepped into the shower and waited for her. Samantha followed him.

They faced each other as the water splashed down their naked bodies. Taking the soap from the tray, he worked his hands into a thick lather.

"Turn around." She did as he requested, facing the shower wall. She closed her eyes when she felt his hands on her back. He massaged her shoulders, back and buttocks as he lathered them with soap. Rinsing her back he turned her around to face him. Their eyes met and held as he lathered her shoulders. When his hands touched her breast, her nipple hardened in response to his caress. He lathered both breasts and moved lower. Her legs parted and she waited. His hand soaped her stomach and then moved lower. He rinsed the soap from his hands and then washed her. She swayed into him when one finger slipped inside her. His fingers worked their magic on her, bringing her to a quick climax. "My turn," smiled Alex, picking up the soap and placing it in her hand.

Samantha took the soap and lathered his chest. She saw him tense as her fingernail scraped his nipple. She saw his body react to the stimulation. Laying the soap aside, she moved down his stomach to his groin. Her hand cupped him and he closed his eyes. Her fingers closed around the hard thickness of him and he moaned. She caressed him until he caught her hand to stop her. He turned around for her to lather his back. She massaged his back and thighs. She cupped the tautness of his buttocks and squeezed slightly.

Turning the shower spray towards him, she rinsed the soap off him and then turned to do the same to herself. Alex grabbed a towel and wrapped it around his waist. Stepping out of the shower, he wrapped her in a towel and lifted her out of the shower.

Removing the towel from her body, he began drying her off, one inch of skin at a time. Samantha followed his lead. He hooked the towel around her and pulled her into the bedroom.

They spent the next hour exploring and pleasuring each other beyond their wildest dreams. Sated and exhausted, they lay quietly in each other's arms.

"Can I ask you something?" Sam asked, sitting up and leaning back against the headboard as she turned to face him. "Can we get dressed and go in the other room? I don't feel comfortable having this conversation here."

"What can't we talk about here?" Alex sat up, frowning.

Samantha was about to leave the bed when he caught her arm to stop her.

"Was Greg having an affair?" Her gaze held his, and Alex was the first to look away. Of all the things he expected her to ask him, that was not one of them. He hesitated briefly before answering her.

"After what just happened, you are bringing Greg into my bedroom." Alex vaulted off the bed and walked over to the window. She stared at his nude body in appreciation. "Samantha, Greg is dead. What's the point of this?" She got out of bed and wrapped the towel around her. "Greg was not having an affair."

Samantha knew right away he was lying. His usually relaxed body was now tense, and he could not meet her eyes. What she didn't know was if he was lying to protect Greg or to spare her feelings. Samantha followed him and turned him around to face her.

"You're a terrible liar, Alex. You have a tic on the left side of your forehead when you lie. It's a dead giveaway. Please tell me the truth," she begged.

"Why, Samantha? Why do you have to know? Why does it matter? Greg is dead. Let the past die with him."

"I can't do that. Your tone and body movements speak volumes. Don't spare my feelings. Tell me the truth. Was Greg having an affair with Vivica Johnson?" Alex visibly relaxed.

"No, he wasn't," said Alex truthfully. Vivica was not the woman Greg had been involved with. "I don't know what you know or what you think you know, but Greg was not sleeping with Vivica. Even if he were, I would not be at liberty to tell you. I do not betray confidences. Greg was my best friend; what he told me in confidence, I would not repeat to anyone, not even to you."

"If he wasn't cheating, there should be nothing to tell. Greg is dead. You won't be betraying his confidence."

"The answer is no, Samantha. No. Greg was not having an affair with Vivica. He loved you. You and those kids were his life."

"But I couldn't give him what he wanted. Because of the pregnancy, I couldn't make love with him. He went elsewhere. I know he did. You know he did. Who was she?"

"A sexless marriage can cause a strain on any relationship. Men are different from women. Women can go long periods of time without sex; some men can't."

"It caused more than a strain, Alex. I was losing my husband and there was nothing I could do about it. Those last couple of months, he couldn't even stand to be near me."

"Samantha, that wasn't because he didn't want to be with you. It's hard for a man to be near the woman he loves day after day, knowing you can't take her in your arms and make love to her. It's torture. No. It's hell. I've been there. I was there a few months ago. I wanted you and I couldn't have you."

"Don't change the subject. We are not talking about us. We are talking about Greg. So tell me, Alex, if the situations was reversed, if you and Kirstin had the problem we did, would you have cheated on her?"

"This is ridiculous. This is not about Kirstin and me. This is about you and your insecurities. You couldn't have sex with your husband. So what? It wasn't your fault. It wasn't anyone's fault. Greg is gone. Let it go with him. Is it going to make you feel any better? No, it's not. I'm through with this whole conversation," said Alex, throwing his arms in the air and storming out of the room.

Samantha followed him down the stairs to the den. She watched him fix himself a stiff drink and down it. When his eyes met hers, she shivered at the anger in them, staring back at her.

"I knew Greg was seeing someone else," said Samantha, sinking down to the carpeted floor. She was rocking back and forth hugging her knees to her chest. "I lost my husband, my sister and my nephew all on the same night."

Alex felt a knot form in his stomach. He wanted desperately to tell her the truth. Her nephew didn't die. Her son did, but he couldn't bring himself to hurt her. She was in enough pain right now.

"Samantha, don't. It wasn't your fault. It was my fault. I'm the one who asked Greg to drop Kirstin at the party for me. I put them in that car together. I sent them to their deaths." The confession was ripped from his throat. She saw the anguish in his eyes. She felt his pain and reached out to him. She never knew until this moment the guilt Alex was carrying around. He blamed himself for their deaths.

"No!" She sat up and looked at him. Kneeling down in front of him, she brought his lips to hers. She framed his face in her hands. "It was not your fault, Alex. Don't do this to yourself. It wasn't anyone's fault. I don't blame you. Please don't blame yourself for this. You are not to blame." She wiped the tears from his cheeks. His lips brushed hers again and again. Her arms went around him and she pressed him down to the carpeted floor. "Let me ease your pain. What happened was not your fault. You did nothing wrong. It was their time to go. I understand that now. I never once blamed you. Let it go, Alex. Free yourself from your guilt. Let me help you." Her mouth touched his again.

She made slow passionate love to him with her hands and mouth. Alex was powerless as her hands moved over his body in a loving caress. As her lips moved down his throat, he inhaled the fragrance that was Samantha. He gasped when she flicked his nipple with her tongue. She rolled the hard pebble between her teeth. Her fingernail scraped his other nipple. She smiled when she felt his arousal pressed against the silk boxers he wore. Her mouth followed the trail of hair down his flat stomach. She slid the boxers down strong, muscular legs. The hair on his legs tickled her breast. Her nipples hardened against his hot flesh.

"Don't stop," said the raspy voice. His hand buried itself in her hair and he pushed her lower. He let out a groan as her hand circled him. He let out a loud gasp as her mouth covered him in a slow, torturous movement. He trembled and then froze beneath her tender assault.

Grasping her hair, he tugged with just enough pressure to bring her back up to face him. He caught the ends of her short nightgown and pulled it up and over her head. Tossing it aside, he brought her mouth back down to his and reversed their positions. His hand moved down her stomach to her parted thighs.

"Now, Alex," she whispered against his throat. Samantha let out a moan of pleasure as his finger slipped inside her wet passage. She arched against him and locked her legs around his waist.

"Not yet. Now it's my turn to pleasure you." He moved down her body and she cried out when his tongue licked her hot flesh. Parting her, his tongue dove deeply into her warm, wet, and inviting flesh. His hands and mouth loved her body as she had loved him. "Don't move a muscle." She watched him run to the bedroom and return with a small package. Taking it from his trembling hands, she opened it and put it on him. In one smooth stroke he was embedded deep inside her. She hugged him to her and held on for dear life. Alex didn't move as he enjoyed the feel of her slick walls encasing him and convulsing around him.

The bold pressure of his mouth parted her lips. As he began to move in and out of her body, his tongue imitated the age-old movement with her mouth. Samantha moved with him. They were one in mind, body and spirit. They clung to each other as shockwave after shockwave rocked them. Together they reached the stars and beyond. The descent back to earth was gradual as they floated on a cloud of pure bliss.

Their labored breathing was the only sound heard in the room. Alex's arms tightened around her as their heartbeats slowed.

"Wow!" Samantha snuggled against Alex's side, feeling safe and secure in his arms. He held her close.

"My sentiments exactly," he said. She kissed his sweat-slick chest. "I think I have carpet burns, but it was worth it. You are worth it."

As he stared at her, his thoughts were jumbled between the past and the present. *You were right, Samantha. Greg was cheating on you, but Vivica wasn't the woman. For your own sake, I hope you never find out who she was. It'll only cause you more pain to know it was the woman you welcomed into your home.*

She snapped her fingers in his face. "Hey, where did you go?" Alex didn't answer. Instead, he pulled her mouth back down to his.

It was another thirty minutes before she showered for the second time, dressed and drove home. Alex followed her to make sure she made it safely inside.

Chapter Ten

Samantha wasn't content to let the subject of Greg's affair drop. She didn't know why it mattered so much to her. Greg was gone and the truth shouldn't matter now, but for some reason it did. She needed to know if everything they shared was a lie. If Greg cheated on her, she was sure her father knew about it. Nathan Thomas knew everyone's hidden secrets.

"Dad, I have to ask you something," said Samantha, nervously playing with her hands. "Did you know Greg was having an affair?" From the uncomfortable flush on her father's face, she had her answer. "So I guess I'm the last to know. Who was the woman?"

"Will knowing make it easier to accept? Honey, this is going to open a whole new set of problems for you. Let the past go. Concentrate on your future with Alex and the kids. Don't bring old baggage into your relationship. You are better off not knowing the truth."

"Why am I better off not knowing?" she persisted. "I know her, don't I? Why are you and Alex protecting her? Who is she, Dad? I'm asking you to tell me the truth."

"It was your cousin Betsy," he said softly. She watched

the play of emotions on her father's face. He sighed in resignation.

Samantha felt all the air leave her. *Greg and Betsy.* There had to be a mistake. Even as she said it to herself, she knew the truth. That's why Betsy had all but disappeared from her life. Samantha hadn't seen or spoken to her cousin since Greg's death. The few times she called Betsy, she always got her answering machine. They had spoken on the phone a few times, but that was the extent of it. Their blossoming friendship died with her husband, and now she knew the reason why.

A million and one questions popped up in her head. Had Betsy only used her to get close to Greg? Sam had a rough pregnancy and could not take care of her family. Her cousin Betsy who recently moved to town offered to help out. She moved in with them and stayed for about three months. When had their affair begun? *Were they sleeping together in my house?*

"I have to go see Betsy," said Samantha, rushing from the house. "I have to know why she did this to me."

"No you don't," said her father, grabbing her. "Don't make a bad situation worse. Sweetheart, think long and hard before you walk out that door. If Alex means anything to you, you will let it go. Greg was your past. Alex is your future. Don't jeopardize your future because of your past."

"He slept with Betsy. How could he do that to me? How could she? She's my cousin." Samantha paced the room in anger. "I don't know if I can just let it go. It's not that easy. I want to go over to her place and rip her heart out. If Greg wasn't dead, I'd probably kill him." She dropped down to the sofa. "You win. I won't confront Betsy. Our five-year marriage was all a lie. He lied to me. He cheated on me. It makes me wonder if Betsy was the only one. Was she?"

"Honey, I can't answer that. I don't know." He sat down next to her on the sofa. "No matter his faults, Greg loved you, and he loved those kids. It wasn't all a lie, Samantha. Don't belittle what you had because of one mistake."

Alex was more than a little surprised when he arrived home to find his father-in-law instead of Samantha watching the kids.

"Samantha knows about Betsy," said Nathan, meeting him at the front door. "She knows, Alex."

"You told her." Alex glared at his father-in-law. "Why, Nathan? Why did you do it? Why couldn't you mind your own damn business for once?"

"So she could put all of this behind her and get on with her life. She needed to know. It was eating her alive, Alex. You should want her to get it out of her system and get on with her life with you. She should be concentrating on you and the kids. She wanted to go confront Betsy, but I talked her out of it. She said she needed some time alone to think." Ignoring him, Alex opened his cell phone and dialed Betsy's number.

"Betsy, it's Alex. Samantha knows about you and Greg." There was silence on the other end of the line. "Did you hear me? Sam knows."

"I heard you," said the soft voice on the end of the line. "I'm glad she knows. Should I expect a visit from her someday soon?"

"I'm not sure. I wanted to warn you just in case she found out where you lived and dropped by. She doesn't know about Joshua, and I'd appreciate it if you didn't tell her right now. I'm not sure she could handle it on top of everything else. Betsy, you owe me," said Alex tightly.

"I know I owe you, but I'm tired of the lies. If she comes here, I'm telling her everything. I will not hide my son. Thanks for the warning." The line went dead.

"Damn!" Alex slammed the phone down. "You've stuck your nose where it doesn't belong, again. Now I have to go do damage control," said Alex, slamming the door behind him.

Alex found Samantha in the den. She was lying on the sofa with her eyes closed. He sat down next to her, and she immediately vaulted to her feet and moved away from him. She walked over to the window and looked out.

"Why didn't you tell me about Betsy?" she asked angrily. "I asked you if Greg had an affair and you lied to me."

"Technically I didn't lie," he shot back. "You asked me if he was having an affair with Vivica. It wasn't a lie."

"A lie is still a lie. So what are you doing, Alex? Are you going behind Greg comforting all the lonely women he left behind? That should keep you busy for a while. There was me, Betsy, and God only knows who else. Forget I said that, you would know. You know all Greg's dirty little secrets. He shared everything with you, even his women."

Alex walked up behind her and turned her around to face him. Raising her chin, his hand wiped the tears from her face. Her eyes were red from crying.

"Don't touch me," she said, pulling away and hugging her arms protectively to her. Samantha felt betrayed and she didn't think she would be able to stay angry with him if he took her in his arms. He dropped his hands to his sides. "Were they sleeping together in my house?"

"Yes." Since she knew part of it, he might as well tell her the rest. If she chose to confront Betsy at a later time, she wouldn't be blindsided. "Samantha, have a seat," said Alex, waving her over to the sofa. "There's something else I need to tell you. I thought I was doing the right thing by keeping it from you, but I realize now I'm being unfair to everyone involved. You deserve the whole truth."

"No more secrets, Alex. I went through it with Greg. I guess I still am. I will not go through it with you. If there's more, tell me."

"I do see Betsy on a regular basis, but it's not what you think," he amended quickly. "We decided it would be best for everyone involved if you didn't find out the whole truth about her and Greg. The timing was off. Now, I think it's time you knew. It's not fair to you and it's not fair to Joshua to keep this secret."

Samantha felt a knot form in the pit of her stomach. She knew she was not going to like whatever it was he had to say. "Can you stop being so cryptic and tell me what's going on? Who is Joshua?"

Alex caught her cold hand and gave it a slight squeeze. "Joshua is Betsy and Greg's son. He's the reason I see so much of Betsy. Josh is my godson."

Samantha stared at him in shocked silence. It took the news a few minutes to register to her brain. Not saying a word, she removed her hand from his and came to her feet.

"So he was not only a lying cheating bastard. He was a lying cheating irresponsible bastard. Are there more children out there I should know about?" Alex shook his head sadly. "Did Greg know before he died?"

"Josh is the only one. As difficult as this may be for you, Joshua deserves the chance to know his sisters and brother. "

"You want me to accept this child into my home. My dead husband's love child, whom I knew nothing about until a few seconds ago." She paced the room at a loss for words.

"No, I don't expect you to baby-sit. That's not what I'm saying. Samantha, you never have to see him if that is your choice, but I want the kids to see him and to know him. He's a terrific little boy."

"I guess I don't have a choice, do I? You've already made up your mind. Whatever Alex wants, Alex gets. You became a substitute father to Greg's children. You seem to be taking on more and more of Greg's responsibilities each day. I wonder if he would have done the same thing for you. Did Greg make any financial provisions for his child, or is that something I'm going to have to do?"

"Samantha, don't make me out to be the bad guy. Don't take your anger at Greg out on me. He left me a sizable life-insurance policy. I put the money in trust for Joshua." Alex pulled her into his arms and held her. The look in her eyes squeezed at his heart. It took Alex a minute to gather his composure. Closing his eyes, he just held her. "I have no idea what you are going through right now. If Greg were here, you'd probably punch his lights out. He's not here, Samantha. I am here. Hit me if you need to. Just this once, I will be your punching bag. I can take it." He framed her face between his hands.

"I'm sorry. I know you're not him," said the anguished voice. "This shouldn't be so important to me, but it does hurt. Greg and I were married for five years, and I can't help but wonder if Betsy was the first affair."

"She was," he assured. "You have to let it go, sweetheart. Don't let this make you doubt yourself. You are a beautiful, kind, and loving woman. Don't ever sell yourself short." His lips brushed hers. "I've wanted to say this for a long time, but the time never seemed right. It seems right, now." He framed her face with his hands. "I love you, Samantha Taylor." Samantha's heart melted at his heartfelt confession. Tears misted her eyes as she smiled up at him. "You don't have to say anything. I know you care. I'm not asking for a declaration of love. I just want you to know how I feel." One tear after another rolled down her smooth brown cheeks. He leaned over and licked the moisture from one cheek and then wiped the other with his thumb. "I'm sorry. I didn't mean to make you cry. You had to know how I felt. I've never made any secret of how I feel about you."

"I know," she hiccuped. Sam chewed on her bottom lip. She wanted to tell him how she felt, but she was afraid. Mastering her fear and calling on all her inner strength, she gazed back at him with all her love shining in her gray eyes. "I love you too," she confessed softly.

"You love me." He smiled. "I kind of figured you did, the night you gave yourself to me body and soul."

She nodded through her tears. Her hand came up to caress his hair-roughened cheek. Tiptoeing, she pressed her lips to his lips in a soft kiss. "I love you," she said again, this time stronger and with conviction. "I love you, Alex Carlisle. What happened with Greg and Betsy hurts. I can't lie about it, but it's in the past. I didn't go to Betsy's to confront her, because although it hurts, it's not that important to me. My pride was hurt more than anything. I'm not in love with a memory anymore. I'm in love with a man who is flesh and blood. The man I love is sitting here beside me. You are my future."

"Prove it," he challenged, touching his lips softly to hers. Her arms linked around his neck and she pulled his head back down to hers. His mouth covered hers in a hungry kiss, blocking out everything else. He swept her up in his arms and carried her upstairs to the bedroom.

That night marked a new beginning for them. The next few days, they were inseparable. Alex and the kids came to dinner at her house every night. After a few steamy good-night kisses, he'd leave. Once home, Alex would call her to say good night and they would talk for hours.

Thanksgiving was spent at Samantha's parents' house. Sam knew Alex felt uncomfortable being there, but he suffered through it for her and the kids. Alex was upset when his brother Keith decided to spend Thanksgiving in Las Vegas with his latest girlfriend. This left him to face his father-in-law alone. Their relationship was shaky at best.

Dinner at the grandparents' was the one tradition both Samantha and Alex wanted to keep for the children's sake. The kids always looked forward to Thanksgiving at Grandpa's house.

Alex picked her and the kids up at five and the housekeeper served dinner promptly at six o'clock. By eight o'clock, Alex was more than ready to leave.

The kids wanted to stay, and Samantha's parents offered to keep them overnight. Alex jumped at the opportunity to be alone with Samantha.

Alex spent the night at Samantha's house. They relaxed in the Jacuzzi with a bottle of wine and talked. After the Jacuzzi, Alex gave her a full-body massage. Samantha was so relaxed she fell asleep.

Alex pulled the comforter over her and eased into bed beside her. She cuddled up next to him, and he too fell asleep.

Chapter Eleven

Samantha put the kids to bed and showered and got ready herself. She was upstairs in her room when the doorbell rang.

She trotted down the stairs and hurried to the door before it rang again. Peering out of the peephole, she was puzzled to see her brother Jason standing there.

"Hi, what are you doing here?" She smiled in surprise, hugging her younger brother. He returned her warm hug.

"I need to talk to you," he said, stepping inside and closing the door behind him. "Are the kids in bed?"

"Yes, I just put them down." She frowned as she watched him. "Hope will be sorry she missed you. Are you staying in town for a few days? Are Debbie and Charlie with you? Are they at Dad's?"

"No, I came alone. I needed to see you." His tone was serious, and Samantha frowned. "I flew in today. Can we sit down?" he asked.

"Sure, have a seat. Jason, what's going on? You sound so serious. Is something wrong? Do you need money?"

"No, I don't need money. My business finally got off the ground and is doing quite well. This is not about me,

Sam. It's about you, and it's about something I did. I don't know how to say this, but there is something I have to tell you. I need you to understand why I did what I did first. Please don't hate me. I couldn't bear it. You are the only person who's ever had faith in me."

"Jason, you're scaring me. What did you do? Please tell me you and Debbie are still together. Losing her would be the worst mistake of your life." Her stomach tightened as she stared at him. Debbie Lawson had probably saved his life. When he fell in love with her, he'd been hanging with the wrong crowd and constantly in trouble. They were all praying they would not receive a late-night call from the police telling them he was dead. That all changed when he met the proverbial preacher's daughter. He started going to church and turned his life around. It was a gradual process, but it did happen.

"Debbie took Charlie and moved back to Oregon with her folks. She won't even talk to me. I miss them so much."

Samantha's heart went out to her brother as she watched the tears fall down his face. "Oh no, not again. What did you do this time? Please tell me you didn't have an affair?" He shook his head. "Do you owe someone money?"

He shook his head sadly. "If only it were that simple, then maybe she would forgive me. I played God," he said softly. "I did something so wrong for all the right reasons. I did it for you, Sam. I wanted to spare you more pain. I knew when you lost Greg and Kirstin you would be shattered. I wanted to ease your pain. I wanted to give you a reason to go on living."

"Honey, I survived. I'm a lot stronger than you give me credit for. Greg and I have two beautiful children. They were my reason for living. They gave me the courage and strength to go on. Why bring it up now? I've finally put the past behind me and gotten on with my life. What ever it was doesn't matter now. I've started over. I have a second chance at love, Jason, and I'm taking it. Alex and I are in love."

"He's been in love with you for years. Do you love him?" She nodded her head. "I'm happy for you. I think you are the only one who didn't know he was in love with you. Your happiness is what made me do what I did." He waved his hand in the air in frustration. "On the plane ride, I was going over in my head what I was going to say to you. I even wrote it down. I thought I was doing what was best for you. I swear I was only trying to help you. I didn't even consider the consequences of what I was doing at the time. I acted on impulse and changed everyone's life forever."

"Spare me the melodrama, Jason. You have never helped me in your life. Your specialty is causing me pain, causing Dad pain. Just when we finally think you have your act together, you surprise us yet again. What have you done now?"

"Because of all the accidents that night, the whole hospital was a madhouse. I was at the nursery looking at Matthew and Michael when the baby went into cardiac arrest. There was nothing the nurse could do to save him. There was nothing anyone could do. She ran out to get help and I walked in. It was so easy."

"I don't want to hear this," she said, turning away from him. "Whatever it is, I don't want to hear it! I don't need to hear the details of Michael's death."

He grabbed her and turned her back around to face him. "You have to hear it, Sam," said the emotional voice. "It's now or never for me. Matthew was the baby who died."

Her eyes met his and she went limp in his arms. "No! You're a little confused about what happened. Matthew didn't die," she said, shaking her head as the tears were already slipping down her cheeks. "It was Michael. Kirstin and Alex's son died that night, not mine." Her tortured eyes begged him to take it back. She didn't believe him. She couldn't.

"No, Samantha. It was Matthew." She felt a chill go down her spine as his words washed over her. He released her and she backed fearfully away from him. She shook her head in denial. She couldn't believe him. She wouldn't. This couldn't be true. Matthew was her son.

"No! I don't want to hear this! You're lying! Why are trying to hurt me?" She screamed at him. "What have I ever done to you? I have helped you out of one crisis after another. I have given you money. I played referee between you and Dad. I would do anything for you, and you stand there and lie to me about something this important. Something that could destroy my whole life."

"I know what you've done for me, Sam. I also know what I did for you. I switched those babies' name tags. I did it to give you a reason to live. You lost Greg and Kirstin. I couldn't bear to watch you lose your son."

As his words really sank in, Samantha started to tremble. Shaking her head in denial, she glared at him. "Get out of my house! I am not going to listen to this garbage. My baby didn't die! He's upstairs asleep!" She launched herself at him in a fit of anger. He grabbed both arms and held her as she struggled to be free.

As their eyes locked, she stopped struggling in his grasp. Samantha saw something in his eyes that scared her. She saw tears. Jason was crying. She saw his pain and it tore at her heart.

"I hate myself for what I did, but I did it! I switched those tags. I gave you someone else's baby. You have had so much heartache and pain. I was only trying to spare you more. I shouldn't have switched those name tags, but I did. He's not your son. Your baby died three years ago. I swear to you I am telling the truth. He's not your son. I swear to you on my son's head. I'm telling you the truth. That little boy upstairs is not yours."

"All right, Jason, let's play this out to the bitter end," she cried, angrily wrenching herself from him and wiping her wet face. "If what you are telling me is true, I should and could have you arrested. If my baby died, then whose child do I have? Whose baby did you give me? Whose child is sleeping upstairs where my son should be? Whose gray-eyed little boy did you give me?"

"Kirstin and Alex's," he said softly. All color left her face and she had to grab the table for support. Jason walked over to the fireplace and picked up the picture of Matthew. "Take a good look at Matthew, Sam. He may have your gray eyes, but he's the spitting image of his father. That was something I had no control over. When Dad told me Kirstin died after giving birth, I knew her child would be better off with you. Her baby needed a mother, and you needed a baby. I switched the name tags to give you and that baby what I thought you both needed. I robbed Alex of his son and I gave him to you. He's Alex's son, Samantha. Matthew Alexander Taylor is really Michael Alexander Carlisle."

"No," she cried, dropping down to the sofa. "Please tell me you're lying, Jason. Please tell me this is a big mistake. I can't lose my little boy all over again. Oh, God," she cried as she rocked back and forth, hugging her arms to her body.

"I did it for you, Samantha," he cried, wiping the tears from his eyes. "I swear I was only trying to spare you more pain."

This couldn't be true. This couldn't be happening. Jason was wrong. Matt is my son. He has to be. I can't lose another baby.

Jason sat down next to her on the sofa. He tried to

touch her, but Samantha jerked away from him. He repulsed her.

"I'll have all the necessary tests done first to either prove or disprove what you are saying, but if what you are saying is true then God have mercy on your soul because I know Alex won't. He will have every reason in the world to have you locked up for what you've done. Get out of my house."

"Sam, I'm sorry. I've already lost my wife, and now I've lost you too. I hope one day you will understand why I did what I did." Samantha said nothing as he left the house.

Matt was Alex and Kirstin's son. Not hers. It explained the resemblance to Alex. It explained so much. The truth was there all along for all of them to see and they ignored it. Nathan had seen it. Who else had seen it? Who else thought she was a tramp for having a child by her sister's husband?

Oh God! What am I going to do? He's not my son. My son is dead. My little baby died. Alex thinks his son died. He doesn't know that Matthew is really Michael and he's his son. I have Kirstin and Alex's child.

Alex and Matthew had a bond, and Samantha had seen it from the beginning. She thought it was because Michael and Matt were born only a few hours apart. Now she knew the real reason. They were in fact father and son.

Samantha closed her eyes, remembering the first time Matt had called Alex "daddy." They had both been a little surprised. This made them both a little uncomfortable at first.

They had tried unsuccessfully to get him to say "Uncle Alex," but he refused. He now called him "Uncle Al."

Please, God, tell me what to do. I can't lose my little boy. He needs me. I need him. I can't let Alex take him from me, but I have to tell Alex the truth. Alex is a great father. He has a right to know he has a son. This changes everything. What do I tell him? How do I tell him?

She was lost in her misery when she heard the door-bell chime. Wiping the tears from her face, she went to answer it. She opened the door, frowning when she saw Dana.

"Jason called me," Dana said. "He thought you might need me." Samantha's face crumpled. The damn broke again and Samantha cried in her best friend's arms. They cried together. When she was somewhat composed, she dried her eyes.

"What am I going to do, Dana? I don't know what to do. I can't lose my little boy. I can't believe this is happening. Matthew is Alex's son. My little boy is dead. I am so confused right now. I need to tell Alex, but I'm scared. In my heart, Matt will always be my son. Nothing will ever change that. What if Alex wants him back? I can't lose another child."

"Ssh," said Dana, hugging her. "That's not going to happen. Alex would never take Matthew from you. He loves you and he loves that little boy. He will do the right thing. You both will."

"What is the right thing? He has every right to take his son. I would if he were mine. I would want him back. Where does that leave me? I can't even face Alex right now. We were getting so close. Now this is going to destroy everything."

"Honey, it doesn't have to destroy anything," she reasoned. "This can bring the two of you closer than ever. You guys are a family."

The days that followed were hell for Samantha. She avoided Alex, because she couldn't face him. She knew she had to tell him about Matthew, but she kept putting it off.

When Alex called, she made excuses not to talk to him. She did the same thing when he came by; she made sure she was never alone with him.

Samantha knew Alex must be confused by her sudden change in behavior, but she couldn't face him yet. She couldn't tell him the truth just yet. She needed more time.

Samantha stared at the telephone for several seconds before she finally picked it up. Dialing Alex's number, she twirled the cord around her finger and waited for him to answer.

"Alex, it's Samantha," she gripped the phone tightly. "I need to talk to you. I need to see you. Can I come over right now?"

"This conversation is improving by the minute. Come on over, I'll chill the wine," he teased, hanging up the phone.

Alex stared at the phone in his hand. He already knew what she wanted to talk to him about. Jason finally told her the truth. It was the only explanation for her strange behavior the past couple of days. She knew Matt was his son.

Pacing back and forth, he waited anxiously for her to get there. Alex prayed he could pull this off. Samantha was smart and she was very perceptive. Would he be able to fool her into believing this was all a surprise for him? To do that, he had to give the performance of his life.

Samantha, forgive me for what I'm about to do. Call me a coward for taking the easy way out, but I did what I felt was the right thing to do.

Alex thought back to the past couple of weeks. He and Samantha had grown closer than ever. They were great together in bed and out. The truth could either tear them apart or bring them closer. He was praying for the second. For Alex, marriage was the logical next step in their relationship.

What will I do if she doesn't want to marry me? What if she wants things to remain as they are?

He was so lost in thought, he jumped when the doorbell rang. Taking a deep breath, he walked to the door and opened it.

"Hi, come in," said Alex, stepping back to allow her to enter. She did so hesitantly. "I've missed you." When he tried to pull her into his arms, she sidestepped him and moved a safe distance away. Samantha knew if he touched her, it would be all over. She would break down in his arms. "Samantha, what's going on?" he asked softly. "Why have you been avoiding me? Everything was fine a few days ago, and now you won't even talk to me. Did I do something wrong?"

Samantha fought back her tears as her eyes met his questioning stare. *I can't do this. I'm not ready yet.* Samantha sailed past Alex to flee the room. Anticipating her move, his arm snaked out around her waist and pulled her to him.

"Alex, don't," she pleaded, staring up into dark penetrating eyes. "Not now. I have a lot on my mind."

"If not now, when would you like to discuss our relationship?" He felt her tense in his arms as she tried to pull away. "Talk to me, damn it."

"We don't have a relationship, Alex," she said miserably fighting back her tears. "We had sex. That's all we had. Things have gotten way too complicated. I can't deal with us right now. Just forget it happened."

"But it did happen," he persisted, catching her face between his hands. "I can't forget it. I don't want to forget it, and if you are honest with yourself, you can't forget it either." She shook her head in denial as his head lowered to hers. When his mouth touched hers, she was lost. Her arms went around his neck, and she returned his hungry kiss. His hands molded her body to his, and she moaned as his hands slid down her waist to her buttocks and he pulled her closer. She felt the evidence of his desire.

"Alex, no," said Samantha, breaking the spell and moving away from him. "That's not why I'm here. We need to talk. There is something I have to tell you. I have to tell you before I lose my nerve."

"Tell me in a horizontal position," whispered the hoarse voice next to her ear. His hands slid around her waist. The cool air hit her skin as her blouse was pulled from the waistband of her jeans. Her hands covered his, and she turned in his arms to face him. "You've avoided me for the past week. You use our kids like shields to keep me at bay. You won't stay in the same room with me for more than two seconds. Today when they are all at school and I'm home alone, you call me and ask me if you can come over. What else am I supposed to think? We shared several wonderful, magical nights together and now you're acting like nothing ever happened. Our nights together are not something I can forget, and neither can you."

"I told you. I need to talk to you, not sleep with you," said Samantha, catching his caressing hands and removing them from her bottom.

"You weren't going to get any sleep," he promised as his mouth planted tiny kisses on the side of her face and down her neck. Samantha trembled as he nibbled lightly at her earlobe. She felt her resolve weakening at his practiced seduction. "I've missed you. I can't stop thinking about you in my arms all hot, wet, and eager. I want you Samantha. I want to feel you naked and panting beneath me. I'm tired of you running hot and cold. I just want you hot." His mouth moved back up to cover hers briefly.

Her breathing became shallow as his words and hands seduced her. "I love you." Those magical three words broke down her remaining resistance.

She watched, mesmerized, as one button after another popped open from her shirt. Her bra was unsnapped and the bra and blouse both fell to the floor. The first touch of his mouth on her bare breast brought Samantha to life. She moaned in pleasure and held his head to her. All thoughts of resisting died on her lips as she surrendered and pulled him closer.

"I love you too," she whispered breathlessly, pulling his shirt over his head and tossing it aside. "Make love to me, Alex."

Within the next few minutes, there was a trail of clothes leading up to Alex's bedroom. Samantha welcomed the weight of his body on hers and parted her legs eagerly for his entrance. Instead, his body slid down hers.

At the initial touch of his mouth on her, she lurched. If he hadn't been holding her down, she would have gone straight through the roof. Her body became a volcano beneath his tender assault, and she moaned loudly and had to bite her lip to keep from screaming out at the intense pleasure.

When Samantha thought she could take no more, he entered her in one smooth stroke. He took her higher and higher. She screamed out as her release came. His soon followed, and he collapsed on top of her.

Still breathing heavily, he rolled to his side, taking her with him. They stayed that way for several minutes, both panting and trying to catch their breath.

"This is so much better than talking," said Alex, absently running his fingers through her tangled mass of dark hair. Samantha lay quietly with her head resting on his chest. She made no reply to his comment. As reality began to sink in, Samantha sat up.

Throwing the covers back, she got up and went into the bathroom. She took a quick shower, dried off and wrapped a towel around her. When she went back into the bedroom, Alex was sitting up in bed.

"Please put something on and come downstairs," she said quietly. "We still need to talk." She closed the door softly behind her and she went in search of her clothes.

Well, Carlisle, you've stalled long enough. You knew this day would come. Go face the music.

He got up from the bed, took a shower, and got dressed. When he went downstairs, Samantha was fully dressed and sitting on the sofa, lost in thought.

She looked about ready to burst into tears. He watched her close her eyes and lean back on the couch. Her eyes snapped open when he leaned over and brushed his lips across hers. She didn't pull away, but she didn't respond either.

Alex sat down next to her. Their eyes met and held. She was the first to break eye contact. Looking down at her folded hands, she took a deep breath.

"Alex I don't know how to tell you this." Samantha stared at him for several seconds. Now that she had his attention, this was harder than she thought it would be. "Alex, this is the hardest thing I've ever had to say." Tears pooled in her eyes. "I don't even know where to begin." She closed her eyes and took another deep breath.

"Come on," he said softly, taking her hand, "it can't be that bad." He already knew what she was going to tell him, but he wanted to make it as painless as possible for her. He knew if she found out he'd been keeping this from her for months, it would be over between them.

"It is for me. It's actually good news for you." Samantha took another deep breath. "Matthew is your son," she whispered past the lump in her throat.

Alex stared at her, not saying a word. His heart ached at the pain in her eyes. Her tears brought tears to his eyes. He knew this was killing her and it was killing him also.

"I don't understand, Samantha," he choked out. "What are you saying?" Alex closed his eyes and prayed he could pull this off. Lying to her and pretending was harder than he had ever imagined.

"Your son lived. My son died. I think this will explain things to you better than I can." She handed him the unsigned confession Jason had given her. Samantha watched him drop down to the sofa as he began to read.

She watched the tears fall from his eyes as he read. Sitting down next to him, she put her arms around him. He returned her embrace and let the letter slip from his fingers.

The nightmare was over. Alex was overcome with emotions. He had wanted to share his feelings with her about his son, and now he could.

"Tell me this is for real," he whispered in her hair. "Tell me someone is not playing some horrible joke on us. He is really my son." Samantha raised his face to hers. Their eyes met and held. She wiped at his tears with her hand.

"It's real, Alex. I thought the same thing at first, but it's for real. I had a blood test done. Matt is not my son. The genetics are similar because Kirstin was my sister, but I'm not his mother. His type is O negative, which means he can't be Greg's son."

He came to his feet and moved away from her. This was even harder than he thought it would be, but he knew he had to be convincing or Samantha would be lost to him. Closing his eyes, he fought for control of his emotions. He was happy, relieved, and very sad for her. His anger was also very real.

"How could someone do this to us? To let me think my son had died. Wasn't it bad enough that I had lost my wife, but to make me think I had lost my son as well? How did you find out about this?" he asked, turning to face her.

"I'm not ready to tell you. I'm still having trouble believing it myself," she said through her tears. Enough lives were affected by what had happened. She didn't want to cause more pain to anyone. She was furious at her brother, but she wanted to protect her niece and sister-in-law. As much as she wanted Jason to pay for his crime, she couldn't hurt him without hurting his family. Debbie and Charlie didn't deserve that.

"Matt is my son," he said aloud. "My son didn't die. He's alive. I want to see him, Samantha. I need to see him. I need to be with him." In truth, he wanted her to see them together now that she knew the truth. He wanted to see her reaction. He wanted her to realize they all belonged together as a family.

The drive to Samantha's house was the longest drive of their lives. Both were lost in thought. Samantha was in turmoil about what would happen next. She had no idea what Alex would do after discovering Matt was really his son. Sam couldn't imagine her life without either one of them.

Alex was also going through his own personal torment. His heart ached to remember the look on Sam's face and in her eyes as she confessed the truth about Matthew. He felt her pain in every tear and expression. They found Matt and Karen in the den, playing with his building blocks. When he saw Alex, he stopped playing and jumped to his feet.

"Uncle Al," squealed the little boy, running to Alex. Alex kneeled down and waited for him with open arms. He lifted Matt in his arms and held him close. His heart melted as it did each time he held his son. It was different this time. This time the truth was out in the open.

Samantha couldn't fight back the tears as she watched Alex embrace Matt for the first time as his father. She hugged her arms to her and turned to leave the room. She couldn't stay and watch. The idea of losing her little boy tore at her heart.

"Don't go," said the emotion-filled voice. He knew her intent without looking up at her. He knew she would bolt. Alex stared at the little boy in wonder. This was his and Kirstin's son. The son he thought he had lost. He watched Samantha watch the two of them. His heart ached for her, but he knew it couldn't be helped. She needed to know the truth. He didn't want it to change in her heart. She would always be Matt's mother. They would be a family.

"Karen, I'm going out for a little while. Go ahead and start lunch. Alex would like to spend some time with his . . . with Matthew," said Samantha as she left the room abruptly. She ran from the room before Matthew could see her crying. She didn't want him to sense anything was wrong. His little world would be turned upside down soon enough.

Chapter Twelve

Samantha drove around for hours before she finally ended up at the cemetery. In the pouring rain, she got out of the car and walked to her sister's grave. Kneeling down by the graves of her sister and her son, she touched the headstone and traced the inscription with her finger. In Loving Memory of Kirstin and Michael Carlisle. Mother and son rest in peace.

"Kirstin, there's so much I have to tell you," whispered Samantha through her tears. "I don't even know where to begin." She took the picture of Matthew out of her pocket and turned it to the stone. "This is your son, Kirstin. He's a wonderful little boy. You see, there was this mix-up at the hospital and we all thought it was your son who died, but it wasn't. It was mine," cried Samantha. "My son is dead. He died the same day you and his father did. Thank you for keeping him safe for me. I'm glad he's got you to look out for him.

"Your son is strong like his father, and healthy. He even looks like his father. I tried to deny it. I didn't want to see it before, but I see it now that I know the truth. I guess it's true what they say about people seeing what they want to see. Before I knew the truth, I thought he looked like Greg. Now I know I was only kidding myself. I should have known. I should have seen Alex in him. I do see Alex in him. You would be so proud of him."

She wiped at the tears with her wet hands.

"How am I going to explain this to Matthew? How am I going to tell him his real name is Michael Carlisle? How do I tell him I'm not his mother and Alex is his father? He's so young. He's not going to understand any of this. I don't understand any of this. Why would God let something like this happen? I have lost so much already. I love him, Kirstin. I love him like he was my own little boy. What do I do now? I told Alex the truth. I had no choice. He deserved to know. I know he's going to take his son. It's only a matter of time before he tells me he wants him back. I don't think I can give him up. I know he's not mine. I know he doesn't belong to me, but I don't know if I can let him go. I can't lose another child!" she screamed collapsing on the ground. "I can't lose my son! He's mine! He'll always be mine!"

Alex stood transfixed, watching Samantha pour out her heart at her sister's grave. Guilt ripped through him like a double-edged sword. He moved into action when her heart-wrenching sobs tore at him. He pulled Samantha to her feet and enfolded her in a raincoat. She looked up into Alex's concerned face.

"I needed to explain to Kirstin what's going on. I had to tell her about her son. I had to see my son's grave. My son is gone. He's dead. I lost another baby, Alex. I can't lose Matthew too. Please don't take him from me. Please don't take my little boy," she begged, near hysteria. "Please, Alex. I'll do anything. Just don't take my son. Don't take him from me."

"Shh. It's okay," said Alex, hugging her to him. "I

would never take him from you." Her pain was his pain as he held her. His own tears mingled with the rain as he held her. "We've got to get you home and out of these wet clothes." She let him lead her to his car and push her inside.

He carried Samantha up to her room and stripped her. After drying her off, he slipped the nightgown over her head and put her to bed. He dried off as well and changed into a pair of warm-ups and T-shirt he left at the house.

Alex was guilt-ridden as he watched Samantha toss and turn on the bed. He gave her a mild sedative to calm her and make her sleep. He lay down on the bed and curled up next to her, pulling her against him, his tears wetting her hair.

I'm so sorry I had to do this to you. If you only knew how much I love you, lady. I will make this up to you if it takes the rest of our lives. I will be the best husband and father you could ever hope to have. How could you think I would take Matt from you? Don't you know me well enough to know that I could never hurt you or my son? You are his mother. He loves you.

The soft rap on the door startled him. He didn't want to release her, but he did. Wiping his face, he got to his feet and went to the door.

"I'm glad you called," Dana said softly, stepping into the room. She looked at her sleeping best friend with concern in her eyes. "How is she?"

"I gave her a sedative. She's falling apart, and it's partially my fault." He waved Dana out of the room and closed the bedroom door. She followed him downstairs to the den.

"Alex, this is not your fault," said Dana, sitting down on the sofa. "Jason is responsible for this mess. He did this to her and to you. How are you doing? This can't be easy for you."

"Dana, you don't know the half of it. I don't know what I'm supposed to do now. Where do we go from here? I thought I had it all figured out. She would find out. We would deal with it and get married. We would be a family. I knew the truth would be hard for her, but I didn't stop to think it would have this effect." Alex stopped talking as Dana stared at him strangely. He closed his eyes as he realized his slip.

"You knew about this?" she asked perceptively. "You knew Matt was your son and you let her put herself through the hell of telling you? Don't lie to me, Alex. I can see the truth in your eyes. You knew he was your son before Sam told you." He nodded and sat down on the sofa. "How long have you known about this? Never mind. I don't want to know. I don't even care. I don't even want to know if Jeremy knows about this. I thought you were in love with Samantha. Do you know the hell she has been through the past couple of days? She thinks you are going to take Matt from her. She thinks she is going to lose her child. How could you do this to her? How could you put her through this agony?"

"I'm not the one who switched the babies," he lashed back. "You can thank her brother for this mess. Do you think it's been easy for me to keep the truth from her? Who do you think made Jason come here and confess? I was tired of living the lie. The truth had to come out."

Dropping down to the sofa, he told her about his suspicions, which led him to have the nursery surveillance tape reviewed from the night of the accident. He relayed to her his confrontation with Jason.

"Sam is going to be furious at you when she finds out you knew about this. She trusts you, Alex. Why would you keep this from her? Telling you the truth had to be hell for her. You've known the truth for three weeks and you didn't tell her. She's known for three days and she confesses to you. It seems to me there is a communication problem here."

"I love Samantha and I want to marry her. I would never do anything to hurt Sam. Keeping this from her was the hardest thing I've ever done in my life"

"Then level with her. Tell her the truth. Tell her you discovered what Jason did and made him confess to her. Don't ruin what you guys have with lies. You love Sam and she loves you. Keeping this a secret is not worth the risk. Alex, you shouldn't build a marriage based on lies. The truth has an ugly way of coming out when you least expect it to."

"I'm not risking anything. I'm going to ask Samantha to marry me at Christmastime. I love her, Dana. Give me a chance to make her happy. If I can convince her to marry me, then she never has to know the truth. If Samantha marries me, then we both win. She gets to keep Matt and I get them both. We become a real family. That's all I've ever wanted. Give us that chance. Give me that chance. You're right. I should and I will tell her the truth. I just don't think she's ready to hear it right now. She's barely holding it together. This year has held a lot of surprises for her, and not pleasant ones."

"I can agree with you there. I'm ready for this year to be over. Give her a little time to adjust to you being Matt's father before you spring this on her, but don't wait too long. The sooner she knows, the better, and the sooner you guys can put this behind you."

The next day, Samantha called an old colleague of hers for lunch. Clint Walker was one of the best child-custody lawyers she knew. She had to find out from a legal standpoint where she stood in case Alex wanted his son back.

Before saying anything, she handed him a dollar. It was a retainer so their conversation would be kept strictly confidential. After he agreed, Samantha explained the situation to him.

"Oh boy. Samantha, I'm sorry to have to say this, but you really don't have a legal leg to stand on. Matthew is Alex's biological son. You have a blood test that proves he is not your son. Alex has a test that proves he is his son. If this goes to court, it could get real ugly. The person who switched the babies would go to prison for a very long time. There would be legal ramifications for the hospital. Not to mention it would ruin any relationship you and Alex have. Even if you got a sympathetic jury, I personally think you would still lose. You have no legal claim to the child."

Samantha's heart constricted and tears welled up in her eyes. "I've loved him and taken care of him for three years. Doesn't that count for something?" Clint shook his head sadly. "Are you saying Alex could just walk into my house and take him from me and it would be within his rights as Matthew's father?" she asked, wiping her tears.

"If you could prove he was unfit to raise Matthew, then you would have a chance. Even then, there are no guarantees." Samantha shook her head. She would never tell that lie. Alex was a wonderful father. He was a father to Hope as well. "You're not giving me much to work with here. Do we have any grounds? How about moral issues?"

She shook her head again. "Alex is a wonderful father. He's Matthew's and Hope's godfather. I can't put this family through a custody fight. It would tear us apart." Samantha closed her eyes as tears fell.

"There is possibly another way you can keep him. How well do you and Alex get along? Do you think he would agree to a joint custody agreement? Matthew could live with you six months and with Alex for six months. That way you could still retain partial custody and have visitation rights."

Samantha shook her head emphatically. "Alex would never go for that. I wouldn't do that to my son. I will not shuffle him back and forth like luggage. There has to be another solution. What am I going to do, Clint? I can't lose my little boy."

"How close are you to your brother-in-law?" Clint asked, watching her closely. Samantha flushed hotly, unable to meet his eyes. "That close. You don't need a lawyer, Samantha. You need a minister. Marry Alex. Problem solved. I hate to skip out on you, but I've got to be in court in an hour. Let me know if you want to pursue this legally, but I have to warn you as a friend I think you would be wasting your money. Marry the man and be happy."

Samantha lay across her bed, lost in thought. She would not put Alex or her family through another custody fight. Everyone still bore the scars from the last one, especially Alex.

Shortly after Kirstin's death, Alex was served with papers. Jack Randolph, Derek's biological grandfather, was suing Alex for sole custody. It didn't matter to him that Alex had legally adopted Derek when he and Kirstin married or that Derek loved his father and wanted to stay with him. Derek was a possession to him. He wanted an heir. Someone he could control.

Sylvia Randolph, Jack's ex-wife, had immediately taken Alex's side. Unlike her ex-husband, she wanted what was best for her grandson. She wanted Derek to have a normal, happy life. She knew Alex and Samantha could give him that.

Jack's private detective was a busy boy digging up dirt on Alex. The local tabloids had a field day with all the stories Jack was feeding them. They had a lot to work with. In Alex's day, he'd been as wild as they come.

The hospital where Alex worked had to hire extra security to keep the reporters out of the ER where Alex was working. Reporters followed Alex everywhere he went.

That was the first time Samantha had seen Alex and Nathan on the same side. Nathan helped the same tabloid do an expose on Jack Randolph.

Things were not looking very favorable when Sylvia suggested to Alex and Samantha they should get married right away. She tried to convince them this would improve Alex's chances of retaining custody. Alex's lawyer and her father agreed with Sylvia, but Alex and Samantha both said an emphatic no. They were both still mourning the loss of their loved ones and would not even consider it as an option.

Samantha didn't go unscathed either. The tabloids had hinted she and Alex were having a hot and heavy affair. The reporters would camp out at her home, hoping to see or hear something.

The judge ordered Derek to have several counseling sessions with a social worker. The same social worker also interviewed Jack, Alex, Samantha, Sylvia, Nathan, and Laura. In her final report, she thought it was in the best interest of the child to remain with his father and sister.

They all went through four months of pure hell. Jack repeatedly taunted Samantha, telling her that when he won she would never see her nephew again.

When the judge made the decision to leave Derek in Alex's custody, they all shed tears of joy. Outside the courtroom, Nathan saved Alex from what would been aggravated assault.

When Jack threw racial slurs at Samantha, Alex lunged for him. Nathan, knowing it was a deliberate attempt to make Alex look bad, grabbed his son-in-law and held him back before he could land a blow.

The nightmare was over, but their lives would never be the same again. Derek would always be scarred by what happened. The memories would always be with them.

Wiping the tears from her eyes, Samantha sat up in bed. Hugging her knees to her chest, she sat staring off into space.

Why not marry Alex? It would solve all our problems. We could raise Matt and all the children together as a family. Why not? I love him and he loves me. Okay, so loving someone and wanting to spend the rest of your life with them are two entirely different things, but it could work. We could make it work.

The more she thought about it, the more sense it made. There wouldn't be a need for joint or shared custody. No more sneaking around. No more stolen moments. They could live together openly as man and wife.

She jumped up from the bed and ran from the room. Trotting down the stairs, she came up short when the front door opened.

"Hi." Alex closed the door behind him. "I rang the bell, but I guess you didn't hear it in your bedroom." Her eyes drank in the sight of him in blue jeans and a black T-shirt. His biceps bulged as his arms swung at his side as he moved towards her.

"I've been meaning to get that fixed. I was coming to see you. I'm glad you're here. We need to talk." He held out his arms to her and she walked into them. Samantha let out a sigh of relief as strong capable arms closed around her.

She needed his love and his strength now, more than

ever. Samantha felt safe and secure in his arms. She breathed in the masculine scent of Alex, which was mixed with her favorite cologne. They stayed that way for several seconds.

"I've missed you. How are you holding up?" Alex asked, leading her over to the sofa with his arms still around her.

"I've been better," she admitted, sitting down next to him. "I can't seem to get my mind to shut off. Alex, what are we going to do about Matt? I've gone over so many scenarios in my head."

"Sam, I have a suggestion. It's three weeks until Christmas. Let's not make any plans until after the holidays. Let's put this on hold for now." She stared at him in surprise. Of all the things she expected him to say, this was not one of them. "No decision has to be made right away. Let's leave things as they are for now."

"You're serious about this?" she asked, looking up at him, puzzled. "You want to put all of this on hold until after the holidays?"

"Totally," he said caressing her cheek. "Honey, no matter what, we will always be family. Let's spend Christmas as a family. I want you and the kids to spend Christmas Eve and Christmas night at my house." His head lowered and touched her lips softly. "Say yes." A smile split her beautiful face.

"I'm still thinking," she smiled pulling his head back down to hers. She rose up and kneeled on the couch, not breaking the kiss. Pressing him down to the couch, her body lay on top of his. Alex let out a groan of pleasure as her firm breasts pressed into his chest. "I'm still thinking. He's aggressive, demanding, and pushy." His hands slid caressingly up her bare calves. "Yet he is also very generous with his favors." Pushing her soft knit dress upward, his hands glided up her thighs. Heat spread quickly through her body under his practiced seduction. "He has a vivid imagination." He slowly peeled the bikini panties down her legs. "He always takes the hands-on approach." Samantha caught his roaming hands and pulled her panties up again. "How can I say no to those qualities? Yes, but no sneaking into my bed when the kids are sleep."

"Deal." He kissed her parted lips as her eyes narrowed on him. "You sneak into my bed," he laughed. Still laughing, they kissed. "Damn, you're easy. I thought you would require more convincing," he said, hooking his fingers in the waistband of her panties and trying to ease them down once again. "Am I going to have to fight you to get these off?"

"I'm starting to have second thoughts. Maybe this isn't such a good idea after all. I think I require more convincing," she responded meeting his hungry kiss. She broke the kiss long enough to pull the shirt over his head and toss it aside. "I'll let you know in about an hour if you've persuaded me." She pulled his head back down to hers.

Alex watched in appreciation as she slipped the dress over her head and smoothed it down. She ran her fingers through her hair to remove some of the tangles. When she looked up at Alex, she smiled and walked toward him.

"Do you have anything planned for this weekend?" She shook her head. "Good. How about a trial run?" he asked, stepping into his jeans and snapping them closed.

"I thought that's what we just had," she laughed, running her hands over his bare chest. She planted small kisses on it. The coarse hairs tickled her face. His arms went around her.

"Not that kind of trial run," he reprimanded, slapping her on the bottom. "I mean a family trip. How about packing up the kids and spending the weekend at my lake house in Palestine? We could take the boat out on the lake, do some fishing, and maybe have a picnic. We need to take games and puzzles, because there is no television."

"Sounds great, but you'd better not tell the kids there's no TV, or they'll try and boycott this trip. We've never been together for the weekend before. It should be quite interesting."

"That's putting it mildly. This will give us an idea of what we're letting ourselves in for at Christmas." Samantha looked down at her watch.

"I'm running late. Can you pick up Matt for me? I love you." Her lips brushed his lightly before she flew out the door.

"Sure." He responded to the empty room as Sam sailed out the door. Alex was smiling as he watched her leave. Things were working out as he'd planned.

Chapter Thirteen

Alex took them out to dinner. After dinner, they went back to his house, where they decorated the Christmas tree and listened to Christmas music.

Samantha smiled as she stood in the doorway with the tray of hot chocolate. Everyone pitched in to decorate the tree. They were all smiles as they sang along with an Oleta Adams Christmas DVD and worked together like a team. Alex lifted Matt to put the star on top of the tree.

This is what family is all about. Samantha prayed things would work out for her and Alex to make their family official.

Over hot chocolate, they told the kids about their weekend trip to the cabin. The kids were excited about the trip. This was their first trip to the country. It was also Samantha's. Alex had grown up in East Texas, so this was like going home for him.

Sam had no idea what to pack for her and the kids until Alex made her a list. He specifically put on the list that no electronics were to leave the jeep. Everyone could play games or whatever on the way there, but once they got there, the no-electronics rule went into effect. He was going to make sure they all got back to nature.

The drive down to the lake was so beautiful and peaceful. Alex hummed along with an old Stevie Wonder song while he drove. They passed several cars on the interstate, but once he turned off the main road, theirs was the only car on the road.

Samantha looked back to see what the kids were doing. Matt, of course, was sleeping. He always fell asleep on long drives. Derek and Lexi were each listening to their Walkman radios, while Hope watched a movie on her portable DVD player.

The cabin was larger on the inside than it looked from the outside. It was actually quite spacious. There were two bedrooms, two bathrooms, a full living room, and a kitchen complete with dining-room table. The furniture was all sturdy wood. The couch folded out into a queen bed.

Alex opened a back door and ushered them all outside onto the deck, which overlooked the lake. He told them they could fish right off the deck.

Alex gave Samantha and Matt the master. He and Derek took the other bedroom, and they put the girls on the sofa sleeper.

The kids threw a fit and pouted upon discovering there was no television and no cable in the cabin. Derek and Lexi both insisted they could not live without television for two whole days. Matt and Hope didn't seem to mind.

Alex woke everyone up bright and early the next morning. After breakfast, he took them onto the deck to fish.

Samantha was glad she remembered her camera as she watched Alex try and teach the girls to bait their hooks. Neither of them wanted to touch the wiggling worms. Derek called them a bunch of wimps, and that was chal-

lenge enough. They all picked one up and at least tried
to bait the hook. Samantha took several pictures of them.

Derek was the first one to reel in a catfish. He held it
up proudly as Samantha took a picture. Not to be out-
done, the girls settled down and tried to outdo him.
They each ended up catching a fish. After the first hour,
the girls went back inside the cabin. Alex caught the
most, while Samantha helped Matt catch his first fish.
The girls came back out a few minutes later with snacks
for everyone.

"Hey guys, who's going to give me a hand cleaning
these babies?" asked Alex holding up the trout line of fish.

"Gross!" the girls chorused, backing away, disgusted by
the suggestion. Alex and Derek laughed at the girls.

"Not a chance, Uncle Alex. I touched a worm. I'm not
touching a dead fish," said Hope, fleeing back to the
cabin with Lexi following on her heels.

"I'm with them." Samantha smiled going back into the
cabin. She showered and changed and started dinner
preparations. She waited patiently for them to clean and
bring in the main course.

"Don't touch those babies," said Alex, putting the fish
in the sink. "I'll cook them. No one can cook fish like a
country boy. I'll do the honors as soon as I shower and
change."

"I'll gladly let you, Mr. Chef," laughed Samantha, wrin-
kling up her nose and holding up her hands in surrender.

He winked as he left the room. Alex took a quick
shower and returned to the kitchen to prepare his feast.
He had changed into a pair of sweatpants and a T-shirt.

Samantha smiled as she watched Alex in the kitchen
preparing their meal. He seemed right at home in the
kitchen. Minutes later, the mouth-watering aroma of
frying catfish and hush puppies filled the cabin.

They dined on catfish, hush puppies, and fries for

dinner. After dinner they played board games. Alex motioned for Samantha to join him out back on the deck.

Pulling on her jacket, she followed him out the door. Alex slipped up behind her, and put his arms around her waist. She hugged his arms to her.

"It's beautiful out here," said Alex, kissing her neck and holding her close. "I'm glad we came. The kids seem to be having a good time."

"So am I." She turned in his arms. "We should do this more often. I love the peace and quiet out here. I also love you." She pulled his head back down to hers and showed him how much with her mouth.

Samantha and Alex had no shared moments alone after that night. He pulled her to him and kissed her passionately in front of the kids. He told the kids they might as well get used to seeing the two of them expressing their feelings. They cuddled on the couch each night before bedtime.

When Alex suggested they make a campfire, the kids loved the idea. He even brought marshmallows and graham crackers for s'mores.

Samantha smiled in remembrance of her Scouting days. She was not in it long, but long enough for it to have had a lasting impression.

She still remembered her first camping trip away from home. Although they were in cabins and not tents, the trip held fond memories. She made some lifelong friends in Girl Scouts.

Alex talked about his Scouting days as a boy. After telling of the fun camping trips and things he did, Derek wanted to join the Scouts. Alex promised to register him when they got back home.

Their weekend trip was a success. They swam, fished and sat around talking. They ate all meals together as a family. Of course, they had a few skirmishes. When didn't Hope and Derek argue about something?

Samantha and the girls took Matt on a nature hike while Alex took Derek out in the boat. She wanted to give them some much-needed time alone.

For the past couple of months, Alex had been working long hours. He needed this weekend to kick back and relax.

They drove back on Sunday afternoon. The kids were all upstairs, and Samantha and Alex were relaxing on the couch after their exhausting weekend. He caught her hand and pulled her to him.

"I would love more than anything to make love to you right now, but I don't have the energy," he laughed.

"Me either." She smiled up at him. "You'll have to settle for a kiss." She leaned over and kissed him on the cheek. "That's the best I can do right now. Even my lips are tired. Could you believe it when the kids asked to go back again? Do you think Derek was serious about Scouts?"

"I hope so. I think it would be good for him. Not to change the subject, but I think we should tell Greg's mother about Matt," said Alex, kissing her hand. "I think we should do it together. Aunt Edna has been a big part of my life. I'll call Ted and have him meet us there. We may as well go tomorrow evening when I get off work."

"Okay, but there is someone else we need to tell as well," she agreed, moving into his open arms. "We also have to tell my parents."

Alex pulled Samantha into his arms for a quick kiss before ringing the doorbell at her parents' house. Her arms went around him and he dipped her.

"What was that for?" she asked, smiling and wiping her lipstick from his mouth. Her hand caressed his cheek.

"Moral support. Courage. Because I wanted to kiss you," he answered, kissing her again and again. His lips had barely left hers when the door opened.

"Hi," said Laura, smiling and hugging Samantha and then Alex. "Come on in. What's going on, you two? Why the mystery?"

"Do tell." Nathan looked from his daughter to his son-in-law questioningly, "What's he done this time?" He nodded in Alex's direction.

"Can we at least sit down before you attack the man I love?" Samantha was ready to do battle for the man she loved. "I think we should all sit down." They followed her parents into the living room and took seats on the sofa. Alex held her hand for support. "Dad, there is something we have to tell you about Matthew," said Samantha, playing with her hands.

"Matthew is Alex's son," Nathan finished, coming to his feet and turning away from his daughter in disappointment. He walked over to the fireplace and took the photo of Alex and Matt down. Walking back to her, he handed it to her. Samantha studied the picture. Now that she knew the truth, she could also see the unmistakable resemblance. "Take a good look." Nathan sat back down. "Did Kirstin and Greg know about your affair? Did they know there was a possibility that your baby could be Alex's?"

"You have it all wrong, Dad, or at least most of it. Of course the baby was Alex's." It took her only a second to realize what he had said and how bad her reply sounded. She crossed her arms defensively and glared back at her father.

"Nathan, you never cease to amaze me," Alex said. "I see you're still holding onto the crazy notion that Sam and I had an affair. You couldn't be more wrong. I was faithful to my wife until the day she died. I thought you knew Samantha better than that. How could you possibly believe she slept with her sister's husband?"

"She wouldn't be the first woman or man to cheat on her spouse. You explain it to me, then. Matthew is your son. That much I've known all along. Didn't you think anyone would notice the resemblance? I'm not stupid."

"That's debatable," Alex shot back, scowling at Nathan. The two furious men stood toe-to-toe, glaring at each other. "You are way off-base, Nathan, in your thought process as usual."

"That's enough from both of you. This is not getting us anywhere." Laura stepped between Nathan and Alex, trying to diffuse the situation. "Nathan, sit down. Alex, sit down. Samantha what is going on? You've just admitted Matthew is Alex's son. Tell us the rest of the story, because unlike your father, I don't believe either of you cheated on your spouse."

"We did not sleep together." Samantha dropped back down to the sofa. Laura came over and sat next to her. Her eyes met those of her stepmother. Taking a deep breath, she looked directly at her father. "Matt is Alex's son, but he's not my little boy. My little boy died. Matt is Kirstin and Alex's son." Her father's head shot up in surprise. Nathan rose to his feet again. "The night of the accident, one of the babies died. Someone was there outside the nursery watching. When my baby died, he switched the name tags. He thought, at the time, that he was doing the right thing for me." She looked up to see the tears run down her father's face.

"Who is responsible for this? I will make sure he goes to jail for a very long time. As district attorney, I will prosecute him to the fullest extent of the law. I promise you he will not get away with this." Torn, Samantha looked away. She couldn't bring herself to tell her father it was his son, Jason.

Alex saw her suffering and as much as he wanted to see Jason pay for what he had done, he didn't want to hurt Nathan any more than Samantha did. He had to stall him.

"I've already taken care of it. Let me handle things my way. I promise you he won't get away with it. Just leave it alone."

"No way! You handle things your way and I will handle them mine. The person responsible for this will not get away with this. He's turned your lives upside down. He should be brought to justice. I will make sure he goes to jail for a very long time. Now, tell me. Who did this? Who switched those babies?"

"Jason." The name was torn from Samantha's throat. She watched all the wind leave her father as he stared from her to Alex. Her stepmother rushed to her father and caught his arm. He dropped down to the sofa shattered. "I'm sorry Dad. I didn't mean to blurt it out like that. Jason came to see me a few weeks ago. He told me what he did and why he did it."

"Jason did this?" said the tortured voice. "Your own brother did this. He took Kirstin's son and gave him to you." His voice faded out as he got up and paced the room. "What possessed him to do something like this? I didn't want to believe you and Alex were having an affair, but I knew Matthew was his son. God, what a mess."

"Jason said he did it for me," said Samantha, fighting back the tears. "Matthew is my son. He will always be my son."

"You are right. He is your son, honey, in all the ways that matter. Kirstin would have wanted him to be with you. She would have wanted you and Alex to raise him. So what happens now?" He turned to face Alex. "I'm sorry." Those two words were filled with pain and regret.

"Now that the truth is out, we take one day at a time. Sam and I are tabling any decision about this until after Christmas."

"Samantha, there is someone else you have to tell. Greg's mother needs to know the truth. If she has this same picture of Alex and Matt, then she might have come to the same conclusion I did. I think you and Alex need to tell Edna the truth as well."

"I know, Dad. Alex and I are going by to see her tomorrow night." She welcomed her father's embrace.

Sam called Karen to come over and sit for the kids while she and Alex went out. On the ride out to Duncanville, they discussed the best approach to telling Greg's mother the truth. Sam thought she should be the one to tell her. Alex thought it might be better coming from him. In the end, they decided to tell her together.

Alex and Samantha sat uncomfortably in Edna Taylor's living room, sipping lemonade. Sam wasn't sure how to bring up the subject of Matt, and neither was Alex. She knew Alex was stalling until Ted and Anita got there.

Ted was Greg's younger brother, and Anita was his wife. Alex had already told them what happened. They knew Edna would need Ted after they told her the truth.

When the doorbell finally rang, Samantha jumped. Alex's hand covered hers and gave it a supportive squeeze. The movement was not lost on Mrs. Taylor as she came to her feet and went to answer the door.

After everyone exchanged handshakes and hugs, they all sat down. Alex didn't even know where to start with the tale. It sounded unbelievable even to him, but he had seen the tapes.

"Aunt Edna, there's something we have to tell you,"

said Alex softly. "I wish for your sake we didn't have to tell you this, but we do. I'll make this story as short as I can. The night of Greg and Kirstin's accident, a baby died in the nursery." Ted caught his mother's hand and put his arm around her. "I thought—and so did everyone else—that it was my son, Michael." He paused briefly. "Someone switched the identification tags on the babies. It wasn't my son who died. It was Greg and Samantha's baby. Greg's son died the night he did. Matthew is really my son Michael."

"Oh God," said the older woman, closing her eyes. Her teary eyes opened and she met Alex's gaze. "That explains a lot. Matt is so much like you. I didn't want to believe that he wasn't Greg's son. I prayed on it and tried not to think bad thoughts about you and Samantha." Her eyes met Samantha's. "Honey, I'm so sorry. I know how much you and Greg wanted a son. Are you okay? This must have been a terrible shock for you." Samantha nodded, not trusting her voice to speak. "When did you find out about this? How did you find this out?"

"A few weeks ago, the person who switched the babies confessed," replied Samantha softly, fighting for control of her emotions. She thought the retelling of the story would get easier, but it hadn't. It still tore at her soul. "It came as a shock to all of us. I didn't see the resemblance either. Now I look at Matt and I can't miss it. He looks more and more like Alex every day." Alex caught Samantha's hand and kissed it.

"There's more, isn't there?" Aunt Edna asked, intuitively looking from one to the other. "Let's hear the rest of it."

"Well, we hope this is good news." Alex smiled. "Samantha and I are in love."

Aunt Edna looked from one to the other in silence. Finally, she smiled and got up and hugged both of them.

"My prayers have been answered. I was hoping you two would get together. I bet those kids are thrilled. I'm happy for you both."

"There's one more thing I need to tell you," Alex said. "Greg had an affair while he and Samantha were married. A son was born from that affair. Is it okay if Betsy brings Joshua by for you to meet him?"

Mrs. Taylor was crying and nodding her head at the same time. She lost one grandson, but gained another one. Her eyes went to Samantha's face.

"It's okay, Mrs. Taylor. I've made peace with it. Joshua is your grandson. You should spend time with him. Greg would have wanted you to."

Chapter Fourteen

The weeks and days leading up to Christmas were hectic for everyone. Laura called Samantha to tell her Nathan had flown out to Oregon to confront Jason. They had a knock-down, drag-out fight, and their father disowned him.

Samantha tried to talk to her father about Jason, but he refused to listen. He made his decision and it was final. He didn't want to see or ever talk about Jason again.

She knew he was upset, so she let the subject drop for now, but she was not giving up on her father or her brother. Samantha realized if she couldn't forgive Jason, why should their father? She made peace with what he did. Part of her even forgave him. She now understood his motives. He wasn't trying to hurt her. In his own way, Jason was trying to help her.

Pushing all the unhappy thoughts aside, she and the kids decorated the house and front yard. While the kids were at school, she dropped Matt off at his Mother's Day Out playgroup and finished up her Christmas shopping. She had to get it done today because today was the last day of school before Christmas break.

She picked up the frozen Cajun turkey for Christmas dinner, stopped by the grocery store and took everything to Alex's house. Samantha gave his housekeeper the night off and set about preparing dinner. She made chicken cacciatore for her and Alex and spaghetti for the kids. Mixing a large salad, she placed it in the refrigerator. She sliced the garlic bread and put in on the tray. She would heat it right before dinner. Turning off the oven, she left the house to pick up the children.

When she'd talked to Alex earlier today, he was having a rough day. His partner and the nurse practioner were both out sick with the flu. He was running the whole show solo today.

Dinner at his place would be a surprise. She told him to call her when he was on his way home. Her plan was to run him a nice, relaxing Jacuzzi bath. She would give him about half an hour in the tub to unwind before dinner.

Alex phoned and Samantha put her plan in motion. She jogged up the stairs to his bedroom and ran his bathwater. She also lit candles and placed them around the tub. Soft jazz filled the air. She set the rum and coke on the windowsill.

Samantha greeted Alex with a kiss. He hugged her to him. Catching his hand, she led him upstairs to his bedroom. The heady aroma of food filled the air. He sniffed appreciatively and smiled.

"You have half an hour to soak and relax." She opened the door and led him into his bedroom. Opening the double doors to the bathroom, she pulled him inside.

"Wow." He looked around the room in amazement. Smiling, he pulled her into his arms. "Thanks. What did I do to deserve this?"

"Everyone needs to be pampered occasionally. You have half an hour, Doc. Make the most of it." She kissed him and moved out of his arms. "Dinner should be ready by the time you're finished soaking. I've given the kids strict instructions not to bother you for at least half an hour. I'm not sure if I can hold them off any longer. If you're not downstairs by dinnertime, I'm coming after you."

Samantha closed the door behind her, smiling. She was glad she'd done this for Alex. He looked tired. She hoped these few minutes of relaxation would help.

She was halfway down the stairs when she heard escalated voices. Samantha rushed down the stairs to the den.

"Derek likes Chelsea," taunted Hope. As usual, she was witnessing an argument between Derek and Hope. They were standing toe to toe glaring at each other.

"I do not!" he yelled, glaring at her. "I don't even like girls. You like David. I saw what you wrote about him in your diary."

"You read my diary? How could you? It's private." She lunged for him and Samantha stepped between the two angry children.

"Derek and Chelsea sitting in the tree," chimed Lexi. Samantha sent her a sharp look and she stopped.

"That's enough!" she whistled. "Everyone sit down and be quiet. Alex is upstairs taking a bath. When he comes downstairs I don't expect him to walk into the middle of a war zone. We are going to have a nice relaxing evening together or you two are grounded. Derek, you had no right to read her diary. It was none of your business." As he started to speak, she held up her hand. "I don't want to hear any more from either of you. I don't care who started it this time. I'm ending it now. I'm going to finish dinner. Derek and Hope, you can set the table."

"Yes ma'am," they chorused, both crossing their arms

across their chest. Giving each other one last glare, they both left the room.

Dinner was ready and on the table, but Alex was a no-show. Samantha decided to go upstairs and check on him.

When she opened the door to the bathroom, she smiled. Alex was asleep in the Jacuzzi. His head was resting on an inflatable pillow and his face was relaxed in sleep.

She quietly walked over to him and kneeled down beside the tub. Her hand reached out and caressed his face.

"Alex, it's time for dinner," she said softly. His eyes came open and he smiled back at her. "I'm glad to see you so relaxed." Sitting on the edge of the tub, she massaged his the stiff muscles of his shoulders. His head rolled from side to side.

"That feels wonderful," he moaned. She leaned over and dropped a kiss on his shoulder. "Ooh, that feels even better. I guess I was more tired than I realized." Standing up, she held out the towel for him. Letting the water out, he got to his feet. Samantha stared at him in all his naked glory. Her heartbeat quickened at the sight of water trickling down his torso. She would never get tired of looking at him naked. He stepped out of the tub and she enfolded him in the towel. He leaned over and gave her a soft kiss. "Thanks for always knowing what I need."

"I laid a pair of warm-ups on the bed for you. I'll see you downstairs." Blowing him a kiss, she sailed out of the room.

They spent Christmas Eve sitting around laughing and talking. They watched *A Christmas Carol* and then listened to Christmas music. The doorbell rang and, smiling, Alex went to answer it.

"I'll get it. Sam, why don't you come with me?" He winked, holding out his hand to her. She caught it and let him pull her to her feet. Outside in the hallway, he took her into his arms. "I thought I'd never get you alone." Their mouths met in a hungry kiss. Her lips parted, and his tongue plunged into her waiting mouth. Samantha clung to him and returned his kiss eagerly. His hands explored her feverish body. He maneuvered them towards the front door without breaking the kiss. The bell rang again.

"You'd better get that," said the throaty breathless voice. "As much as I would like to finish this, I don't want to shock the children if one of them should happen to come to investigate."

"I know you're right, but it's been weeks since we've made love. If you don't find a way to be alone with me soon, I'm going to explode." He pressed a hard kiss to her lips before taking a step back. Catching her hand, he pulled her with him to the door. Still smiling, he opened the door.

"Looks like I missed all the fun," teased Keith, looking from one to the other. "That shade of lipstick does nothing for you bro."

"Very funny." Alex smiled, wiping his mouth and then embracing his younger brother warmly. "You're late. What kept you, or should I say who kept you?"

"I'll never tell, but believe me when I say she was well worth it. Hello, beautiful." Keith smiled, hugging Samantha.

"Hello, Keith," she said returning his warm greeting. "It's good to see you again. I left a plate for you in the refrigerator if you're hungry."

"A woman after my own heart. Samantha, I still think

you are with the wrong brother," he teased. "I could show you the world."

"I kind of like my feet being firmly planted in one spot," she teased. "The minute I started talking about marriage and more children you would run for your life and you know it."

Keith backed away holding up his hands in surrender. They laughed at the truth behind her words. They all knew Keith was gun-shy about commitment.

Alex slipped his arms around her waist and pulled her against him. Samantha's hands caressed his at her waist.

"You two look happy. I'm glad. It's about time. So, bro, when are you going to make an honest woman of her?" Samantha blushed and Alex kissed her neck.

"You'll be the first to know little brother. Follow me," said Alex, changing the subject. "The kids can't wait to see you."

Samantha and Alex stood back as they heard the excited squeals of the children at seeing Keith. He hugged each of them. They adored their Uncle Keith, and the feeling was mutual.

They talked for hours until it was bedtime. Samantha went upstairs with the kids to tuck them in. This gave the brothers time alone to catch up.

"You look happy." Keith smiled as he surveyed his older brother. "I'm glad. You deserve it. You both do. You know I think the world of Samantha."

"I know you do. I think the world of her too, but I guess I don't need to tell you that. Tomorrow night, I'm going to ask her to marry me," confided Alex.

"I think it's wonderful. From the look on her face earlier, I'd say you're a shoe-in. You are one lucky man. Samantha is one in a million. Are you going to tell her you uncovered the truth about Matt?"

"Eventually," said Alex coming to his feet. "Keith, I

know I'm digging myself into a hole, but I don't want to lose Sam."

"You won't. She loves you. Alex, I don't think you should start off your engagement with a lie. She needs to know the truth. You've got to tell her. Think about how bad it will turn out if she doesn't find out the truth from you, but from someone else. What if Jason tells her it was you who uncovered his plot?"

"Jason's in enough trouble right now. I don't think he will say anything to her." Alex took a deep, steadying breath. "Enough about me. How are you?" Alex asked changing the subject. "Are you still running from commitment and sticking to your two-date rule?"

"I should have, and then I wouldn't be rethinking my life right now," Keith laughed uneasily. "I let my guard down and met someone."

"What do you mean let your guard down? Your guard is never up and you're always meeting someone," Alex laughed.

"This time is different." Keith held up his hand to silence the retort on his brother's lips. "I know I've said this before, too, but this time is different. Candace is different from any woman I've ever met before. She's so like me it scares me to death. She's more afraid of commitment than I am. We've gone out for about a month." Alex's brow rose in surprise. "That's right, one month exclusively dating the same woman."

Alex tried unsuccessfully to control himself, but he couldn't help it. It started out as a snicker and turned into sidesplitting laughter. He doubled over with laughter as he stared at his younger brother.

"I don't see a damn thing funny," said Keith.

"I do," laughed Alex, wiping the tears from his eyes. "You know what they say about payback." Keith rolled his eyes at Alex. "You have played this game for how many years with how many women?"

"Where's the sympathy I'm supposed to get from you?" asked Keith getting to his feet and pacing the room in frustration.

"What sympathy? I love you kid, but you get as good as you give. Your comeuppance is long overdue." Keith dropped back to the couch. "I am just glad I'm still around to see it happen." Alex started laughing again. He couldn't help it. It was about time his little brother got what was coming to him. "So is she a beautiful airhead like the rest of your harem?"

"I don't have a harem. I consider myself a collector. No, I'm a connoisseur of women. You collect sports cards, while I collect beautiful, sexy women. To answer your question, no she is not like all the rest. Candace is a psychiatrist."

Again Alex doubled over with uncontrollable laughter, slapping his leg. "You've got to be kidding, you and a shrink? Boy, does she have her hands full. I can see why she has a problem with commitment if she's dating you. She probably sees right through your bull."

"Thanks, bro. I knew I could count on you to have my back. Where's the love around here? I am not feeling it."

"Hey, I'm being honest. You're my brother and I love you, but I'm not wearing blinders. You've broken heart after heart. Every dog has his day. No pun intended. There's plenty of love, kid. There's also honesty. I know you and I know your track record. If Candace is wise, she will run as fast as her feet can take her in the opposite direction."

"Gee, thanks," said Keith sarcastically. "Since you are not taking this conversation seriously, let's talk about something else. Let's talk about you and the gorgeous Samantha. So when are you proposing?"

"Tomorrow night. Can you entertain the kids for at least an hour before the proposal and for the rest of the night after we tell them?"

"Not a problem. Maybe I'll invite Candace over. She flew in with me. She's spending Christmas with her brother. He lives in Plano."

"Invite her over. I'd love to meet her. I can give her my condolences," teased Alex, smiling at his brother.

Christmas morning the kids woke the adults bright and early to open presents. Alex held the camcorder while Keith took pictures. He set the camcorder on the tripod and joined in the fun.

The girls had stacked the presents by name the previous night. Alex dove into his pile of presents with the zest of a child.

Samantha smiled as she watched her family. She and Alex hadn't discussed their future, but Sam was sure a wedding was in the plan. It was their logical next step.

After the holiday, she and Alex would have a serious discussion about the past, present and future. Marriage seemed like the only logical avenue for them to take. It was surely the only win-win situation.

"Hey, Samantha, get in the picture," said Keith, motioning her over to her family. Smiling, Samantha moved quietly on slipper-covered feet to join the group. Her red silk pajamas swished as she walked.

Catching her hand, Alex pulled her down on the carpeted floor beside him. The kids covered her in her untouched stack of presents.

"Pick one, Mom," said Matt, excitedly holding out a present he obviously wrapped for her. Smiling, she took the package out of his hand. Samantha ripped into the paper with Matt's help. She laughed when she saw the Betty Boop nightshirt. She held it up to her.

"I love it. Thank you, sweetheart." She hugged him to her. "Who's next?" she asked, smiling and waiting for someone to hand her another present. Matt assisted her in opening all her presents. Her hand shook when she got to the small box from Alex. In her heart she was praying for a ring, but instinct told her it wasn't. She unwrapped the box and opened the lid. She gasped at the beautiful heart-shaped diamond necklace twinkling back at her. "It's beautiful." Her eyes met Alex's. She took the necklace out of the box and put in on.

"You will always have my heart," said Alex leaning over and planting a soft kiss on her lips. "Always," he promised.

"And you have mine," she smiled. Their lips met again in a soft kiss. They were oblivious to the camera flashing around them.

"Okay, enough with the mushy stuff. Who wants breakfast?" asked Keith. "I'm cooking. Kids, why don't you guys come out and help me?"

Samantha and Alex were looking at each other and barely noticed everyone leaving the room. Alex leaned over and kissed her again. This time there was no rush in the lazy exploration of his mouth and tongue.

"Merry Christmas, my love," he whispered against her lips. Alex got to his feet and pulled her with him.

"Merry Christmas," she repeated. Hand in hand they walked out to the kitchen to help with breakfast.

Her father and stepmother called after breakfast to wish them a Merry Christmas. They were spending Christmas in Hawaii. He and Laura spoke with each of the kids.

The girls pitched in to get everything ready for Christmas dinner while Alex and Keith set the table. Derek kept Matt entertained and out of the kitchen.

Later that evening, they all sat around the beautifully decorated formal dining table. It was set with the good china and crystal glasses. A beautiful poinsettia floral arrangement decorated it.

The heady aroma of turkey, corn-bread dressing and pecan pie filled the air. They held hands as Alex said a prayer of thanks. He carved the turkey to perfection.

They ate until they were all stuffed. After helping clean up the kitchen, the kids went upstairs, while Alex, Keith and Samantha went to the den.

Samantha didn't stay long when they turned on the football game. Giving Alex a quick kiss, she told him she forgot something at the house and needed to run out to get it.

She hid a secret smile as she left the house and headed for home. Turning off the alarm, she went to the den. Dropping her coat on the sofa, she lit the fireplace. The soft glow of the flames did a seductive dance.

Samantha went upstairs to get the throw blanket from her bed and one from the closet. She took two pillows off her bed and carried her loot back to the den. Making a pallet on the floor in front of the fireplace, she smiled in satisfaction.

She proceeded out to the kitchen. Taking the ice bucket out of the pantry, she set it on the counter. She took a bottle of champagne from the wine rack and placed it in the refrigerator. She opened the plastic wrapper on the strawberries, washed them, put them into a bowl, and place them back in the refrigerator.

Walking out to the den, she looked around the room and smiled. Dimming the lights, she placed a soft jazz DVD on the console. It was the perfect seduction. Peering down at her watch, she grabbed her purse and left the house without resetting the alarm.

When she got back to the house, Alex and Keith were

still in the den watching the game. She went upstairs to get Matt ready for bed.

Once dressed, she carried him downstairs to say goodnight to Uncle Al and Uncle Keith. Samantha tucked him in and kissed him goodnight. She lay with him until he fell asleep. Exhausted, she too fell asleep.

Alex looked around the room and smiled in satisfaction. Everything was perfect. He went out the door closing it softly behind him. He told Keith to keep Sam distracted for about an hour. When he came for her, Keith was supposed to watch the children for the next hour or so.

Alex found her an hour later, sound asleep in bed with Matt. He smiled as he looked down at them. His heart melted at the sight of the two of them.

Walking over to the bed, he kneeled down beside it. He leaned over and brushed his lips across Samantha's forehead. She stirred and turned towards him.

Smiling, she sat up in bed. She caught his outstretched hand and he pulled her to her feet. Without a word, they tipped out of the room. He led her to his bedroom.

"What are you up to now?" she asked stopping outside the door. "Are all the kids in bed?" He placed a quick kiss on her lips.

"No, not yet. I have a surprise for you. Don't you trust me?" he teased winking at her. Her eyebrows rose in suspicion. "Come on. Close those beautiful gray eyes and let me be your guide. I promise not to let you walk into the walls."

Samantha laughed at his playful attitude. "I trust you with my life and my love, Dr. Carlisle. Don't ever disappoint me. I don't know what I would do without you." Her words came straight from the heart. "If you make me walk into a wall, you will have to cook and do the dishes for the next month."

"Trust me now. Close your eyes and hold out your hand." Samantha did as he instructed, and smiled when he took her hand. He opened the door and gently led her inside the room. "Open your eyes." Samantha let out a startled gasp as she looked around the bedroom. The floor and bed were completely covered in rose petals. "Don't move." He flipped a switch and then turned off the lights. Alex moved within arm's length of her. "I want to give you the stars and the moon. I think I am off to a great start. Look up, sweetheart. This is my gift to you."

"Oh my God," gasped Samantha, looking up at the ceiling, which was covered by the solar system and about fifty twinkling stars. "It's beautiful. When did you have time do all this?"

"It's not as beautiful as you are. I wasn't really on the phone with a patient earlier. I was setting the stage for this. I love you more than life itself. I want to spend the rest of my life with you. I don't know if I deserve a second chance at love, but I found it with you." Taking her hand in his, he kneeled down on one knee. All the air left Samantha's lungs as she gazed down at the man she loved. He opened the small red velvet box with a click. The shimmering two-carat diamond ring winked at her. "Samantha Thomas Taylor, will you marry me?"

She smiled down at him with all her love shining in her eyes. Unshed tears made her gray eyes sparkle like diamonds. She nodded, not trusting her voice to speak.

"Not good enough sweetheart. You are going to have to say the words." He took the ring out of the box and slipped it onto her finger. He brought her hand to his lips.

"Yes!" she cried through her tears. Launching herself into his arms, they landed on the carpeted, rose-covered floor. He broke her fall by pulling her on top of him. "Yes, I will marry you." Her mouth lowered to his and she kissed him hungrily. "I love you. I love you. I love you." She covered his face in kisses.

"I love you too, and if you keep wiggling like that you are going to find yourself flat on your back," he teased.

"I wouldn't mind," she teased, rubbing her breasts against his chest. Rolling over, he reversed their positions.

"Nothing would give me more pleasure, but I'm not sure how long Keith can keep the kids entertained. Alex caught her hands and kissed them. "I have an idea," he whispered kissing her neck. "After we put the kids to bed, let's slip over to your place and have our own private celebration. Keith will look after the kids and I will look after you. How does that sound?"

"You read my mind. Can you guess what else I'm thinking?" Her hand caressed his razor-stubbled cheek. "Tonight, Alexander Carlisle, I will make all your dreams and fantasies come true," she whispered seductively. She felt his body react to her words and planted a path of fiery kisses down his throat.

"My bed is two feet away, and if you keep this up, you'll find yourself on it in the next few minutes." Her hand moved down his stomach and he caught it. "Okay stop," said the breathless voice, trying to gain some control over his warring emotions.

"Those are words I never thought I would hear coming out of your mouth." She smiled, buttoning his shirt.

"And before this night is over, they will be coming from yours," he promised, silencing her with a steamy kiss. "Let's go make our announcement, shower, change, and get out of here."

They made their announcement, and the girls let out bloodcurdling screams that had the rest of them wincing and covering their ears. Laughter, hugs, and questions soon followed.

The kids fired questions at them about when was the big day, where were they going to live, and so on. Samantha and Alex assured them they had not made any decisions yet.

When the kids went upstairs to get ready for bed, Samantha and Alex both hit the shower. After saying good night to the kids, they left the house.

Samantha opened the double doors to the living room. Alex looked at the scene in front of him and then at her in surprise. He stepped into the room, shrugging off his coat. The soft glow from the fireplace cast a sultry atmosphere throughout the room.

"Welcome to paradise." Samantha smiled, unbuttoning her black leather coat. It slid from her shoulders slowly and she let it slip to the floor. She stood before him in a sheer black, thigh-high nightgown and black high heels. She walked into his open arms and met his hungry mouth.

Alex kept his promise to her. Less than an hour later, she was begging him to stop in one breath and to continue in the next. Samantha was more than happy to return the favor as Alex lay panting and gasping beneath her tender ministrations. She made slow, tortuous love to him with her hands, mouth, and body.

Chapter Fifteen

Things went pretty much back to normal after Christmas. Samantha continued to take all the kids to school and pick them up. She carted Derek off to karate and soccer practice and the girls to tap and jazz.

The whole family had dinner together at least twice a week. Alex would take them out to dinner on Friday night.

They finally agreed on a wedding date: Valentine's weekend. The wedding would be a small affair consisting of family and close friends, held at the Baptist church they both attended.

Samantha put her house on the market, since Alex's house had more space and bedrooms. She expected to feel a great sense of loss at selling her home of five years, but she didn't. She was tired of living in the past and couldn't wait to start her new life with Alex.

Tonight she was cooking dinner at Alex's house. The kids were upstairs finishing their homework while she started dinner.

She was coming from the restroom when the phone started ringing. The closest phone was in Alex's office. Opening the door, she walked inside. The office was a mess, as usual. Sitting down at the desk, she picked up the telephone.

"Hello," she said into the receiver as she began to straighten up the desk. Stacking papers into neat piles, the phone rested easily on her shoulder.

"Alex Carlisle, please," said the sultry female voice on the other end. Samantha frowned and dropped the papers in her hand.

"He's not in at the moment," she said warily. "Would you like to leave a message for him? I expect him in the next half hour."

"Please tell him Chloe called and I enjoyed being with him last night. I'd like to get together again soon." Samantha froze. Alex said he had an emergency at the hospital last night. *Who was this woman and could this be true?* "Tell him next time, dinner is my treat. Are you still there? Did you get all that."

"Just a minute. Let me get a pen," said Samantha past the catch in her throat. She found a pen on top of the desk. Samantha fumbled through the desk in search of a pad. Frowning, she picked up what looked like a lab report and her blood ran cold. Her hand trembled as she stared at the paper. "Please call him back later this evening and tell him yourself." She replaced the receiver, numb. The caller was now the furthest thing from her mind.

Samantha stared at the blood test results in her hand. Not believing what she was seeing, she read over the paper again. The date caught her attention and she trembled even more. It was dated two months before Jason had come to see her.

Please tell me this is not what I think it is! Please God, don't let this be what I know it is! He knew!

If this were the only evidence she had she would have shaken the thought away of Alex forcing Jason's hand.

Wiping the tears from her eyes, she picked up the discarded airline ticket stub, which was also in the drawer. The ticket was for a flight to Oregon made out to Alexander Carlisle. Jason lived in Oregon. This couldn't be a coincidence. She recalled Jeremy's words on the day of Matt's party. *Alex is out of town on business. He will be back today. He wouldn't miss Matt's party.* She shook her head wildly. Her hand trembled and the documents tumbled from her fingers.

Alex wouldn't do this to me! He wouldn't hold something like this from me!

Samantha closed her eyes and took several deep breaths. She didn't want to believe all the damning evidence in front of her. She wanted to believe in Alex. She needed to believe in him. He wouldn't lie to her about something like this. He couldn't.

Opening her eyes, she looked down at the documents on the desk. There was no other explanation except for the obvious one. Alex knew about Matthew at least a month before Jason came to see her. Somehow, Alex found out what Jason did and went to Oregon to confront him. He made him confess to her about the switch. Alex had lied to her again and again.

She reflected on the heartache she felt in telling him the truth. She had struggled for days, with when and how to tell him the truth about Matt. A truth he already knew. A truth he kept from her.

Her confession to him ripped out her heart. His reaction, his tears. It had all been a lie. Alex had faked the whole thing. He knew Matthew was his son and he let her put herself through the hell of telling him.

I thought we had something special, Alex. I thought we had a chance. I love you. I trusted you and you betrayed that love and trust in the worst possible way. Samantha wiped angrily at her wet cheeks. *How could you do this to me, to us? I am*

so sick of lies and secrets. Why couldn't you be honest with me?
Why couldn't you tell me the truth?

She went upstairs to get her purse. Finding Jason's number, she called him. She tapped her hand on the desk as she waited for someone to answer.

"Jason, it's Samantha," said the teary voice. "How are you? How are things going?" She wiped the tears spilling down her cheeks.

"Sam, hi. I didn't expect to hear from you ever again." She closed her eyes at the sadness in her brother's voice. "I guess you know Dad paid me a visit and disowned me."

"He told me. I'm sorry. Give him some time and he'll come around. He always does." She held the phone tightly in her hand and bit her lip to keep from crying out.

"Not this time. I've really blown it with everyone this time. Debbie is at least talking to me now. She won't let me come see her, but we're talking."

"That's a good sign," she sniffed. "Maybe with time you two can work things out. When is the baby due?"

"Just a few weeks. I'm hoping she'll come home before then. I want to be there when our son is born. I love her and I'm not giving up."

"Good. Don't give up. She loves you. Jason, I need to ask you something. Why did you tell me about the baby switch?"

"I couldn't keep the secret any longer," he said evasively. "You had to know the truth, Sam. I'm so sorry. I truly did what I thought was right at the time. I was trying to protect you."

"I know Jason. I understand why you did it. If you want a fresh start with me, then be honest with me now. Why did you come here and tell me, three years later?"

"I'd like to say I would have eventually told you, but that's not true. I would have taken the secret to my grave, but the truth was discovered. Someone found out what I did."

Samantha wiped at her tears. Jason was trying to spare her more pain. They both knew who that someone was. "Stop trying to protect me, Jason. Tell me the truth. Alex found out what you did and he came to see you. He made you tell me the truth. How am I doing so far?"

"Sam, the guy is in love with you. He would do anything for you. Talk to him. Ask him for the truth. I don't think he'd lie to you."

"You're wrong, Jason. He's been lying to me for months," she said softly, twisting the engagement ring on her finger. "Alex proposed to me at Christmas and I accepted. It's all been a lie. He knew the truth about Matthew and he didn't tell me. Yes or no: Did Alex fly to Oregon to see you?"

"Yes, but . . ."

She couldn't stop the cry, which was ripped from her soul. She already knew the answer to her question. She interrupted him. "Please, don't defend him to me," she snapped. "He lied to me and he forced you to tell me the truth."

"Alex was trying to do the right thing. He knew the truth should come out and it should come from me. It wasn't his place to tell you. It was mine. If he had told you what I had done, would you have believed him?"

"We'll never know, will we? He didn't give me the opportunity to decide. He took that away from me too. I can't talk about this anymore. I'll talk to you soon." Samantha stared at the telephone and then dropped it back to the cradle.

Alex knew about Matt. He has been lying to me for months. He knew and he said nothing. He could have prepared me for the truth, but he didn't. He let me be blindsided by this whole situation.

Samantha laid her head on the desk and cried her eyes out. Her whole world was crumbling down around her. She had put her love, faith, and trust in the wrong man again, and now she was paying the price for it.

She was in a fog as she went up to Alex's bedroom and lay across the bed. She cried herself to sleep.

She was awakened an hour later with a kiss. As her eyes focused on the man beside her, she cringed away from him.

"What's wrong?" Alex asked, sitting down on the bed beside her. He took in her red puffy eyes. "You've been crying. Honey, tell me what's happened?"

"Wrong?" Samantha asked sitting up slowly. Her voice cracked and her throat hurt. "What could be wrong? First some woman calls here to thank you for the wonderful evening the two of you had last night and then . . ." Her voice trailed off and she looked away from him.

"Stop right there. What woman? You believe I was with another woman. Is that what this is all about? Sam, I was working at the hospital last night."

"Were you? I don't know what to believe anymore. I want to believe you Alex. I really do, but I can't. You keep so many secrets from me." Her red eyes met his and Alex held her gaze.

"What secrets are you talking about?" Even as he asked, he knew from her expression she knew the truth. He didn't know how she knew, but she knew.

"How long did it take you to plan your strategy? How long have you been lying to me? How long have you known or suspected Matthew was your son?" Climbing out of bed, she picked up the papers and threw them at him. "Next time you decide to hatch a scheme, make sure you get rid of all the evidence—that way your unsuspecting victim won't stumble upon the truth. Truth and honesty, what a concept! Ever heard of it, Alex?"

"Samantha, hold up a second and listen to me," he said, moving towards her. "Let me explain. It's not what you think."

"Oh really, then what is it? I'm all ears," she said in a raspy voice, holding up her hand to stop him from coming any closer. She knew if he touched her she would fall apart. "Please don't come any closer or I won't be responsible for my actions. Tell me how you plotted and schemed to get us to where we are today? Don't try and lie your way out of this one. Tell me the truth or I walk out that door and never come back. I want the truth, Alex, or we are finished. I told you I couldn't live with lies and secrets again. I meant that. Tell me everything." He waved for her to take a seat on the bed. When she did, he sat down beside her.

"About six months ago when Keith was here, he picked up the photograph of me and Matt. He asked me straight out if we had an affair and if I was Matt's father. I denied it, but he kept pointing out similarities between us. My brother wasn't the first person to ask me that same question. Your father was always hounding me about doing the right thing by you and Matt. He knew Matthew was my son. At first, I ignored the speculation. Then I started to notice things myself. Matt has eyes like yours, but he has my facial features. I took out my baby pictures and compared them to Matt's. The resemblance was too close for me to ignore.

"The day I kept him while you and Dana went shopping, feeding time became a real mess. Afterwards, I had to give Matt a bath." He paused and pulled his shirt out of the waistband of his pants. "Does this look familiar?" asked Alex, holding up his shirt. Samantha took two steps forward and paled. On his left side was a birthmark that almost resembled a half moon. The same mark Matt had on his side.

"You have the same birthmark," she said quietly. She thought she knew every inch of his body. How could she have missed the birthmark? Samantha closed her eyes. She hadn't even noticed the mark on Alex until now.

"I was a bit shocked myself. I didn't know how it was possible, but I knew at that moment, he was my son."

"So you did nothing and you said nothing," she whispered, hugging her arms to her body protectively. "You said nothing, Alex. Why didn't you come to me? Why didn't you say something? Anything."

"Because I needed more proof. I took Matt to the lab and had blood drawn. I didn't want to say anything to you until I was sure. I needed proof from the blood test."

"Yet, when the results came back, when you had proof he was your son, you still said nothing to me. Instead you started to plot and plan. You set out to seduce me. You made me fall in love with you."

The knock on the door interrupted her. She turned her back to the door as Alex opened it. Samantha didn't want the kids to see her looking like this. She wiped at her wet cheeks with her trembling hands.

"Dad, I need money. The pizza guy is here," said Derek, looking past him to Samantha. "Is Aunt Sam okay?"

"She's not feeling well." Alex lied. Taking money out of his wallet, he gave Derek two twenties. "This should cover the pizza. The 'buy one get, one free coupon' is on the counter. Go ahead and eat. Sam and I are going to be a while." He closed the door and leaned against it.

"How did you find out about the baby switch? How did you put it all together?" she asked softly, turning around to face him.

"I've known the security guy at the hospital for a long time. I had him pull and check the nursery security tapes from the night of the accident. They showed everything."

"You saw my baby die," she whispered through her tears. Alex nodded, not trusting his own voice to speak. "And you saw Jason switch the babies." Again he nodded. "Then what?"

"Then I walked to the nursery window and saw what I thought was Michael already dead. I had to relieve the pain of losing my son all over again."

"But you didn't lose your son. I did." She turned away from him. "So begins the seduction of Samantha. I never stood a chance, did I? You knew what you wanted and you knew how to get it. You knew I would marry you to keep Matthew. You used my love for your own son to trap me." She saw him flinch at her cruelty, but she didn't care. She was too upset to care.

"Is that why you agreed to marry me, to keep Matthew?" asked the devastated voice. "What about love, Sam? You pledged your love to me. Was it all a lie to hold on to our son?"

"Why couldn't you tell me the truth?" she asked, not answering his question. "Why did you have to play this stupid game with me? We were friends and then lovers. You could have told me the truth. Why didn't you just tell me?"

"Because I didn't want to be the one to break your heart. I didn't want to be the one to cause you that kind of pain. I've answered your question. Now it's your turn to answer mine. Do you love me, or did you agree to marry me to keep Matthew?" Their eyes locked.

"I agreed to marry you because I love you and because I trusted you," she admitted, wiping at her tears. "I keep forgetting the two don't necessarily go hand in hand."

"You needed to know the truth. I wanted to tell you, but I couldn't bring myself to do it. If I had told you what your brother did, would you have believed me? Would you have taken my word over his without seeing the tape for yourself?"

"We'll never know. Tell me, Alex. The first time we made love, did you know about Matt?" He closed his eyes and turned away from her and she had her answer. "I pledged my heart and soul to you. I gave you everything I had to give. You are the reason I started living again. You gave me hope and faith. When you told me about Joshua, I asked you if there were any more secrets and you lied to me. You held me in your arms. You looked me straight in the eye and lied. The foundation of our relationship has been a lie. Everything has been a lie. I thought you were different, Alex. I thought you were the man I wanted to spend the rest of my life with. Now, I'm not so sure. You're just like Greg and my father. You will do and say whatever is necessary to get what you want." His expression went from one of shock, to hurt and then to rage.

"I'm not Greg, and I'm certainly not your father. I didn't trick you Sam. I didn't manipulate you into accepting my proposal. You did it because you love me, or were they just words on your part? I am not perfect by a long shot, but don't ever compare me to Greg or your father again."

"Where's the difference, Alex? You all lied to me. You betrayed me. What happens next? What do you expect from me?"

"I expect you to try and understand why I did what I did. I never meant to hurt you. Honey, it was killing me inside not being able to tell you the truth. I have lived with this lie for months and it's eaten me alive. I love you and I know we can get past this."

"I'm not so sure we can. I'm not sure *I* can. I can't marry a man who lies to me. Who is Chloe, and what does she mean to you? You were with her last night."

"Chloe is a nurse who was working in the ER last night when I was called in. She means nothing to me, Samantha." Alex was furious now. "Why am I explaining this to you? If you don't believe me, call the hospital and verify it. I was there, Samantha."

Twisting the ring nervously, she slid it off her finger. Her hand trembled as she reached out to him. "I can't marry you," said the choked voice. "I don't trust you, and I don't believe anything you say to me. I think we need to take a step back. I need to take a step back."

Alex felt his heart being ripped out of his chest as he stared at her and then the ring. He couldn't take it. He wouldn't. He bought it for her and he would make her see they belonged together. Samantha was upset and needed some time to think. They could get past this. He knew they could. "The ring is yours, Sam. Keep it. When you change your mind, put it back where it belongs. I love you and you love me, walking out on me won't change that. We belong together. I waited for you once. I can wait again. In the meantime," he said, grabbing her and pulling her into his arms, "here's something to re-member me by." His mouth covered hers in a hungry kiss. Samantha tried to push him away, but he was relent-less as he kissed her into submission. Her arms went around him and she kissed him back. His tongue plunged into her mouth, seeking and searching. His mouth demanded a response and she gave him one as her tongue teased his. His hands moved over her body in an equally hungry exploration as if imprinting her body in his mind forever.

When he finally released her, they were both breath-less and shaken up. Samantha took a step back from him and her hand went to her bruised lips. "I don't think I should keep the ring." Again she held it out to him. He shook his head. "Please take it."

"Everything is not black or white, Sam. There is a gray area. I made a mistake. It's not worth losing you. Nothing is. I admit it was wrong to lie about Matt, but I swear to you, I was not with Chloe or any other woman." Sam looked skeptical. It was clear. She didn't believe him. "I love you. I can't make you believe me, but at least give me the benefit of the doubt. If you don't believe me, then call the hospital. I was there all night."

Minutes ticked by without either of them saying a word. Sam wouldn't even turn around to look at him. When he tried to touch her, she shrugged him away. Alex grabbed his jacket off the bed and stormed out of the room.

A few minutes later, she jumped when she heard the garage door open and then close followed by the screeching of tires. She sat down on the bed with the engagement ring cutting into her palm. Getting up from the bed, she placed the ring in Alex's jewelry box.

Samantha went to the bathroom to wash her face in cold water. She knew she had to go downstairs to see the kids. Staring at her reflection, she grimaced. Her eyes were still red, and so was her nose.

She was only going through the motions when she helped the kids with homework. As soon as she heard Alex's car in the garage, she ushered her kids into the car. Neither Samantha nor Alex said a word as she left the house.

The following days were rough on everyone. The kids wanted to know where Uncle Al was and why he hadn't come by. Alex's kids wanted to know the same thing about their aunt. Samantha simply told her children she and Alex had a disagreement.

Derek and Hope were the first two to ask if the wedding

was off. Samantha had no answer for them. She wasn't sure what to tell them.

When Alex came by after work to pick up Derek and Lexi, he didn't stay long. He spent a few minutes with Matt and Hope and left. He said nothing to Samantha other than a casual hello.

Samantha's heart was breaking as she watched him leave each evening. She wanted to say something, but didn't know what to say. She was still furious at him for lying to her.

Even her father came over to plead Alex's case. Sam was so angry, she threw him out of the house for defending what Alex did.

Dana sat at the bar while Samantha made dinner. Dana kept steering their conversation to Alex, and Samantha kept moving away from the subject.

"I knew this would happen. I should never have become involved with him. This has ruined our friendship. We can never go back to the way it was."

"Good, because the way it was sucked. Have you talked to Alex?" Dana asked, sipping her ice tea. "I can't believe it's over. You and Alex hit a speed bump in the road, that's all it is."

"Speed bumps have been known to wreck a car." Samantha put the lid back on the pot of spaghetti, walked over to the kitchen table, and sat down. "Dana, what am I going to do?"

Hopping up from the bar stool, Dana came over and sat down at the table. "Sam, talk to Alex. You love him and he loves you. He may have gone about everything wrong, but I believe his heart was in the right place. You guys can get past this."

"I'm not so sure we can. What about this Chloe person? Where does she fit into the picture? Why would she call the house looking for him?"

"Maybe she wasn't looking for him. Maybe she wanted to speak with you. Maybe this Chloe woman wants Alex and is out to cause trouble for the two of you. Don't let her win, Sam. He's worth fighting for. At least call the hospital and verify his story. Tonight when he comes for the kids, dress to seduce. Greet him at the door with a steamy kiss. Don't give him a chance to put up his guard. Are you going to just let him walk out of your life without a fight?"

Samantha stared at the telephone in her hand. She threw caution to the wind and dialed the hospital emergency room. When she hung up the phone, she was laughing and crying. She sat down and the desk and lay her head facedown. Now she was more confused than ever. Alex was telling the truth. He'd been working and Chloe was a nurse in the ER on the night in question.

Alex slammed the door behind Chloe. He was so sick of her coming on to him. He couldn't have been any clearer, having thrown her out of his office. He tried to be nice, but she wasn't taking no for an answer. She wanted him, and was determined to seduce him in his office. She didn't even seem daunted when he threw her out.

He wasn't in the mood to deal with Chloe or anyone else at the moment. He was too furious at Samantha.

Alex was lying back on the couch in his office when the door opened. He looked up to see his father-in-law standing there. He closed his eyes, hoping the man would go away. It was obviously wishful thinking on his part. Nathan was there for a reason. Alex didn't need to guess what that reason was.

"Don't get up on my account," said Nathan sarcastically, folding his arms across his chest and leaning against the desk.

"I wasn't going to," replied Alex closing his eyes again. "Tell whoever let you in to let you out. I've seen my last patient for the day. I'm tired and I'm not in the mood to trade insults with you today."

"Damn, just when I was beginning to appreciate your witty repartée. I heard about the shortest engagement in history, and I'm willing to put in a good word for you."

"Good news travels fast, Pops. Nice to see you. Have a good day. Goodbye. I thought for sure you'd be jumping for joy and breaking out the fine china."

"Why would I do that? I may not be your biggest fan, but I want you and Samantha together. You, Samantha, and those kids are a family. I'm here to help you get them back."

Alex opened one eyes and peered at Nathan. "Said the spider to the fly." Alex met the serious eyes of his father-in-law. "Why would you want to help me with Sam? I know you can't be doing it out of the kindness of your heart, Dad."

"I'm trying to keep you out of trouble, son. I see this as a temporary separation between you and Samantha. I'm just protecting my daughter's interests until the two of you kiss and make up."

"Nathan, you don't like me and I don't like you, so why are you trying to help?" Alex stated honestly. "I don't trust a word that comes out of your mouth. I think you're an arrogant, egotistical snob—or you could take the *n* out of snob and that would fit you just as well."

"There's that sense of humor I've come to appreciate. Look, Alex, I'm on your side. I understand why you did what you did. I would have done the same thing. I've done a lot worse. I'm a businessman. You wanted Matthew and Samantha. I admit I was wrong about you and Sam having an affair. I know you were trying to do what was best for everyone by manipulating her to the altar. I think you could have been a lot smoother, but I also think she overreacted. Samantha just needs a little time to cool off, and she'll come to her senses. Just give her some space and time. She told me the reason you and I don't get along is because we are too much alike. Personally, I don't see it. I would have been smart enough to get rid of all the evidence, instead of leaving it lying around the house. You were sloppy and you got caught. I would have given you credit for being smarter than that."

"Gee, thanks. That makes me feel much better. I'm sure I could learn a lot about scheming and manipulation from you, Nathan. You are the master of deception. Just for the record, I'm nothing like you. I was not trying to manipulate Sam to the altar. I love her and I would never use my son to get what I want. If you want to see a carbon copy of yourself, look to your son. Jason is just like you. He always has been. He's selfish and he's ruthless, just like good ole dad. He acts without thinking about consequences. Like father, like son. Instead of disowning him for what he's done, I'd think you'd be cheering him on for ingenuity. I bet if you had made it to the hospital in time, you would have done the same thing he did."

"You're right. I probably would have done the same thing. It took me a while, but I understand why he did it. He saved Samantha's life. I don't know if she would have made it through without Matthew. What do you think, Alex?"

Samantha was headed out of the garage when she heard the doorbell ring. Setting her purse on the kitchen counter, she walked to the front door. Peering out, she saw Jeremy.

"Jeremy, what are you doing here?" Samantha asked, closing the door behind him. She knew that look, and she was not in the mood for another Alex-is-great pep talk. "You have five minutes."

"Samantha, give the guy a break. You are being unreasonable. He did what he did out of love for you and Matt."

"That would be your way of thinking. Are you sure you are not Nathan Thomas's son? Of course you don't see anything wrong with what Alex did. I'm sure any one of you would have done the same thing in his shoes. Tell Alex sending you and my father to talk for him is definitely not helping his cause."

"Alex didn't send me here. I came because I care about both of you. Alex loves you. He would never do anything to intentionally hurt you. Everything he has done has been for love."

"You knew about the baby switch, didn't you?" Jeremy neither admitted nor denied the allegation. "Never mind. You don't have to answer that, of course you knew. You are Alex's friend first and my cousin second."

"That's not fair. I love both of you. I want you both to be happy. You pushed him away. You have been pushing him away for the past three years. Have you ever thought maybe there's something wrong with *you*, Samantha? You set such high standards no one can meet your expectations. We can't live up to your larger-than-life expectations. We are all human, and we all make mistakes. We learn from our mistakes and we move on, but not you. You let things eat away at your soul. They leave you bitter and alone. Is that how you want to live the rest of your life? You pushed Alex away. It's up to you to get him back. The next move is yours. If you want him in your life, you are going to have to give a little."

Chapter Sixteen

Samantha thought long and hard before accepting the party invitation from Dana. All things considered, she was not in a partying mood.

It didn't help matters when Alex showed up. He nodded in her direction, but didn't come over, which infuriated her even more. Within minutes he was the life of the party.

Samantha was standing by the patio doors looking out when Jeremy walked up. She warily faced her cousin.

"Hello beautiful. Enjoying the party?" he asked, kissing her cheek. He followed her eyes to Alex with apprehension.

"Not as much as he is," she replied, glaring across the room at Alex. Their eyes met briefly before his attention was diverted by one of the four women surrounding him.

"Okay," said Jeremy smiling. "How are things with you and Alex? Have you spoken to him tonight?" This time, she glared at him. "Not exactly keeping the lines of communication open, I see. If it bothers you that much, go over there and let them all know he's already taken. Go over there and flash that rock you're wearing on your ring finger. Oh, I forgot. You're not wearing it anymore. You gave up your right to be jealous, kiddo."

"Did you come over to cheer me up or depress me? I could care less if Alex is over there making a fool of himself with four girls who are probably half his age."

"He's having a good time. He's just talking. There's no harm in talking. So what."

Samantha's eyes narrowed to gray slits.

"There's no law against flirting. Forget I said anything. I pity Alex," said Jeremy shaking his head and walking away.

Alex raised his glass to her in salute. Samantha turned her back on him. The least he could have done was come over and speak to her.

Why am I the one expected to make the first move? I'm not the one who lied.

Someone calling her name startled her. She turned around to see a sight for sore eyes. Her face lit up in recognition. They embraced warmly.

"How are you?" asked Drew Thomas, smiling and hugging her again. "It's good to see a friendly face."

"I'm fine. How are you? Where the heck have you been?" laughed Samantha. "You dropped off the face of the earth a few years ago."

"I went wherever business took me. California, Las Vegas, Oregon. You name it. Now I'm back home to stay. How are things going with you? Are you still married?"

"No," she said softly, looking down at the glass in her hand. "Greg was killed three years ago in a car accident."

"I'm sorry. I'm sure it was rough on you. You look great. So tell me, Samantha, are you involved with anyone?"

"Not anymore," was her slow reply. She held up her hand. "No ring on this finger. I'm free as a bird."

"Then who is the guy watching us?" Drew asked, looking

past her to Alex. She flushed and then laughed. "He hasn't taken his eyes off you since I've been standing here. Who is he?"

"That would be Alex, my ex-fiancé, as of a few weeks ago," she said not bothering to turn around. "Ignore him."

"Recent breakup. Should we give him something to think about? How about a dance for old time's sake?" Drew asked. His eyes twinkled with mischief, and he held out his hand to her. "So now that I'm back in town, we are not going to lose touch again, are we?"

"No. I need all the friends I can get." She put her hand in his and let him lead her toward the dance floor. "What about you? Are you married? Divorced? Do you have any kids?"

"No to all of the above. I really haven't been in one place long enough to form a steady relationship, but I'm still looking." The song ended, and they walked over to the sofa and sat down. They were inseparable the rest of the evening.

Drew pulled Samantha to her feet when a slow song came on. Before they made it to the dance area, Alex was blocking their path.

"I'm Dr. Alex Carlisle," said Alex, holding out his hand to Drew. "I don't believe we've met." Samantha rolled her eyes at his arrogance. He had ignored her for the past couple of weeks, and now when someone showed an interest in her, he was ready to step up to the plate.

"Drew Thomas." Drew took his outstretched hand. The silence stretched on as they sized each other up.

His eyes moved to Samantha and he broke the silence. "I believe this is our dance, Samantha." He held out his hand to her.

Samantha was fighting the waging war inside her. She wanted to take his hand, but she was still angry. She wasn't ready to forgive him yet. She looked at Drew, and he took the decision away from her by placing her hand in Alex's. She trembled when his hand closed around hers. They were staring at each other as Drew moved away unnoticed.

When Alex pulled her into his arms, Samantha closed her eyes, momentarily savoring the feel, the sensation of being in his arms again. She almost moaned aloud as her arm went around his waist.

"So who's your friend? You two looked pretty chummy," said Alex, pulling her closer. "He doesn't seem your type."

"It's none of your business what I do or whom I do it with. You don't share my life or my bed anymore," she stated sarcastically, trying to put some distance between them. Alex continued to hold her close. "We're not engaged anymore, remember?"

"You may have given back my ring, but I still have your heart, and you still have mine." Samantha froze at his words. She couldn't deny them. She did love him. "You stopped dancing. Did I hit a nerve?"

"Please let go," she whispered. He released her, and she took a step away from him. She wasn't sure when his arms had dropped from around her, but she felt cold and empty without them. "So which girl are you taking home tonight, the redheaded bimbo or the brunette?"

Alex stared at her in hurt and disbelief. To know she had so little faith in him caused his heart to constrict. She had no idea that she and the kids meant everything to him. "Why don't you choose one for me, since you know me so well?" he shot back furiously. "You know my likes and dislikes."

"I'd take the brunette," she said flippantly. "She's not as obvious as the others, although she does look at least ten years younger than you."

"Done," he snapped, turning away from her. "Since

your father has the kids tonight, maybe I will take her home with me."

Her anger flared out of control. "Do me a favor, Alex. Unlike Greg, be more responsible and use some protection when you're out there catting around. I refuse to take care of another accident."

"You are some piece of work," he hissed between clenched teeth. "Do you ever stop and think before you attack? Whatever comes up comes out. I don't even know why the hell I bother wasting my time with you. You don't trust me. You never wanted me in the first place. You just wanted my son and a stud in your bed." She winced at his hurtful words. "The old adage 'Be careful what you wish for' keeps popping into my head. I wonder why?"

The song ended and Alex walked away, leaving her staring after him. Without saying anything to anyone, he went out the front door and slammed it shut. "Damn her!" Alex got into his car and drove away.

Samantha flinched when the door slammed shut. Alex's angry words were ringing in her ears. She found Drew talking with Jeremy and Tomas.

"Great party, guys, but I'm taking off," said Samantha hugging each of them. "I'm going to find Dana and say good night."

She found Dana making more sandwiches. Dana waved for her to take a seat. She sat down at the butcher-block table.

"I'm taking off. As usual, I've made the situation worse with Alex. We had a fight a little while ago and he left, furious with me."

Dana laid the knife on the table. "Samantha, do you want a future with Alex?"

Samantha nodded slowly.

"Then stop pushing him away. You're going too push too hard one day and he's not going to come back."

Drew caught her at the door. He escorted her outside. She and Drew stood by the car catching up on old times. Samantha missed his friendship.

"I'm glad you're back," said Samantha. "I could use an impartial friend. Alex and I have the same friends. They don't see the situation the way I see it."

"How do you see it? Spill it, Samantha. I'm a good listener if you want to talk. I'd be happy to lend you a shoulder to cry on."

Over a cup of hot chocolate, Samantha related the story to Drew. When she finished a few hours later, Drew was speechless and she was exhausted.

"Wow. That's some story. You should consider writing a book. I'd buy it," he smiled. "I don't know what else to say."

"Alex plays by his own rules. I thought I knew him. I thought I knew how his mind worked. Well, the scary part is maybe I do. This is just the kind of stunt he would pull and he doesn't see anything wrong with what he did. You see the ends always justify the means. Am I totally over reacting? Am I being that unreasonable?"

"I saw the way he looked at you tonight. He loves you. As hard as it is for you to admit, you know you were wrong." He raised his hand to silence her. "You were both wrong. He should have told you about Matthew as soon as he found out. You should have believed him about this Chloe woman. As a woman you should know some women will do and say anything to get what they want, and so will men. She wouldn't be the first woman to lie to the competition."

"She did lie," she admitted. "I feel terrible for checking out his story. I shouldn't have to verify what he tells me. I should be able to trust him, and he should trust me."

"Ouch. I bet it made you feel this tall." He smiled, separating his fingers by an inch. "You love this guy. You're miserable and he's miserable. You want him back. All you have to do is swallow your pride and tell him."

"Easier said than done. Would you like to come by for dinner one night? I'd like for you to meet the kids."

"I like the way you changed the subject," he smiled. "I'd love to come to dinner and meet the kids."

Samantha cooked dinner while Drew sat at the bar and kept her company. They chatted about everything and nothing in particular.

The kids were in the living room playing and watching television when the door to the garage opened. Piercing screams where Samantha and Drew both flinched followed this.

"Daddy! Daddy!" chorused the kids excitedly. Matt jumped up and down in excitement as Alex walked through the door.

Samantha froze momentarily before walking over to the sink where she could see Alex. He was on the floor covered in little bodies. They were all laughing in merriment.

Samantha smiled without even realizing it. She knew how much the kids had missed Alex. Drew smiled too, at the warm reception Alex received from the children.

When Alex finally made it to his feet, he had Matthew still clinging to his leg. He lifted him up in his arms and started towards the kitchen. He stopped when he saw Drew sitting at the end of the bar. His eyes locked with Samantha's. She was the first to look away.

"I'm sorry, I must have gotten my dates crossed." Samantha looked at him, puzzled. He looked great as usual in a pair of khaki pants and a tan polo shirt.

"What are you doing here? Your dates crossed about

what?" she asked, embarrassed. "I invited Drew to dinner tonight."

"I see," said Alex in a tight voice, setting Matthew on his feet and turning away. "My mistake. It won't happen again."

"There was obviously a mix-up. Why don't I leave, and let you guys have a nice family dinner?" Drew suggested, coming to his feet. "I'll talk to you later."

Samantha's eyes darted to Derek's flushed face. Now she knew who had invited Alex. He must have overheard her invite Drew to dinner and had invited his dad also.

Samantha decided not to embarrass him in front of everyone. Instead, she would deal with him later. For now, she would deal with the situation at hand.

"Dad, don't go," said Derek following Alex to the door. Matthew started screaming at the top of his lungs for his uncle. Alex reached down and picked him up and soothed him. He immediately quieted, but held on to Alex for dear life.

"Mom, please let Uncle Alex stay." Hope begged, hugging Alex. "We hardly ever see him anymore. You may not miss him, but we do." Sam cringed at her daughter's response.

"Guys, I promise I'll come back another day," said Alex, hugging each one of them. "Take care of your mom for me." He couldn't hide his unhappiness from her or the kids, much as he tried. Samantha saw the pain in his brown gaze as their eyes met.

"This is ridiculous. Drew, sit down. Alex, sit down. You are both welcome to stay. There is more than enough food," said Samantha, smiling tentatively. "Please stay, Alex." Samantha wasn't sure if she was asking for the kids or for herself, but she had missed him.

Samantha finished dinner while Alex helped the kids

with homework. He helped Derek with his science project before helping Lexi with her spelling words.

"I like him. He's a great father," noted Drew watching Alex and the kids interact. "He's good with kids. I can see why he has a thriving practice."

"Yes, he is a great father," agreed Samantha. "He has more patience than I do when it comes to helping with homework. By the way, Alex didn't get his days crossed. I think Derek overheard me invite you to dinner so he took it upon himself to invite his dad."

"I don't blame him, Samantha. Maybe he feels threatened by me. He wants you and his Dad back together. They all do."

"I realize that, but he needs to learn that for every action, there are consequences. I don't want him trying to manipulate others the way his father does. He is so much like Alex it scares me to death."

"Dinner was wonderful," said Drew, putting on his coat. "I'm going to take off. Go talk to your fiancé," he whispered, kissing her cheek.

"Ex-fiancé," she amended, smiling. She hugged Drew. "Thank you for coming tonight. It's good to have you back in town."

"Go talk to the man, Samantha. I'll talk to you later." Samantha stood in the doorway and waved to him. Once the car was out of the driveway, she locked the door behind him.

"I like him. He seems like a nice guy," said Alex from behind her. She turned to face him in surprise. "I would probably like him better if I didn't think he was after you."

Samantha didn't see the twinkle in Alex's eye as she walked past him and into the kitchen. She put the leftovers in the refrigerator and put the dishes in the dishwasher. After finishing in the kitchen, she went in and sat down and watched a movie with them.

"That's it, guys. It's time for bed," said Samantha, coming to her feet. The whining started immediately.

"You heard her, guys and dolls," said Alex, sternly. "Everyone upstairs. We'll be up in a little while to make sure everyone has had a bath and tuck you in."

"Derek, stay," said Samantha. His eyes met hers, and he flushed hotly and sat back down on the couch. She watched him fidget with his hands before sitting on them. She waited until the kids were all upstairs before speaking, "So Derek, I bet the evening turned out a lot different from what you had planned." He flushed again under her close scrutiny. "You are the one who called and left the message with your dad's answering service about dinner, aren't you?"

"Yes ma'am," he replied softly, not meeting her eyes. Samantha's heart went out to her nephew.

"Why did you do it?" Alex asked, staring at his son. Derek's head dropped. "Look at me when I'm speaking to you." Derek raised his face to his father's. "Talk to me."

"I was only doing what you asked me to do. I was looking out for Aunt Sam and the others. We don't need another man here. We only need you, Dad. If Aunt Sam has a new boyfriend then you need to know about it. We don't want another father."

His words sent a wave of cold fear washing over Alex. He was not about to lose Samantha or his family. He stared from Sam to his son at a loss for words.

"Derek, Drew is not my boyfriend. He's just a friend. No one can replace your dad. Drew is not trying to replace him. It was wrong for you to invite Alex without letting me know. You made all of us uncomfortable. You know your Dad is welcome here anytime, just let me know when you ask him to come. If I invite Drew or anyone else to dinner it is none of your business. It has nothing to do with you."

"I don't want to stay here. I hate it here. I want to go home," Derek said angrily. "I want to sleep in my own home, in my own bed."

"You know I'm working a double shift tomorrow and Sunday," Alex said. "You will come home on Monday. While you are here, you will respect your aunt and her house rules. Samantha has the right to invite anyone she pleases into her home, and you, young man, had better deal with it. You don't make the rules."

"I know this situation has been hard for you, but it's equally hard for us," said Samantha, sitting down next to Derek on the sofa. "Let Alex and I work this out by ourselves. We don't need your help. We don't need you trying to play matchmaker. If it was meant to be, your dad and I will find our way back together."

"Samantha is right. You were playing a game with us, and I for one don't appreciate it. Son, you can't manipulate people to make them do and act the way you want them to. Believe me, I know. I've tried and it always backfires." Alex and Samantha's eyes locked. "I'm living proof of that." Samantha was the first to break eye contact. "I think you need to learn from your mistake. You just blew the game on Saturday. You're grounded."

"But Dad! That's not fair," he cried, looking to his aunt for support. "Granddad and I have been planning this for months."

"Then you should have thought about that before you started lying. You are grounded for one week. No karate class on Tuesday and no soccer practice on Thursday. Don't pull another stunt like this again. Now go on up, shower, and get ready for bed."

"Don't you think you were a little hard on him?"

Samantha waited until Derek was out of earshot, before moving next to Alex.

"No, I don't." Alex leaned back and closed his eyes. "I guess I haven't set a very good example for him."

"Don't," chided Samantha, softly. "You have been a wonderful father." Samantha stared at his stiff profile. "You look tired."

"Long shift. It's my week to be on call." Opening his eyes, he sat up. "Let's go say goodnight. Then I'm going to take off and get some rest."

When they got upstairs, the girls were bathed and in bed. Derek had just gotten out of the shower. Matthew was lying across Lexi's bed, playing.

Samantha ran the bathwater for Matthew, and Alex carried his giggling son into the bathroom. The phone rang and Samantha left Alex to finish Matthew's bath. By the time she got back to the bathroom, Alex was soaked. They dressed Matt in his pajamas and put him to bed.

"You can't leave like that," said Samantha pointing to his wet clothes. "It's cold outside. Come on," she said catching his hand and leading him into her bedroom. "Please put on some dry clothes before you leave."

She sat down on the bed and turned on the radio. As the ballad filled the room, Samantha closed her eyes and lay back on the bed.

Images of Alex naked filled her mind. She could clearly see his broad torso; hair-roughened chest and flat stomach. As her eyes moved down his flat stomach . . .

"Samantha. Samantha," repeated Alex, standing over her. Her face flushed hotly and she stared up at him with glazed eyes. He was now dressed in a pair of light blue scrubs. "I'll drop by tomorrow or Sunday to see how things are going with Derek."

Saying nothing, she hugged her knees to her chest. She wanted so badly to reach out and touch him. She wanted more than anything for him to take her in his arms. Him being near was pure torture. "Are you okay?" he asked touching her forehead. Samantha trembled at his touch and then pulled away. She nodded, not trusting her voice to speak. He looked at her one last time for any sign she wanted him to stay. When he saw none, he left.

Samantha sat there trembling until she heard the garage door open. Hopping up from the bed, she went and took a shower. She did her usual bedtime routine of putting on lotion and brushing her hair out. She stared at her sad reflection.

Why didn't I ask him to stay? I need you, Alex. You make this family complete.

Throwing down the hairbrush, she slipped on a red nightgown and climbed into bed. She was about to turn off the radio, when she heard the garage door again.

What did he forget tonight? Last night it was his beeper, and two nights ago it was his cell phone. He really is working too hard. He needs a break.

She walked over to the window and looked out. When the bedroom door opened, she turned in surprise to see Alex standing there.

Alex stared at the vision before him in the sexy red satin nightgown. His mouth watered as his eyes devoured her.

"What did you forget this time?" she asked quietly. "You never seem to leave here without forgetting something." Alex moved towards her slowly.

"This." He pulled her to him, and his mouth covered hers in a hungry kiss. Samantha responded just as passionately. Her arms went around him and her lips parted beneath his as he swung her up in his arms and carried her to bed.

Their clothes melted away and they clung to each

other. No preliminaries were needed as her body met his eagerly. She held nothing back as her body joined his again and again. This was what she wanted, what her body craved.

Samantha lay sated and content in the arms of the man she loved. Their lovemaking was intense. It was a little over a month, and neither one of them could wait. Her head rested easily on his chest.

"Welcome home," said Samantha, kissing his chest. "I've missed you." She felt Alex tense beside her. "What's wrong?" She asked looking up at him and meeting his eyes.

"Samantha, this doesn't make things right between us," he said softly. It was her turn to stiffen in his arms. She sat up, pulling the sheet up to cover her breasts. "We still have some unresolved issues. You still have some unresolved issues. I want you to do something for me. No," said Alex, turning to face her, "do it for yourself. I want you to talk to a psychologist." Samantha stared at him blankly.

"You want me to see a psychiatrist?" she asked, unbelieving. "You think I'm the one who needs therapy?"

"Samantha, you need to talk to someone. You have had more pain than most people will in a lifetime, starting with the death of your mother. You had to deal with Greg and Kirstin's deaths. Followed by finding out about Greg, Betsy, and Joshua—and to top it all off, you find out the truth about Matthew. That's a lot to deal with on your own. I think it might help you to talk to someone. It's obvious you can't talk to me about it."

"You forgot your betrayal, Alex. I think that one hurt the most. So now you think I'm crazy?" she asked, leaving the bed.

"No. I don't think you're crazy and I'm not denying what I did." He climbed out of bed and caught her arm, stopping her from leaving the room. "Samantha, if our relationship stands any kind of chance, you are going to have to deal with the past. You need to deal with it and then let it go. I want a future with you, but I don't see that happening unless you get some help. I've tried, but I can't help you. I don't know what else to do. I know someone who can help you deal with this. Give her a call."

"Is this an ultimatum?" she asked angrily, glaring up at him. "I either see a psychiatrist or we are over?" When he made no reply, she jerked her arm from his grasp and stomped into the bathroom. She resisted the urge to slam the door.

Sinking down to the carpeted floor, she hugged her knees to her chest. *I'm fine. I don't need help. I'm dealing with my grief in my own way. He's wrong. I'm not crazy. I can handle this. I have always handled things on my own.*

When Samantha came out of the bathroom, Alex was gone. She walked over to her nightstand and picked up the business card he left. REGINA MADISON, PHD. Holding the card in her hand, she sat down on the bed.

Chapter Seventeen

Alex sat at a bar table and ordered a drink. He waited patiently for Drew. This little meeting was long overdue. He needed to make a few things clear to Samantha's friend and confidante.

"Looks like you started without me," said Drew, shrugging off his coat. "Since I know this isn't a social visit, what do you want, Alex?" asked Drew, getting straight to the point. "Why am I here?"

"Drew, glad you could make it." Alex waved to the vacant seat at the bar. "I think we need to talk." Alex set his rum and Coke on the bar. "I think it's important we know exactly where we each stand in regards to Samantha." Drew's eyebrows rose and he smiled.

The waitress came by to take his order. "I'd like a Miller Lite, please. Where do you stand, Alex? That's a million-dollar question."

"That's easy. Samantha is the woman I love. She's the mother of my children. We are having some problems and I don't want you or anyone else to try and take advantage of her. This situation is only a temporary one. I have every intention of marrying her."

"She may be a substitute mother to your children, but

last time I saw the lady, she wasn't wearing a ring on her finger. Do you love her the way she deserves to be loved, or do you simply take her for granted?"

"I love her. Samantha is mine and will always be mine. You don't want to make an enemy of me, that I promise you. Don't try and come between us," warned Alex.

"I'm not the one who lied to her," Drew shot back. "Samantha is my friend. We have never been any more than friends. She needs a friend right now, and I'm not going to turn her away. She's hurting and she's confused."

"I intend to be there to ease her pain. If you go after her, I will go after you. I don't mince words and I always keep my promises."

"I've been warned," said Drew, taking a sip of his beer and sitting it back on the table. "Alex, I'm not afraid of you."

"You have no reason to be afraid of me, unless you're after Samantha. What you need, Andrew, is to meet some beautiful unattached women. So, I'm going to do you a favor. Samantha tells me you're a nice guy. She is a pretty good judge of character for the most part," he amended. "I've decided to help you out. Let's face facts. You are not going to meet any single women sitting around Samantha's house. I'm a true believer in the fact that men and women can't be just friends. It never works; either one or the other ruins it. Samantha and I are a perfect example. We tried it for three years and now look at us. Samantha is a beautiful and desirable woman. You'd be crazy not to make a play for her, eventually. So to take temptation out of your way, I've got some friends I want you to meet."

"You're serious," laughed Drew, taking a swig of his beer. He saw the seriousness in Alex's eyes.

"I've never been more serious," said Alex waving his hand to the group of women he had waiting in the wings. "Samantha is off-limits. These beauties, on the other hand, are very much available." Drew's brows rose in question as they were soon surrounded by a bevy of beauties. "Drew, meet Jennifer, Melanie, Suzette, Leeza, Chelsea, Heather, Stephanie, Stacie, Tara, Jessica, Sandra, Brandy, Meagan, Cindy, Chloe, Karen, Robin, and Rachel." Drew smiled in appreciation at each and every one of them.

"I think I've died and gone to heaven. Samantha was right. You are full of surprises." Alex finished off his drink and came to his feet.

"Dr. Carlisle, why don't you hang around for a while?" asked Chloe, brushing up against him suggestively and loosening his tie. Alex knew an open invitation to bed when he saw one.

"Chloe, you know I'm committed," said Alex, taking a step back and removing her hands from his person.

"I don't see a ring on your finger yet. How committed are you? How committed is she?" she inquired, caressing his cheek. "I could make you forget her. I can make you unbelievably happy."

"I will be unbelievably happy tonight," he winked, removing her hands from his face. "Chloe, how do I put this delicately? I'm not interested. Samantha is woman enough for me. Why eat out when you have lobster waiting for you at home?"

"Touché," she quipped. "Samantha doesn't have to know. What she doesn't know won't hurt her." He caught her hand and pulled her away from the group.

"Chloe, I don't know what game you are trying to play with Sam and I, but it won't work. I'm still not interested. I love Samantha, and I'm going to marry her."

"Only time will tell. Your fiancée is a lucky woman. Maybe I should call her up and tell her sometime," she smiled coyly. "We could maybe do lunch and discuss your likes and dislikes."

"Stay away from Samantha and stay away from me. I don't know how I can be any clearer than I have been with you. You're a beautiful woman, Chloe, but I'm not interested. I didn't invite you here tonight, but you are more than welcome to stay. I'm leaving." He left her standing there and walked back over to the table. "Drew, old buddy, looks like you'll be busy this evening" He smiled, slapping Drew on the back. "Don't do anything I intend to do tonight. I think I'll go over and keep Samantha company, in your absence. If things don't work out for you with these ladies, I've got one more lined up for you. You may want to steer clear of Chloe. She's a wee bit too possessive for my taste. Some might even say she's a psycho."

"Thanks," said Drew, staring at the beautiful blonde gazing at Alex. "She looks harmless enough. Forget I said that. The way she's looking at you, I don't think I would stand a chance."

"Looks can be deceiving. She may look like an angel, but she's pure devil. If you're smart, you won't give her a second look. She's lethal. Don't say I didn't warn you."

Whistling, Alex left the bar. He was still smiling when he pulled into the garage at Samantha's house half an hour later.

Samantha put the kids to bed and was lying on the couch with a bowl of popcorn. The fireplace was lit, but she still had a blanket draped over her. Her hand rested lightly over her stomach. She was thankful her cycle had come and gone. She'd been a few weeks late and had panicked that she might be pregnant.

"Samantha," said Alex, coming into the room. Startled, she sat up, and her hand dropped to her side. "Glad to see you back in cotton and fleece. At least I know you are not playing the seductress for anyone."

"Talk like that could turn a girl's head." She set the popcorn on the coffee table. "What are you doing here? The kids are already in bed. Since you don't talk to me anymore, I know you didn't come by to talk about old times," she said sarcastically. He sat down next to her and picked up the discarded bowl of popcorn.

"I was in the neighborhood and I thought maybe you could use some adult company. Where's your friend Drew? He seems to be underfoot every time I come by. The man is in desperate need of a social life."

"That's a good question. He was supposed to come over tonight, but I haven't heard from him. It's not like Drew not to at least call."

"I guess he got held up." Alex smiled knowingly, popping a handful of popcorn into his mouth. Samantha looked at him suspiciously. She knew that look, and it usually meant Alex was up to something.

"What did you do?" she asked, folding her arms over her chest. "Did you let the air out of his tires or something? I realize that's juvenile even for you, but I wouldn't put it past you."

"What makes you think I did anything?" he asked innocently, holding up two fingers. "Scout's honor. Your mistrust in me hurts."

"I know you, Alex. Put your fingers down. You are full of tricks. Where's Drew? What have you done with him? Is he locked in the trunk of your car?"

"That's an idea. Maybe I'll try that next time. He's not coming tonight. He has other plans." He tossed more popcorn in his mouth, and she stared at him waiting for him to continue. "We met for drinks a little while ago, and some of the 'single' nurses dropped by."

"Why would you and Drew be meeting for drinks? Some of the single nurses just happened to drop by," she repeated, "I'll bet they did."

"He was still engaged in conversation with them when I left," he concluded picking up the remote and hitting play. Samantha took the remote from him and hit stop. "You said yourself he didn't have many friends in town. So I took it upon myself to introduce him to about fifteen to twenty single women. He was in heaven when I left him. You should be thanking me for giving your friend a life. He definitely needed one. You did the same thing for me if you recall. Hey, maybe I should have set him up with Linda. He'd love her. She's so . . . "

"All right already," said Samantha, interrupting him. "I don't need to hear how great she is or anything else." Alex smiled at her jealousy. He knew Linda was still a sore subject with Samantha.

"I never kiss and tell. You know that, Samantha." She didn't know whether to kiss him or strangle him. She surprised him and herself when she leaned over and kissed him on the cheek. "I know why you did it, but I don't care. Drew needed to meet some women and you made it happen. Thank you." Samantha snuggled up against him. Alex's arms went around her and she hit play on the VCR.

When the movie ended, Samantha excused herself to go to the bathroom again. Alex watched her suspiciously.

Lately, he noticed her attire. The last time he was at the house, she was wearing a loose fitting denim dress, almost like a smock. Now she wore a loose-fitting pair of warm-ups. He picked up the empty glass of milk on the table. Samantha hated milk.

She's pregnant. She has to be. Everything pointed to it, the loose-fitting clothes, frequent urination, and her drinking milk. He set the glass back on the table.

Okay, Samantha so when are you going to tell me? You are not going to be able to hide your condition for very long.

When she came back into the room, she had a small bowl of black-walnut ice cream. He watched her devour two spoonfuls before looking up at him.

"Would you like some?" she asked, smiling, and holding out the spoon to Alex. He moved closer to her.

"That depends on what you're offering me." His mouth opened for her to place the spoon between his lips. He licked his lips in appreciation. "Delicious."

"Everything I have is yours. All you have to do is reach out and take it." She ate another bite and fed him another.

"Maybe I don't want to take anything. Maybe I want it given freely." She watched him walk over to the door and close it. The soft snap of the lock filled the room. Alex took the blanket off the couch and spread it out in front of the fireplace.

"That's being a bit presumptuous," said Samantha softly, setting her empty bowl on the table.

"Is it?" he asked with raised brows. Samantha slowly shook her head. Her heart was pounding wildly as she walked the short distance to where he was standing.

"What do you want from me, Alex?" Kneeling down on the blanket, he pulled her down in front of him. The fireplace cast a soft glow over the dimly lit room.

"I want all of you, heart, mind, body, and soul. I especially want your heart. I want everything you have to give and more. I want your love and your trust." Samantha pulled her sweatshirt up and over her head and tossed it in the general direction of the couch.

You have everything already. Well, maybe not my trust, but I do love you. Maybe I always have.

One long finger traced the outline of her breasts through the red lace of her bra. Taking the initiative, she pulled his shirt out of the slacks and unbuttoned it. When at last all the buttons were free, she pushed the shirt from his broad shoulders.

Her hands trembled as they reached out and touched his hair-roughened chest. His skin was hot to the touch as she ran her fingers through the hairs on his chest. As gentle hands made contact with his nipples, they hardened in response to her touch. Her hands moved down his naked torso to the waistband of his slacks. Without any hesitation, she unbuttoned and unzipped his pants.

Pushing the offensive material to his knees, her hand reached out to touch him. Alex inhaled sharply, his head swooped down, and his mouth covered hers as he pressed her back onto the blanket. Samantha returned his hungry kiss with a fever that matched his own. Alex rolled to his side and Samantha stared at him in confusion.

"Strip for me." She saw the seriousness in his eyes as he watched her. She nervously got to her feet. "Slowly," said Alex, removing the remainder of his own clothing.

Her eyes never left his as she slid the warm-up pants down her legs one at a time. She pushed the straps of her bra down her arms, before unsnapping the front clasp. When her breasts sprang free from the red lace, Alex moaned and his eyes darkened.

His eyes followed her hands to the waist of her matching red panties. Hooking her hands into the band, she slid them down her long legs and let them drop to the floor.

Alex groaned and closed his eyes. Coming to his knees, his hands slid up her calves to her hips. Pulling her closer, he buried his head between her parted legs.

Samantha gasped in pleasure as his mouth did incredibly wicked things to her. She had to bite her lip to keep from screaming out in pleasure. Her trembling hands grasped his head as she began to spin out of control. His mustache and beard tickled her creamy thighs as he worked diligently to bring her pleasure. Samantha reached peak after peak of sheer ecstasy. When she thought she could stand no more, Alex proved to her time and time again that she could.

When her legs buckled from exhaustion, Alex pulled her down to him. The plastic crinkled as he tore open the condom wrapper. He quickly applied it and entered her hot, wet body in one quick stroke. She gasped and held on to him as he lifted and lowered her body to meet each penetrating thrust. Alex stopped moving and Samantha looked down at him with questioning gray eyes. He pulled her head down and her mouth covered his.

"You set the pace." She needed no further instructions as she moved above him in a slow methodic pace that drove him wild. Within minutes, he rolled over on top of her and took control again. This time, when she reached out and touched the stars, she wasn't alone. Alex collapsed on top of her and Samantha held him to her. Rolling to his side, he pulled her with him. They lay that way for several minutes in silence. His warm hands glided over her body. When his hand moved to her stomach, her hand covered his. "I know your body almost as well as I know my own." Samantha held her breath. "You've gained weight." His hand moved back up to her breast, and she slowly let out the breath she was holding.

"I've gained about five pounds," she confessed, not meeting his eyes. She tried to read his mind but failed.

Alex's sharp gaze rested on the slight rounding of her abdomen. If he hadn't been looking for it, he would have easily missed it. His eyes moved back up to the breast that rested in his hand. It was also fuller, and tender, he had guessed, from her earlier response when he had taken her nipple into his mouth.

"My guess is all those late-night cravings for ice

cream." Samantha's eyes locked with his at the mention of the word "cravings." "I'm not complaining about your weight. You could stand to gain another five pounds."

She pulled his head down for a quick kiss. He nibbled at her lips before covering her mouth in a kiss so deep and penetrating that it made her toes curl up. His body covered hers again and Samantha welcomed him home.

Samantha sat nervously in the doctor's office. She crossed and uncrossed her legs for what seemed like the twentieth time. She picked up the magazine and then laid it back on the table.

What am I doing here? I don't need a psychologist. Okay, I admit, I have a problem with forgiving and forgetting. That doesn't make me crazy. It makes me human. The things we do for love.

"Mrs. Taylor, Dr. Madison will be right with you," said the receptionist. Samantha nodded past the lump in her throat.

An hour later, when Samantha left the doctor's office, she felt better about herself and about the past. She made another appointment for the following week.

Alex was surprised when he got the beep from Dr. Madison's office. He called the office and asked for Dr. Madison.

"This is Dr. Carlisle," he said, jotting something down on a chart. He handed the chart to his nurse. "Did someone page me?"

"Alex, it's Regina. Samantha Taylor came in for her first appointment a little while ago." Alex sighed in relief. He'd been hoping Samantha would take his advice and go.

"Yes," he said breathing a sigh of relief. "Thanks for letting me know. Did she make another appointment?"

"Yes as a matter of fact, she did, for next week. You know I can't share the session with you."

"I don't need to know what she said. I only needed to know she went. Thanks for letting me know she kept her appointment. I owe you one."

The following Monday, Alex phoned to tell her not to prepare dinner; he would bring it with him when he came over.

She figured he would bring Chinese, which was his favorite. Samantha didn't particularly care what he brought as long as she didn't have to cook anything. She was battling the flu bug and nothing sat well in her stomach right now.

Samantha was setting the table when the garage door opened. Alex sailed into the room carrying a large brown paper bag. The sight of him made her heart accelerate.

He was dressed in a dark blue button-down shirt and a pair of matching slacks. These were, of course, clothes she had purchased for him because she had gotten sick of the basic-black look. Alex made anything look good.

"Hi," said Alex setting the bag on the bar. He smiled when he noted her attire. Samantha was wearing a red knit jumpsuit, which hid the curves of her body. She was still trying to hide her pregnancy from him.

"Hi," she responded shyly. "Let me give you a hand with that." She walked towards him slowly. She hadn't taken more than two steps before the aroma of Chinese food greeted her. Her face paled and her stomach immediately revolted against the smell.

Putting her hand to cover her mouth, Samantha ran from the room. She ran straight up the stairs to her bathroom.

* * *

Samantha lay across the bed drained after emptying the contents of her stomach. The smell of Chinese food was nauseating. She pulled herself up from the bed and opened the window.

The gust of cold air made her shiver, but the smell was heavenly. She breathed in and out deeply and sat down on the carpeted floor by the window.

Alex saw it coming a mile away. The minute Samantha got a whiff of the Chinese food, she turned pale and then green. He hid a smile as he watched her flee the room.

Check and checkmate, my beautiful fiancée. Let's see how you get out of this one without spilling the beans.

He would give her a few minutes to collect herself before he went in to see if she was okay. Alex helped the kids fix their plates and sat them down at the table before he went in search of Samantha.

Samantha thought she was alone in the room, until a burgundy throw blanket was draped around her shoulders. Alex silently sat down next to her on the floor.

"So, how pregnant are you?" he asked, lifting her face to his. Their eyes clashed. His were questioning. Hers were amused.

Samantha started to laugh. She couldn't stop herself as she doubled over with laughter. Her amusement was cut short, when she started coughing. Hacking coughs shook her body and she gasped for air. Taking several deep breaths, the coughing finally subsided.

"You think I'm pregnant," she wheezed for air. Alex watched her with concern. "Is that the reason you're here?"

"Sam, if you are pregnant. I will stand by you," he assured her. "We will get married immediately. I'd marry you in a heartbeat."

"You would marry me for our baby's sake?" That was not exactly the answer she wanted to hear. "Let me see if I've got this straight. You think I'm psycho, but you would marry me if I were pregnant. How noble of you? Would the wedding take place before you deemed it necessary for me to seek psychiatric help?" she asked, sarcastically turning away from him. "Would that be a clause in the prenuptial agreement?"

"I don't think you're crazy, Sam. You just need someone to talk to. Okay, this does complicate things a little." Samantha got angrily to her feet. "Sam, I know this is an emotional time for you. Your hormones are out of whack."

"Get out," she fumed, pointing at the bedroom door. "There is nothing wrong with my hormones. I don't know where you came up with the idea of me being pregnant, but you're dead wrong. I'm not pregnant Alex. My cycle was two weeks ago." He eyed her in disbelief. "The weight gain is due to me snacking more than I should and not exercising. The nausea is because I'm fighting the flu bug, you idiot. In case you haven't noticed, I have a stupid cold. If there is nothing else, please leave my room." Samantha swayed on her feet and grabbed the bed for support. She felt hot and sweaty. "Alex, I think . . ." Her words trailed off as she collapsed on the carpeted floor.

Alex rushed to her and lifted her in his arms. He laid her on the bed. Touching his hand to her forehead, he frowned. She was burning up with fever.

"Sam, can you hear me?" Kneeling over her, he checked her eyes. Sweeping Samantha up in his arms, he rushed down the stairs with her. "Kids, let's go! Samantha's sick. We have to get her to the hospital. Everyone in the Expedition, now!"

There was complete silence in the SUV while Alex silently prayed all the way there. Alex called ahead to alert the ER team they were en route. He also called Nathan and Laura to let them know what was happening.

Alex felt powerless as he stayed with the children in the waiting room while they rushed Samantha back into a room. On edge, he paced the room. Nathan and Laura came shortly after they arrived.

When Dr. Sanders came out to see them, Alex was the first one to reach him. He waved for them all to sit down.

"Mrs. Taylor has the flu. It's borderline pneumonia, so we are going to keep her a few days. Her lungs are a little cloudy. We are trying to lower her temperature right now. It's spiked at 104." Alex closed his eyes. He didn't want to say anything that might frighten the children, but he knew they had to get her temperature down fast. "I have to get back to my patient. I'll let you know if there is any change." He walked away, leaving Alex stunned and speechless.

"How could you, not know she was sick?" charged Nathan, glaring at Alex. "You see her every day."

Alex took his father-in-in-law's anger because he knew what Nathan said was true. He should have seen Samantha was sick. He was kicking himself, because he'd known something wasn't right with her, but he'd thought she was pregnant.

"Alex, you are not responsible," defended Laura. "Samantha is a grown woman. She knew she was sick and didn't say anything or go to the doctor. This is not your fault."

"Is Mom going to be alright?" asked Hope, sliding her arms around Alex. He returned her warm hug.

"Your mom is a strong woman. She'll be fine," he whispered past the catch in his voice. All the kids went to him and hugged him.

An hour later, they all breathed a sigh of relief when the nurse came out to tell them Samantha's temperature was down to 100. Laura took the kids home with her while Alex and Nathan waited to see Samantha.

They got to see her briefly before she was admitted and moved to a private room. Samantha was sound asleep, so they didn't wake her.

As Alex sat by her bed, he slipped the engagement ring onto her finger. He couldn't imagine his life without her. He had come close to losing her, and it terrified him. He would not lose her again.

Nathan stayed a while longer and then took a cab home. Alex had the nurse bring him a blanket and pillow. He had no intention of leaving Samantha's side.

Samantha slept through the night, and Alex slept on the couch in her room. When he woke, he was stiff as he got to his feet. He went into the bathroom and came out feeling somewhat refreshed. The nurse had left him a toothbrush and toothpaste.

He was sitting in the chair beside the bed watching the morning news when Samantha moaned. Turning his head, he locked eyes with her.

She blinked a couple of times to clear her vision. Looking around the hospital room, she tried to sit up in bed, but found herself too weak to move. "What happened?" she asked past the dryness of her throat. Seeing her discomfort. He poured a small amount of water in a glass and held it to her lips.

"Take a small sip," he instructed. Samantha obeyed and then relaxed against her pillow. "Why didn't you tell me you were sick?" He sat back down in the chair beside her bed.

"It was just a cold," she said, wheezing, and then

erupted into a fit of coughs. Alex watched her feeling guilty all over again.

"No, it wasn't a little cold," argued Alex shaking his head. "Honey, you have borderline pneumonia. You're going to have a hospital vacation for the next couple of days."

"I can't stay here," said Samantha, attempting to get up from the bed. Alex pushed her back down. "I have too much to do. The kids . . ."

"Will be fine. You need your rest. Honey, I will take care of the children, and you will take care of Samantha."

"Alex, you can't take care of the kids," she coughed. "You wouldn't know where to begin. I have to keep a calendar just to keep up with soccer, karate, dance, and basketball."

"Yes, I can," he argued. He wasn't convinced he could do it either, but Sam needed the break. "Sam, you need to rest and recover. I'll take some time off and take care of the kids. A missed basketball or soccer practice will not be the end of the world. Stop worrying. Let me take care of the kids and take care of you."

"I'm more worried about you," she admitted. He caught her hand and held it up so she could see the ring. Tears smarted in her eyes as she fingered her engagement ring. "I don't remember putting that back there."

"Lady, you scared ten years off my life." He brought her hand to his lips. "I almost lost you. I don't ever want to feel like that again. I love you, Samantha." Mindful of the IV in her other hand, he got up and sat down on the edge of the bed. "I don't know what I would do if I lost you. You are my life, Samantha Taylor. You make me whole. I know we have problems, but we can get through them. Honey, together we can get through anything."

Tears ran freely down her cheeks as she smiled at him.

She raised herself into a sitting position and hugged him. Alex's arms closed around her and he held her close.

"I love you, Alex," cried Samantha as fresh tears rolled down her cheeks. "I'm sorry." He eased her back on to the bed and dropped a kiss on her forehead.

"Does this mean the next time I tell you to go take the flu shot you will?" he teased, brushing the hair back from her face. Samantha laughed and winced. "I'm sorry, sweetie." He planted a kiss on her forehead. "Rest. I'll be right here when you wake up."

"I'll make you a deal. You go home, shower, and change, and I will rest easy." She silenced him by placing her hand against his lips. "Go take a nap in your own bed. Come back later this afternoon when you are well rested. We can't afford for you to get sick as well. Go get some rest. I'll see you later. I'm not going anywhere," she smiled.

"Okay, I'll go." Alex said, touching his lips to hers and then to her forehead. "I'll see you later. Get some rest."

"You too. You're going to need it." As the door closed, so did her eyes. She fell into an exhausted sleep. Minutes later, she was awakened to have her temperature and blood pressure checked. She drifted off to sleep again as soon as the nurse left.

The following few days were pure hell for Alex. He had no idea what he had let himself in for by keeping all four kids. After two days, he was ready to strangle both Derek and Hope. They were at each other's throats twenty-four-seven. Matt whined and cried himself to sleep because he missed his mother.

Lexi wasn't one to share her feelings. She kept everything locked inside until she blew up. She was angry at the world right now. After days of pouting, she finally asked Alex if Aunt Samantha was going to die like her mother did. He finally convinced her it wasn't the case.

"As soon as you are on your feet lady, we have a wedding to plan. I'm not letting you get away from me again."

She put her arms around him. "And I'm not letting you out of it this time," she smiled up at him. "Consider yourself off the market permanently. You are mine."

"I've always been yours. You just couldn't see the forest for the trees." Looking into his eyes, she saw the truth of his words.

Sam wasn't sure what disturbed her sleep, but when she opened her eyes, she wasn't alone. A tall, slender woman in scrubs stood inside the closed door. The look on her face did not set Sam's mind at ease. She sent Samantha a look of pure venom and without a word, slipped out the door.

Samantha stared at the closed door. She had no idea who the woman was or what she wanted. She buzzed the nurse.

"Keri, there was a nurse in my room a few seconds ago. She didn't say anything, but left as soon as I woke up."

"You're not scheduled for any medication. Maybe she had the wrong room. Your next dose of medicine isn't until morning."

"Thanks, Keri. It was probably the wrong room." Samantha released the buzzer unconvinced. She had a feeling it was more to it than that. She did not mistake the woman's look of loathing.

Chapter Eighteen

A few weeks later, when Dana called them to come over for their monthly get-together, Samantha jumped at the opportunity. She and Alex could use a little distraction right now. They were at each other's throats, disagreeing about wedding plans. She wanted small and simple. He wanted a big wedding and reception. Samantha had been there and done that, and had no desire to do it again. It was way too overrated and entirely too much money and hard work on her part.

"I'm teaching my husband to speak Spanish," said Alicia, smiling. "You can imagine the challenge I'm having."

"Oh, brother," laughed Alex, turning to face Jeremy. "That's just what he needs, another language to slaughter. He has yet to master the English language, and he's been speaking that for thirty-four years."

"Hey, Angel-face, are you going to let him talk to your man like that? I thought you had my back."

"I've got your front and your back, sweetie, but if the shoe fits," replied Alicia, silencing him with a kiss.

"Since I'm teaching the kids Spanish and English, we

thought it might be a good idea for Jay to learn Spanish as well," explained Alicia.

"The real reason is so I can understand when her father curses me out in Spanish. At least then I'll know what the hell he's saying. He's gotten away with it for years, and no one will interpret for me. It will be a big surprise for Hector when I respond," he winked.

"Jay," admonished Alicia, "If I had known the reason for your sudden interest in Spanish, I wouldn't be teaching you."

"I know. Here's my song," said Jeremy, dancing around the room, singing. The popular oldies Sam & Dave hit "Hold on, I'm Coming" filled the air. They all watched the show Jeremy put on for them. He was an excellent dancer and had more rhythm than any white man she had ever seen. Alicia hopped down from the bar and started dancing towards him. Their bodies brushed together suggestively as they danced.

"Don't you two have a bed somewhere?" yelled Tomas good-naturedly. This only made the situation worse. They started dirty dancing at this point. When it was over, everyone was laughing and applauding.

Between the two of them they had no shame. They were two of the most outgoing people Samantha knew. Alicia and Jeremy were perfectly matched. Alicia was as dark as he was fair. Jeremy was a blond-haired, blue-eyed, fair-skinned Adonis. Alicia was a deep brown, with brown eyes and long, curly dark hair. She had an exotic look to her.

"Jeremy and I are going upstairs to play pool," said Alex, kissing Samantha's parted lips. "Want to come up and cheer me on?"

"No thanks. I think I'll stay here with the girls. We have a lot of catching up to do." She watched in appreciation as he took the stairs two at a time. *What an ass!*

The women were sitting around chatting when the doorbell rang. Excusing herself, Dana went to answer it.

Samantha stared in horror as Drew strolled into the house escorting Betsy. Samantha's blood began to boil as she watched them together. She stood in the doorway to the kitchen, not moving.

Propelled by anger, she sailed into the room toward the smiling couple. She saw the smile disappear from Betsy's face as she stopped directly in front of her.

"Samantha, hi," said Drew kissing her cheek. "I want you to meet someone very special to me. This is Betsy."

Samantha's eyes shifted to the woman in question. Betsy stared back at her with fear in her eyes. Folding her arms over her chest, Samantha looked from Drew to her cousin.

"How did you two meet?" she asked between clenched teeth. She already knew the answer to the question, but she wanted to hear it from Drew. Considering all the things she wanted to say, she surprised herself by remaining so calm. She held up her hand to silence him. "No, let me guess. 'Alex,'" repeated Samantha, softly biting her lip, "somehow, I knew you were going to say that. This is definitely status quo for Alex. This is some of his best work yet. I bet he had a good laugh about this one."

"Come again?" Drew said, confused. He put his arm around Betsy, and kissed her cheek. Samantha stared at them, shaking her head.

"You don't know who she is, do you? Alex failed to tell you what she did to me. I'm not surprised."

"Samantha," said Dana, walking over to them and trying to lead her away. "Hi, Drew. Hi, Betsy. Can you come into the kitchen with me for a minute, Samantha? I need to talk to you, now."

"No, Dana. Nice try, though. I think Drew should know exactly whom he's escorting around town on his arm."

"Samantha, please don't do this," whispered Betsy, softly. "Let me tell him. I promise you I will tell him everything."

"There's no time like the present. I really hate secrets, don't you? They always come back to bite you when you least expect them."

"Did I miss something?" asked Drew, looking from Betsy to Samantha. "Do you two know each other?"

"Quite well, actually. Betsy is my first cousin, Drew. I guess Alex forgot to mention that little tidbit. She's also the woman my husband had an affair with. Her son, Joshua, is the product of her affair with Greg. She delivered Joshua about four months after I delivered my child. Isn't that right Betsy? As a favor, my dear cousin moved in with us to help me out. Boy did she ever help herself to everything in my home, including my husband." Drew stared from an angry Samantha to Betsy, who was on the verge of tears. "I guess Alex forgot to mention all of this to you."

Alex and Jeremy were playing pool when Alicia rushed into the room. One look at her face told them something was wrong.

"Alex, I think you should come downstairs. Drew showed up a few minutes ago with Betsy. Samantha was headed their way when I came up here." Alex was out the door and down the stairs in a flash, followed by Jeremy and Alicia.

"This is the woman, and I use the word loosely, who was sleeping with my husband in my own house. She's the woman who . . ."

"That's enough, Samantha," warned Alex, coming to stand directly between the two women. He faced a furious Samantha.

"No, it's not enough. I've only begun," seethed Samantha, glaring at Alex. "You did this deliberately. How dare you set my friend up with Greg's mistress? Did you do it to spite me, Alex? Did you have a good laugh about it? You set Drew up with her and neglected to tell him what she's done. She is not good enough for him. He deserves better than a lying, cheating witch like Betsy."

"This has nothing to do with you," he charged, glaring back at her. "Everything is not about you, Samantha.

"Let's go," said Betsy turning to Drew. Alex caught her arm to stop her from leaving. Drew stood there motionless, not knowing what to do next.

"Nobody is going anywhere!" yelled Alex in frustration. "I've had it with this whole situation. I think it's time we all cleared the air. We'll start with you, Betsy. Everyone here knows you had an affair with Greg. God knows Samantha's harped on it enough since finding out. We also know you had a child by him." He saw the pain in her brown eyes. He caught her hand and gave it a squeeze. "I'm not condemning you. We are all human. You made a mistake. You fell in love with a married man. You are not the first woman to do so. We all make mistakes. No one is perfect, least of all me. I've made my share of mistakes and so has Samantha."

"She seduced my husband, in my home!" seethed Samantha glaring at Alex. "It's not exactly something I can get past easily. You are just one surprise after another. You've lied to me repeatedly and now you set up my friend with my dead husband's mistress. You have quite a sense of humor. So what do you do for an encore, pull a rabbit out of a hat?"

"Samantha, I'm sorry," cried Betsy. "I never meant for any of it to happen. I never meant to hurt you."

"What did you mean to do, Betsy?" Samantha asked furiously. "You slept with my husband in my home. You had a child by him. Am I just supposed to forgive and forget because you're my cousin?"

Betsy looked from Samantha to Drew and ran out the front door. To Samantha's frustration, Drew went after her. "I'll take a cab home."

"I brought you, and you will leave with me." Alex followed her out the front door. "Samantha listen to me," said Alex catching her arm to stop her. "Stop." She stopped and crossed her arms over her chest.

"How could you do this? How could you set him up with Betsy, of all people? There are over a million women in this city and you set him up with her."

"Yes, I set him up with Betsy. I didn't tell you because I knew you would take it as a personal affront. Sam, this has nothing to do with you or with us. Drew is an adult. Betsy made a mistake with Greg. I don't think she deserves to be punished the rest of her life for one transgression."

"I can't talk about this right now, Alex." She walked over to his car and waited for him to unlock the door.

They were both silent on the drive home. Samantha was fuming inwardly at what Alex had done. She did not find at all amusing the fact Alex set Betsy up with Drew. Betsy didn't deserve someone as loving and kind as Drew.

When Alex pulled into the driveway at Samantha's house, she got out of the car and marched to the front door. Unlocking the door, she went inside.

"I didn't expect you back this early." Karen, the babysitter, picked up her purse and keys.

"I'm not feeling well," Samantha lied, removing money from purse. She paid Karen and left the room. "Alex, can you make sure she gets home safely?"

Alex came inside and left the door open for Karen. He watched her cross the street and go inside her parents' house before closing and locking the front door. He followed Samantha into the den, where he knew all hell was about to break loose.

"Okay, let's hear it. I set Betsy up with Drew." He closed the door behind him and waited for the explosion.

"He's too good for her. He deserves better." Alex said nothing as he listened. He saw no point in interrupting, so he let her get it out of her system. He sat down on the sofa and peered up at her without saying a word. "Don't just sit there! Say something!"

"What would you have me say, Sam? I know what she did to you was wrong, but she is not a bad person. She and Drew are good together. Drew and Betsy are adults. They don't need our permission to see each other." Catching her hand, he pulled her down onto his lap. His mouth covered hers smothering her gasp of surprise. His tongue plunged into her mouth and he kissed her until they were both breathless. "Isn't this better than talking?" His mouth covered hers again and she returned his kiss. She pulled her mouth from his.

"This conversation is not over," she said breathlessly. His hot mouth trailed kisses down her throat. He unbuttoned her blouse and pushed it from her shoulders.

"I locked the door behind me," he whispered against her throat. He unsnapped her bra and slid it from her shoulders.

"This isn't over, Alex. You are only shutting me up temporarily." She gasped in pleasure as he took her breast into his mouth.

"My sentiments exactly, sweetness. It's only the beginning. Forget about everything except pleasing your man." His hand slid under her skirt. He smiled in surprise at what he found. Not only was she hot and wet for him, she wasn't wearing any underwear.

Much later, Alex refused to apologize for setting them

up. Finally, they agreed to disagree on the subject of Drew and Betsy.

Samantha knocked nervously on Drew's door. One week had passed since the incident at Dana's. Samantha felt guilty about hurting him.

"Hi," said Drew, opening the door allowing her to enter. "This is a surprise. Come in."

"Thanks," said Samantha, stepping inside the townhouse. "I was hoping I was still welcome. I came by to apologize for my behavior at the party. I shouldn't have gone off on Betsy in front of you and everyone. My problem is with Betsy, not with you. It just so happens that particular night was the first time I've seen her since finding out about her affair with Greg. When I looked at her, I completely lost it."

"It's understandable under the circumstances. Have a seat." They both sat down on the sofa. "You were trying to protect me."

"I wanted to hurt Betsy. I wanted her to feel some of the pain I felt. When I saw the way you looked at her, I wanted to rip her heart out. I think I succeeded by exposing the truth. I'm sorry you were hurt in the process."

"Talk about being blindsided, I had no clue there was a connection between you two. Alex never said a word. Neither did Betsy, for that matter. It must have been quite a shock for you seeing us together."

"That's the understatement of the year. I had no idea you even knew her. She was probably equally shocked to see me. She couldn't have known you were bringing her to Dana's house or she wouldn't have come."

"No, she didn't know. I told her I had some friends I wanted her to meet. The minute Dana opened the door

I sensed something was wrong. It's all a moot point now. Betsy and I are not seeing each other any more."

"Because of me?" asked Samantha, feeling guilty. It was obvious by Drew's reaction he cared about Betsy.

"No, because of Betsy. I know what she did to you was wrong, but that doesn't stop me from caring about her. I love her, Samantha, and you have to deal with it. I haven't seen her since that night. She won't take my calls. When I go by, she won't let me in. We talked about it briefly the night of the party, and then she brushed me off."

"Maybe she thought you were going to give her the brush-off. Maybe she thought she was beating you to the punch? Don't ask me why I'm saying this, but if you really care about her don't give up on her." He looked at Samantha in surprise. "You are the best thing that has ever happened to her. Believe me, I know. If she lets you get away, she's crazy."

"I can't believe you are saying this. Why the sudden change of heart?" he asked curiously, watching her closely for a hint into what she was thinking.

"It's not a change of heart. I still despise her, but I do care about you. Maybe Alex knew what he was doing when he put you two together. Drew, I want you to be happy. If Betsy makes you happy, then who am I to stand in the way of true love? Don't give up on her."

Samantha later told Alex what was going on with Drew and Betsy. After their discussion, Alex left the house to go see Betsy.

"Alex, what are you doing here?" asked Betsy, hugging him. He returned her warm greeting. She closed the door behind him and followed him into the living room.

"You know I'm not a small-talk kind of guy, so I will get right to the point. How are things with you and Drew?"

"Drew who?" she asked, turning away from his questioning eyes. "You're right. You don't beat around the bush. Sometimes I wish you would."

"Why won't you talk to Drew?" he asked without preamble. "I hear he's been by a couple of times to see you. Why did you bail on him?"

"What would be the point of talking to him? You saw the look on his face after Samantha's little announcement. He couldn't even look at me. He gave me the silent treatment all the way home. I didn't bail on him. I just beat him to the punch. I dumped him before he could dump me."

"How do you know he was going to dump you? Maybe, just maybe, you are wrong. He was surprised. Be honest with yourself, what man wouldn't be surprised? It just took him off-guard. Betsy, the man is crazy about you."

"Past tense, Alex. Whatever he felt died when he found out what I had done. Samantha wanted to hurt me, and she did. She wanted me to feel her pain, and I do. Why do I keep being punished?" she asked, close to tears. "I'm never going to be able to live down my past mistakes. I don't want to be hurt anymore." Alex pulled her into his arms and held her as she cried. "Why do I always choose the wrong men to love? First Floyd, then Greg, and now Drew." Alex raised her chin to look into her misty brown eyes. "I love Drew," she said.

"I don't think you chose the wrong man this time. I think Drew is exactly what you and Joshua need. For your sake Betsy, talk to Drew before you let him walk out of your life. Don't give up on him. Don't give up on yourself. You do deserve a chance at happiness. Everyone deserves a second chance."

"Your little matchmaking couldn't have helped your relationship with Samantha any. Is she even talking to you? Had I known whose party Drew was taking me to, I never would have gone."

"That's a given. Forget about it. Betsy, there is nothing you can do to change the past. You and Samantha both have to move past this. Don't focus on Samantha. Focus on Drew. He's the one you love, and he loves you. Don't let him get away. He's worth the fight."

"Thanks, Alex." She hugged him. "I need to go find Drew. I'll see you soon. Lock the door on your way out."

Samantha dropped by Alex's office to take him to lunch. Tina had her wait in his office while he finished up with his patients. She studied the various degrees on his wall. Sitting down, she looked at the family pictures on his desk.

"Hi, what are you doing here?" asked Alex, opening the door. She was in his arms in a flash. His lips brushed hers.

"I came to take you to lunch," she smiled, kissing him again. "Can you take a lunch break, or am I out of luck?"

"It's a lovely thought, but I can't. I'm running behind and I'm booked solid for this afternoon. I've got to run. I have patients waiting." The intercom paged Alex to examining room one. He looked down at his watch and cursed. "Samantha, read my lips. I'm busy. I have patients to see. I can't do this right now. I'll come by as soon as I get off work. I've got to go. I'll see you later." He left the office abruptly.

Chapter Nineteen

Samantha was furious when she left his office. She went home and poured herself a glass of wine, and was nursing her third glass when Dana got to her house. She emptied the glass and sat it on the coffee table.

"Sam, why are you drinking? What's going on with you? Has something happened with you and Alex?"

"You mean the on again, off again engagement? I don't know. What day is it?" Samantha picked up the bottle of wine, and Dana took it from her.

"I think you've had enough," Dana said, carrying the bottle to the other side of the room. "Did you and Alex have a fight?"

"That's putting it mildly. He thinks of me as a trophy wife already. I take care of his children. I'm his damn cook, lover, and child-care provider. How much more useful can I be? It's not like I sit around all day eating bon bons and watching soap operas. He has taken me for granted for the last time. He can cook his own meals and pick up his own children from now on. I've had it with being taken for granted." Dana said nothing as Samantha vented. "Dana, what am I going to do?" asked Samantha, laying her head in her hands. "My life is so screwed up. I can't trust my fiancé to be honest with me. I never know when he's telling me the truth and when he's lying. He's nothing like Greg. With Greg I at least knew when he was lying, or at least I thought I did. But Alex is so good. Maybe I shouldn't marry him. I should try to work out some sort of visitation with Matt. We don't belong together. Sure the sex is great, but that's all we have. I could get the same thing from a male prostitute. Where are the feelings? The emotions? Oh, I keep forgetting his emotions are all below his belt. Whenever we have a problem, his answer is to take me to bed."

"Samantha," interrupted Dana softly. "You don't mean that. It's the alcohol talking."

"Yes I do mean it. I'm through being his doormat and girl Friday. He doesn't love me. He doesn't even know what love is. I was convenient and handy. I'm through being his little baby-sitter and love toy."

"Samantha, stop," pleaded Dana softly. Samantha raised her head and looked up at Dana. Following Dana's eyes, she looked towards the door to the den.

Alex stood there with a bouquet of flowers in his hands. Samantha's heart stopped at the pain in his brown eyes. He laid the flowers on the table by the door and left the room. She jumped to her feet and went after him.

"Alex! Alex!" As she opened the front door, she heard the tires screech as he drove away. Hugging her arms to her body, she stared after him. Dana pulled her back inside the house and closed the door.

"That's strike two for me," said Samantha sadly. "I keep hurting him and he keeps coming back. What if he doesn't come back this time?"

"Alex, I'm sorry," said Samantha closing the door behind her. "I was upset about what happened earlier in your office and I had a little too much wine. I didn't mean the things I said."

"The flowers were an apology," he said staring off into space. "I wanted to apologize for my earlier outburst. I was having a bad day and I took it out on you. You think I see you as some domestic goddess sex toy. You believe I take you for granted."

"You take it for granted that I will always be around to look after Derek and Lexi. You take it for granted I will have dinner for you when you get here. Yes, Alex. You do take me for granted."

"And you think I'm a great stud, but I can't be trusted. Bottom line is, Samantha, I'm not Greg and I will never be Greg."

"I know you're not Greg. I don't want you to be Greg. I want you, Alex. Why can't you be honest with me?"

"Maybe because you can't be honest with yourself. I'll admit I went about everything the wrong way. I should have told you about Matthew as soon as I found out. That is the only thing I have ever lied to you about. I have tried to be patient with you. I have tried to give you space and give you time, but I've had it. I refuse to live like this. Life is too short. You need to decide if you want me in or out of your life. Say the word and I will walk out that door. I want a real wife and a real marriage. You are Matt's mother and I would never try and take him from you." She met his solemn stare with tears in her eyes.

"I love you," she said softly. "I know you probably don't believe me right now, but I do love you."

Alex closed his eyes against the pain and fear he saw in her eyes. As much as he wanted to believe her words, her actions were not those of a woman in love.

"They are only words. You don't treat someone you love the way you have been treating me. Talk is cheap at this point. You say I haven't given you a reason to trust me. Well, you haven't given me any reason why I should trust you either. Your words and your actions to this point have been near-fatal blows. You have done everything in your power to push me away. Now you say you want me. How can I believe you mean it? You may mean it today or tonight, but tomorrow you could change your mind again. I have never given up on anything in my life," said Alex in a defeated voice, "but I'm giving up now. I give up, Samantha. I give up on you and on this relationship. I'm at my wits' end. I don't know what else to do." Her heart broke into tiny pieces at his declaration. "For the first time ever, I'm admitting defeat. I'm tired. I'm unhappy and I quit." He wiped the tears from her cheek. "I don't blame you for any of this. This is my fault. I created this situation. I thought I could make you fall in love with me. I thought I had enough love for both of us. I was so wrapped up in what I wanted and I was determined to make you love me."

"I do love you," she cried. "I love you more than you could imagine. We can work through this. I know we can."

"I'm not so sure anymore. If you need anything, I will be here for you and the kids. I can't promise you any more than that."

Her heart was breaking as she stared at the man she loved. Samantha made a vow to herself that she would prove to Alex she loved him. She couldn't let it end like this. She knew she had a battle ahead of her, but she was determined to win his love and trust again.

The following weeks were miserable for everyone. The harder Samantha tried, the more resistance she met. The tension between Samantha and Alex was so thick the kids picked up on it immediately.

Samantha and Alex were both lucky they hadn't told

the kids the engagement was back on. Now they wouldn't have to disappoint them again.

Alex was exhausted as he finished his shift. He couldn't wait to get home, shower, and collapse on the sofa.

He unlocked his car and got in. He frowned when someone tapped on his window. Alex was stunned when he saw two police officers. Panic set in—something was wrong with Samantha and the kids. Alex quickly got out of the car, facing the officers.

"Dr. Alex Carlisle?" one of the officers inquired. "Please place your hands on the car," the officer instructed, taking a step back. "Dr. Carlisle, we have a warrant for your arrest."

"What?" Alex asked, unbelieving. "That's impossible," he said placing his hands on the car. "There's been a mistake. What am I being charged with?"

"Sexual assault." Alex stared at him, dumbfounded. "Please place your hands on the car," the officer repeated sternly.

Alex was in a state of shock as they put on the handcuffs. "You have the right to remain silent." Alex faded out as he was read his Miranda rights. He had no idea what was going on or who made the charges against him. He was still dazed and confused as they booked him an hour later.

"You get one phone call, doctor. Make it count," said the officer, setting the phone in front of him.

Alex picked up the phone, immediately thinking of Samantha. He held the phone in his hand. No, he couldn't call her. He dialed a number and waited for the phone to be answered.

"I need your help," said Alex into the receiver. "I know

I'm the last person you would ever expect to hear this coming from, but I need you. I'm in jail. I've been arrested for sexual assault."

"What? Who? Never mind. I'll be there in thirty minutes or less," said the voice on the other end of the phone.

Alex paced the cell as he waited for his attorney. He still had no clue who made the charge against him. Samantha was the only woman in the past three years he made any sexual advances towards. This was a nightmare. This could ruin his career and his family. He prayed the press wouldn't get hold of the story.

Alex breathed a sigh of relief when he saw Nathan with a policeman. The policeman unlocked the cell.

"I posted your bail," said Nathan. "Let's get out of here." Alex followed his father-in-law to pick up his personal possessions. Once in the safety of the Mercedes, Nathan exploded. "What the hell is going on, and who is Chloe Bell?"

"Chloe is behind this?" Alex exploded. "That lying witch!" he snarled. Chloe, the head case was not going to get away with this. "When I get my hands on her—"

"No, Alex, you will stay away from her! You are in enough trouble as it is. Tell me the truth. Did you have an affair with her?"

"No, I didn't have an affair with her," replied Alex furiously. "Samantha is the only woman I've made love to since Kirstin's death. I love your daughter."

"Loving her has nothing to do with an affair. One has nothing to do with the other. If you want me to represent you, then you will have to tell me the whole truth. Lie to Samantha if you have too, but tell me the truth."

"I didn't sleep with her!" he denied hotly. "You can damn me for my past, but don't damn me for something I didn't do. I was faithful to Kirstin and I have been faithful to Samantha. Chloe is nuts. She's obsessed with me. She keeps leaving me sexy messages on my cell phone. If anyone is being harassed, it's me. I never hit on her or flirted with her. I rebuffed her advances and this is her revenge."

"Did you save any of these messages?" Alex shot Nathan a dirty look. "Of course you didn't. Did anyone hear you turn her down? Has anyone commented on her interest in you?"

"Drew and several nurses a few weeks back heard me turn her down. She was coming on to me and I told her I wasn't interested. I told her I was committed to Samantha."

"It's a start. The first thing we have to do is have her investigated. I have a PI who can find out anything about anyone. I'll give him a call right now. You need to prepare Samantha for what is to come. Right now she's only after you, but if she sues the hospital, it will make headlines."

"I cannot believe this is happening. I haven't touched her, yet. You'd better hope she doesn't cross my path."

"Stay away from her. Do not under any circumstances go near her. Are you listening to me Alex? Leave her to me."

Nathan drove Alex to pick up his car. From there they went back to Nathan's to plan a strategy for dealing with Chloe.

Alex drove home slowly. His thoughts were filled with different scenarios. In one Samantha wouldn't believe Chloe's allegations and rallied behind him. *What were the chances of that happening? Slim to none was his guess.* In another, she believed it and told him she never wanted to see him again. He didn't know which scenario would come true.

He went in and checked on the kids before walking down the hall to his bedroom. Pushing the door open, he came up short when he saw Samantha lying in his bed. He stood there several minutes not saying anything.

"Hi," she smiled, meeting his eyes. "What took you so long? I was about to call out the calvary looking for you. You left the hospital hours ago."

"It's a long story. I'm going to take a nice, relaxing shower and then I'll tell you all about it." He grabbed a pair of pajama bottoms out of the dresser drawer and headed for the bathroom.

He took a long, leisurely shower. His body and his mind were exhausted and now he had this one last hurdle to cross.

"There's something I have to tell you." He turned to face her. "The reason I didn't come straight home is because I was arrested for sexual assault." Samantha felt the air rush out of her lungs as she stared at him. Their eyes locked. "It's a lie. I didn't assault Chloe and I didn't have an affair with her." Samantha continued to stare at him in shocked disbelief. "I know with all the problems we are having you have no reason to believe me or trust me."

"I believe you," she said quietly. Her gaze held his and he saw the truth in her eyes. She did indeed believe him. Her hand covered his and squeezed. "How did you get out? Why didn't you call me? Who bailed you out?"

"Your father. He's representing me. Nathan is doing a background check on Chloe to see what he can dig up. I can't believe this is happening. I swear to you Sam, I never touched her."

"I believe you." She moved into the circle of his arms and returned his hug. She proved to him again and again how much she did love him.

Nathan warned Alex to stay away from Chloe, but he'd said nothing about Samantha staying away. He didn't want any confrontations at the hospital. He told Alex to keep a low profile until his PI finished checking into

Chloe's past. Thus far, the PI discovered Alex was not the first man she stalked or the first man she pressed false charges against.

Samantha did her own legwork and found out where Chloe lived. Against her better judgment, she drove to Chloe's apartment complex. She sat in her car and waited for her to come home from work.

This was one confrontation long overdue. Sam let her get away with calling her home on a pretense of looking for Alex, but this was the final straw. She was not about to stand aside and let some crazy woman ruin the life of the man she loved. This was war.

When Samantha spotted the leggy blonde going into her apartment, she got out of her car and followed her. Ringing the doorbell, she waited patiently for the door to open.

"Hello, can I help you?" asked the pretty woman, smiling. Her look changed immediately when she recognized Samantha. "Let me guess," she said in a sneer, "you are here to defend your boyfriend. You have my sympathies."

"I don't need your sympathy, but you obviously need mine. You seem to have some delusion about Alex. I'm here to make sure you see the light." Samantha barged into the apartment. "You are the one who will need more than sympathy when my father gets through with you. He will wipe the floor with you. Every detail of your miserable life will be exposed in the courtroom. Every guy you stalked. I'm sure Alex isn't the first, but he will be the last. You won't be able to show your face in this town again when we are finished. You will lose everything the way you tried to make Alex lose everything. You and I both know he didn't touch you, and it will be proven in court. Everyone knows you've been chasing Alex around the hospital like a dog in heat." She watched the expression on the woman's face go from fear to anger in the space of a heartbeat. "Alex didn't rape you. He wouldn't spit on you if you were on fire. You are a liar. He kicked you to the curb and now you are out for revenge."

"Are you sure about that?" Chloe challenged. "Lonely men do stupid things all the time. How do you know what he did? You two weren't even together at the time. He said he loved me. I believed him. Alex told me he would never marry a head case like you. You're just a baby-sitter. You take care of his house and his kids. Any paid nanny can do what you do."

"And you would like the job. Would you like to trade places with me, Chloe? Isn't that what this is all about? You love Alex and he loves me. You are living in a fantasy world if you think you can win him like this. Alex would never walk away from his family. When my father is finished with you, you will be the laughingstock of this town."

"Get out of my apartment! You shouldn't even be here!" said the crazed woman, becoming unraveled. "I have a restraining order against your fiancé. Do I need to get one for you as well?"

"If you go through with this farce, you better believe it," Samantha warned. "Alex told me he rebuffed your advances and you didn't take the rejection very well. You would ruin a man's life and reputation because he won't sleep with you. How sick can you be? Speaking of restraining, that's exactly what's going to happen to you once they have you in a straightjacket in a padded cell."

"He did sleep with me! He is not going to get away with what he did to me!" She kicked the door shut with her foot and then locked it. "He's mine and you are not going to take him from me. No one is going to take him from me." She took a gun out of her pocket and aimed it at Samantha.

Samantha gasped in surprise and her heart nearly

stopped as she stared down the barrel of the gun. "I could have given him everything. I wanted to give him everything. He chose you. I still don't know why. You love him. You love him not. Have you finally made up your mind, you dumb twit? And to think he chose you over me. He's the real loser here. He rejected me. He said he loved you. I told him he would pay for rejecting me. No one rejects me and lives to tell about it." Chloe waved the gun at Samantha. "Go sit over there. I have to think about what I'm going to do with you."

"Chloe, let me go. Alex will come looking for me," reasoned Samantha softly. Her eyes were glued to the gun. "This will not accomplish anything. It won't make him love you. It will make him hate you."

"Alex doesn't even know you're here." She read the surprise in Samantha's eyes. "No one does. See how stupid and useless you are? That will work to my advantage. We'll just tie you up to keep you out of harm's way. Don't worry, Samantha. It's not you I'm going to kill. Someone has to be left behind to look out for the children. My vote is for you. You can have the job. That's probably the only job you are half good at. Besides, I don't want the kids. I want Alex. Alex and I will be together, one way or another—if not in life, then in death." Samantha's look went from anger to stark fear. Chloe was planning to kill herself and Alex. She opened her mouth to speak.

"Save it or I will gag you. I don't want to hear another word from you. Now we wait for Prince Charming to ride up on his fiery steed." Chloe laughed, and her maniacal laughter sent chills all over Sam.

Chapter Twenty

Alex was making rounds when he received a stat page. He called the nurses' station, and they told him to call his father-in-law immediately. He called the number from his cell phone.

"Alex, something is wrong. Samantha was here around noon, and she dropped off the kids. She said she had an errand to run and she would be back in about an hour. That was four hours ago. I've been trying her cell phone and it's going straight to voice mail. Have you talked to her?"

"No," said Alex gripping the phone. He had a bad feeling something was wrong. "Do you have any idea where she went?"

"We were talking about Chloe Bell and I received a phone call. When I came back to the room, she was gone. You don't suppose she went to see Chloe?"

"God, I hope not. Let me check on something and I'll call you back." Alex took his cell phone out of his pocket and checked it. He had four missed calls and one new message. Praying it wasn't who he thought it was, he dialed his voice mail.

"Hello lover. Did you miss me? I miss you. I had a visitor today. Your fiancée and I had a real interesting talk about you.

We compared notes, and you've been a very naughty boy. You've been playing games with both of us. It's time to make a choice between us, lover. You can no longer have it your way. Today you get to decide which one of us you want to be with. We'll be waiting at my place with bated breath for your decision. I love you, Alex. I've always loved you. I'll see you soon. If you know what's good for Samantha, you'll come alone. I'm just looking for an excuse to shoot her."

Alex sprinted down the hospital hallway. Crazy Chloe had Samantha. He had to find her and save her. He bypassed the elevator and took the fire exit. The door banged behind him as he took the stairs two at a time. Alex raced up to the fourth floor. He rushed towards the nurses' station.

"Janet, is Chloe Bell working today?" he asked breathlessly. Fear more than anything else had his heart accelerating.

"No, she's not here. I don't know what happened to her," said the head nurse angrily. Alex's heart fell. "She was supposed to come in at three and she hasn't even called. She better have a good explanation or she's fired. I've had it with her odd behavior."

"Thanks." He took the elevator down to Human Resources on the first floor. "Brenda, I need a huge favor. I need Chloe Bell's address."

"Dr. Carlisle, you know I can't give that kind of information out," she said, eyeing him strangely. "Is something wrong?"

"Brenda, it's an emergency. I think something's happened to Chloe. She wasn't feeling well when she left yesterday and she didn't come in for her shift or call. I think someone should check on her, and I happen to be leaving for the day." She wrote down the address on a Post-it and gave it to him. "Thanks, Brenda." He rushed out the back door of the hospital to the parking lot while dialing Nathan's numbers. "Nathan, I need you to meet me at 5515 Gaston, apartment 5. If you beat me there, wait for me. Chloe didn't show up for work today and she didn't call in. She also left me a cryptic message. I think Sam is with her."

Alex sped out of the parking lot at breakneck speed. He had a bad feeling about what he would find at Chloe's apartment. He felt from the beginning Chloe was a little unstable, but he had no idea how out there she was. Her obsession with him now gave him chills. He prayed Samantha wasn't with her.

Nathan and Alex pulled up at the same time. Alex's heart stopped when he saw Samantha's car. He laid his hand on the hood and frowned when he found it cool. This meant Sam had been there for a while.

"Call the police," Alex instructed, looking toward the front door of the apartment. "She's not playing with a full deck. She thinks we are in love and having an affair. I'm going up to try and talk to her. I have to find out what she did to Samantha." Nathan nodded in agreement.

Alex knocked on the door. When there was no answer, he rang the doorbell. He pounded on the door. "Chloe, it's Alex. I know you're in there. Let me in. We need to talk. I came alone like you asked. Don't play games with me, Chloe! Open the damn door!"

"Alex, sweetheart, what are you doing here?" she asked innocently. "It's open, lover! Come on in and join the party." Alex turned the knob slowly and opened the door. His heart almost stopped when he saw Samantha tied to a chair. Chloe was standing beside Sam's chair holding a gun pointed at her head. "We've been expecting you." She pointed the gun at Alex. "Close the door." Alex closed the door and moved towards Samantha. "That's close enough," warned Chloe. He took another step and stopped when he heard Chloe cock the gun. "I said that's close enough! Why is it men never listen?"

"Samantha, are you okay?" he asked worriedly as his eyes devoured hers. He searched her body for signs of injury, and sighed in relief when he found none.

"I'm fine," she whispered in a choked voice, meeting his eyes. He sadly watched the tears rolling down her cheeks. He had never felt so helpless in all his life as he did now.

"How touching," sneered Chloe. "Tell me what is it about her you love so much? Look at me and look at her. Am I not more glamorous, more beautiful? I would do anything for you," she cried. "I have loved you for years. I wanted you when you were with your first wife. I waited years for you and you have the nerve to propose to her! It's not fair! It should have been me! I should be Mrs. Alexander Carlisle. Why couldn't you love me?" screamed Chloe, glaring at Alex.

"Chloe, let Samantha go," he reasoned. "This is between us. We can talk about this, just the two of us. You're sick. You need help. You don't want to hurt anyone. I'll help you."

"I'm sure you will help me right into an institution because you think I'm crazy. I've been there before. It's horrible. They kept me drugged. I was strapped to the bed at night. I can't go back there. I can't. I'll die in there. I love you. We belong together. We can be together at last, just you and me. I have it all planned."

"Chloe, it will never work. You deserve more than I can give you. You deserve someone who loves you. I don't love you. I love Samantha. I can't leave her or my children. They need me."

"I need you! What about me? What about my needs? Why do my needs always come last? Your children will be fine with her. They are always with her anyway. They will be fine without you. I won't! I can't let you go. I know you love me. I've seen the looks you send me. I know you want me. Every man wants me."

"You're right Chloe, every man wants you." He decided to change tactics with her. "You are a beautiful woman. I choose you, sweetheart. We don't need Samantha. I'm asking you to let Samantha go," he said calmly. "We can stay here and talk, just the two of us. We don't need her here."

"No!" cried Samantha, trying to get free from the ropes. She wouldn't leave him. "Alex, she's planning to kill you! I won't leave you!"

"She won't hurt me. She loves me. You do love me, right Chloe?" She nodded and relaxed her hold on the gun. "I'll stay, if you let Sam go." Chloe moved away from Samantha and stood in front of the window. "Chloe, we can sit down and talk once she's gone."

"All right," she said, shaking. "Untie her and get her out of here."

Alex quickly came forward and untied Samantha's hands and feet. She launched herself into his arms. He held her close.

"That's enough. Stop touching her. Get away from her before I change my mind and shoot her."

"I love you," Samantha cried, clinging to Alex. "I can't leave you here." He unclasped her hands from around his neck and pushed her towards the door.

"No! No! No!" Chloe turned the gun on Samantha. "It's no use. He'll never love me as long as you are alive. You have to die. It's the only way he'll ever love me." She cocked the gun, and everything happened in slow motion.

"No!" Alex shouted and dove in front of Samantha just as Chloe pulled the trigger. Samantha screamed as the impact of Alex's body sent her tumbling backward to the floor. They heard several shots being fired and the sound of broken glass.

When the smoke cleared Alex crawled to Samantha, fearing the worst. He only spared a glance for Chloe's facedown, unmoving body. He barely felt the wound to his arm as he pulled Samantha against him.

"Samantha!" he cried, shaking her. He looked over her expecting to find a bullet, but found nothing. "Open those beautiful gray eyes, sweetheart." Her eyes opened and she flew into his arms. "Are you okay?" She nodded, not trusting her voice to speak. He held her, too choked up to say anything more.

The door flew open and police filled the room, followed by Nathan. He helped Alex and Samantha to their feet and hugged his daughter.

"Sweetheart, are you okay?" She nodded, returning her father's hug. "Don't ever pull a stunt like this again. You could have been killed," he reprimanded.

"Dr. Carlisle, you're bleeding. We'd better get you to a hospital," Samantha looked down at the blood covering Alex and fainted. He and Nathan caught her, and Alex weakly collapsed under the strain of her weight.

Samantha rode in the ambulance with Alex, while her father followed in his car. They were halfway there when he came to.

"Sam," he whispered through the pain. His arm felt like it was on fire. "What happened? Are you all right? Where am I?"

She put her finger to his lips to silence him. "Easy. I'm right here." Her hand covered his and she gave it a little squeeze. "Lie still. You've been shot."

"Is that all?" he said through gritted teeth. He gasped as the ambulance hit a bump. "I guess that explains the severe pain in my arm."

A few hours later, Samantha was on pins and needles

as they wheeled Alex into the operating room to remove the bullet still lodged in his left arm. She sat by his hospital bed and prayed.

Nathan tried to get her to go home and rest, but Samantha wouldn't budge from his side. She had to know Alex would be okay. Early the next morning, Alex was released.

For the next week, Samantha and the kids spoiled and waited on him hand and foot. They were all relieved that he was on the mend.

Samantha smiled as she looked around the decorated room. The dark blue and white streamers crisscrossed the ceiling. In the middle of the room was a revolving disco ball. Jeremy, Alicia, Dana, Keith, Candace, and Tomas had helped her decorate the house.

The plan was for Alex to go over to Jeremy's after work to shower and change. From there, they were going out for a couple of drinks. On the way to the bar, Jeremy would call her. The phone would, of course, give a busy signal. With call waiting, there shouldn't be a busy signal. He would suggest to Alex that they swing by to make sure everything was okay. She asked all the guests to be there by 7:45. Jeremy was bringing Alex home around 8 P.M.

Samantha went back upstairs to shower and change. After her shower, she stared at the two dresses lying on the bed. She couldn't decide between the dark purple and the red. They were both form-fitting and totally out of character for her. They would also knock Alex's socks off.

Finally deciding on the purple dress, she slipped it over her head. She sat down at the dresser and applied a light base and purple eye shadow. To that, she added a touch of plum lipstick.

Taking the rollers out of her long hair, she ran her fingers through it. Combing the front, she put a clip in it and let the back hang down. Applying lotion to her legs and feet, she slipped on a pair of spike-heeled sandals.

Staring at her reflection in the mirror, she hoped Alex was as pleased with her appearance as she was. She also hoped he would have a good time tonight. The past couple of months for them had been a nightmare. Now it was time to put the past behind them and start afresh.

Everyone arrived right on schedule. There was a tense, uncomfortable moment when Drew and Betsy showed up, but Samantha was a gracious host.

She had taken Betsy completely off-guard when she had invited her and Drew to Alex's birthday party. At first, Betsy thought she was joking, and then she became suspicious. Finally, Samantha assured her she was sincere in the gesture.

She beeped Jeremy to let him know to come on over. She turned the lights out, and everyone remained silent as they heard Alex's key in the door.

"Surprise!" the crowd yelled as the door opened. Alex was stunned and speechless as he stared around the decorated room. His eyes locked on a smiling Samantha. She moved forward and brushed his lips with hers.

"Happy Birthday, my love," she said softly, smiling up at him. She watched the smile spread across his face as he pulled her into his arms and kissed her properly. His hungry mouth devoured hers. Samantha's arms went around his neck, and she returned his kiss. It seemed like weeks since he had held her or kissed her like this, and she was like a starving woman.

"I love you," she whispered against his lips. Samantha hoped that at least her eyes could tell him what she was feeling in her heart. She did love him, and she wanted the whole world to know it.

"I love you." He brushed a flyaway strand of hair from

her cheek. Their blissful few seconds were shattered
when everyone moved in on Alex with birthday wishes.

Alex was surprised and pleased to see Drew and Betsy.
He stared thoughtfully at Samantha. He knew what inviting Betsy into her home had cost her, and he was touched
by her gesture.

Throughout the night, Samantha and Alex made constant eye contact. They were never really out of each
other's sight.

Shortly after 9 P.M. trouble arrived wearing a short red
minidress. Samantha had no idea who the woman was,
but she knew she looked like disaster wrapped up in a
tight little package.

Samantha's feelings only intensified when the woman
hugged Alex and kissed him on the cheek. For the next
hour, Samantha fumed while she watched the woman
touch and caress her fiancé at every opportunity.

"Who is she, and are you going to let her get away with
fondling your man?" asked Dana, also watching her with
disgust. "What she is seems to be pretty obvious.

Tina, the nurse from Alex's office, walked over and
joined their circle. She eyed Samantha expectantly as
she shook her head in disgust.

"What a tramp!" Tina said, glaring at the other woman.

"Okay, Tina, who is she? Give us the scoop," said
Samantha.

"That's Leah Guthrie. She should just carry a mattress
around attached to her back. Telling you she wants Dr.
Carlisle is like telling you your carpet is tan. I think you
can see that for yourself. Successful black doctors are a
rarity at the hospital. She's a nurse there, and she's decided Alex is the man for her. Everyone knows she has
Alex marked as her next victim. He blows her off, but
she doesn't give up easily. She sees him as a challenge."

"I'm not going through this again. I think it's time

Leah and I had a little chat," said Samantha, walking away and heading straight for Leah.

"Hello. I'm Samantha Taylor," she said, holding out her hand to Leah. She watched the hesitation on the woman's face before she took her outstretched hand.

"Leah Guthrie," she responded, taking the offered hand. "You have a beautiful home."

"Thank you. Would you like a tour?" Sam asked cordially. She was determined to get Leah alone to have a few words with her. "I'd be happy to show you around."

"Maybe Alex can give me one later." She took a sip of her drink and met Samantha's angry gaze. The two women faced off.

It took every ounce of self-control Samantha had not to slap the smirk off the other woman's face. "I don't think so, but I can. Let's start with the kitchen. Would you give me a hand in there, now?" asked Samantha, pasting on a smile. It wasn't really a request, and everyone standing there knew it.

This was followed by hoots of laughter from the guys surrounding her. Most of them worked at the hospital and knew this was not one of Leah's favorite rooms.

"You obviously know nothing about me, or you would know I don't know the first thing about cooking."

"Improvise," Samantha said, waiting patiently for Leah to follow her. "I think it's time we had a chat."

"Sure, why not?" When the door closed behind them, Leah crossed her arms expectantly over her chest and turned to face Samantha. Samantha stared back at her just as intently. "So let's hear the speech, Samantha."

"Great party." Keith smiled. "Samantha went all out for this one. I hope you appreciate her hard work."

"I do appreciate it. Candace is wonderful," Alex said,

turning in her direction. "If I were you, I'd hang on to her, little brother."

"I intend to. My player days are over. Did you notice her finger when you came in?" Alex looked at his brother in shock.

"You're kidding me." Laughing, Keith shook his head. Alex looked from his brother to Candace showing off her engagement ring. "You're not kidding me."

"No, I'm not. I asked Candace to marry me. She said yes. It would make a great book, wouldn't it, the shrink and the executive?"

"Congratulations!" Alex smiled, hugging his brother. "I'm in total shock, but I'm happy for you guys."

"Did I hear someone mention me?" Candace asked, sliding her arms around Keith's waist. Catching her hand, he held it up for his brother's inspection. Alex whistled in appreciation.

"You're blinding me," he teased. "Congratulations, Candace." He embraced her warmly. "Welcome to the family. I wish the two of you nothing but the best. When's the big date?"

"After going back and forth with my parents, we've decided to fly off to Jamaica at the end of this month to get married."

"That's great." He looked around the room. "Candace, you haven't by any chance seen Samantha, have you?"

"The last time I saw her, she was headed toward the kitchen with 'your touchy-feely girlfriend' in tow. From the look on Samantha's face I'd say she's getting an earful right about now." Alex's eyes narrowed. "Watch out for the flying fur when you open the kitchen door."

Alex made his way to the kitchen. His hand froze on the door when he heard Sam's voice. He knew from her tone she was pissed off.

* * *

"I'm not going to give you a speech. I'm going to talk to you woman to woman. I've met a lot of brazen women in my time, but you take the cake. You have the audacity to waltz into my home, and try and seduce my man, in my face."

"What can I say?" Leah asked, looking down at her long, red, manicured fingernails. "I like to take the direct approach. I have nothing to hide."

"You have plenty to hide, but you choose to display it for all to see. I'd rather not have to stare at your nipples all night. Have you no shame?"

"None at all. Some of us were not born with a silver spoon in our mouth. Some of us have to work with what we were born with. I have a beautiful body, and I love showing it off. Dr. Carlisle is a handsome man. Any woman in her right mind would find him attractive. I'm not Chloe Bell. I'm perfectly sane. It's harmless flirting."

"I doubt there's anything harmless about you. Women like you see something you want and you go after it. Normally, I wouldn't see anything wrong with that, but we are talking about my man. I don't believe in playing games, and I don't share. Alex is mine."

"That all depends on Alex. Since we're taking the gloves off, I have a few things to say to you, Samantha. For the sake of his children and yours, he keeps you hanging around. You're nothing but a sniveling unpaid domestic. You keep his house, take care of his kids, and warm his bed on occasion. That's not love. That's called convenience. You're handy, Samantha, nothing more."

Samantha didn't even flinch at the verbal attack. "All relationships have problems, Leah, but if you think for one minute I will let Alex go you are sadly mistaken. Alex is mine. I love him and he loves me."

"Love him? Samantha, you are tearing him apart. Even someone as selfish and self-centered as you should be able to see what you are doing to him. When he finally realizes you are not worth all the trouble and unhappiness you have caused him, he will come to me. If he does, I won't turn him away. I will take him any way I can get him."

"Alex would not risk losing his family over sleeping with you. It doesn't matter how skillful you are in bed. He may flirt and he may look. He may even be tempted to touch, but he won't. Do you know why? I'll tell you why. Alex is an honorable man. He loves me. Alex would never walk away from me. He would not throw what we have out the window for a night of cheap sex with you or anyone. You're as deranged as Chloe Bell if you think so. Keep dreaming, little girl, because that is all you will ever have of him."

"Time will tell. I don't see a wedding band on your finger yet. Until there is, he's a free agent as far as I'm concerned."

"Do your worst, Leah. Alex won't take the bait. You're not his type. You're way too obvious. I trust him and I believe in him. I refuse to share him with you or anyone else, and furthermore, I will not continue to watch you paw him in my house. Alex may be too much of a gentleman to throw you out, but I'm not. Keep your hands off my fiancé or leave. If you don't have enough decency to respect me in my home, then there's the door. It does in fact swing both ways. So which will it be? Are you going to stay and behave yourself, or are you going to leave? The house rules are simple. Keep your hands off my man, or don't let the door hit you on your way out."

Alex felt a warm feeling spread over him at her words. He had waited a lifetime to hear the inflection of love in her voice. Samantha trusted him. She was standing up to Leah and putting her on notice to stay away from him.

Unable to suppress the smile spreading across his face, he pushed the door open and stepped inside. Both women turned to face him. "What's going on in here?" Alex looked from Samantha's furious face to Leah's angry one. Leah looked about ready to tear Samantha's head off.

"Just girl talk." Samantha smiled smugly. "Leah was trying to decide if she wanted to abide by the house rules or leave. She's decided to start paying rent for the condo. Isn't that wonderful? We can use the money to pay for our honeymoon." The two women's eyes locked in silent combat. Alex didn't need to be told what the house rules were; he already knew. "What have you decided, Leah?"

"You win," said Leah, turning to face Alex. She walked over to him. "Your loss, Dr. Carlisle. I would have rocked your world." Smiling, she left the room to rejoin the party.

When Samantha turned around to face Alex, he was smiling at her. He held out his hands to her, and she caught them and he pulled her to him. His lips brushed hers lightly. "You handled her admirably. Have you ever thought about a career in public relations?"

Samantha couldn't suppress her laughter.

"You look remarkable tonight. You're beaming."

"I'm beaming because I'm happy." Her lips touched his tenderly. "Happy birthday, my love."

They all gathered around the table and waited for Alex to cut the cake. After cutting himself a slice, he cut the rest in neat squares.

"Hey, you're pretty good with that thing," teased Tomas. "I bet you could make a living with a knife."

"All in a day's work." He fed Samantha a piece of cake. He moaned as she licked the icing from his fingers. "Shall we save some of this for later?" he whispered in her ear. Samantha blushed, looking around to make sure no one else had heard him.

The party was a huge success. Everyone had a great time, especially Alex. Samantha nervously watched the last of the guests leave. The kids were spending the night with their grandparents, and the two of them were all alone in the house.

"Thank you. The party was great. I think everyone had a good time," said Alex, leaning against the closed door. He was still smiling when his eyes met hers. "It's good to have something to smile about. You look tired. Why don't you go up and shower, and I will do a little picking up down here?"

Samantha was disappointed he was ending their evening. She'd had such high hopes for the rest of the night. Alex didn't miss the look of disappointment on her face as she turned to walk away.

Don't worry, sweetheart—the night is far from over!

Samantha was sitting up in bed when Alex came out of the shower. He had on a pair of paisley boxer shorts and nothing else. Her heart did a little flip-flop as she stared up at him. Her heartbeat quickened when he slid into bed beside her.

As they held each other's eyes, he leaned over and buried his hand in her thick, dark hair. His mouth fused with hers in a hot kiss. When she responded, he pulled her closer and deepened the kiss. He pressed her back onto the bed, and Samantha relished the physical contact. Her arms held him close as she returned his kiss. Samantha withdrew her mouth from his with much regret.

"You have one present left," she said softly, coming to a sitting position and forcing him to one as well.

"I'm trying to unwrap it," said Alex, pushing the thin straps of her nightgown off her shoulders. The heated look he gave her made her nipples harden in anticipation.

Samantha reached over and picked up the envelope off the nightstand. Holding it out to him, she waited impatiently for him to open it.

When Alex finally looked up at her, he had tears in his dark eyes. He pulled her into the circle of his arms and held her. They were both too choked up for words. He closed his eyes and held her close.

"I don't know what to say," said the strangled voice. He pulled back slightly so he could see her face. He held the adoption papers tightly in his hand.

Something painful squeezed at his heart to know she would do something like this for him. Changing Hope and Matt's last name was severing her last tie to Greg.

"Don't say anything. I was going to have the papers drawn up for Matthew months ago, but never got around to doing it. I talked it over with Hope, and they were all for you adopting them as well. You are their father, Alex. You have been for the past couple of years. In a few weeks, we will be one family. One name will suffice. I wanted to make it legal."

"Thank you. You have no idea how much this means to me."

He proceeded to show her.

Chapter Twenty-one

The two weeks passed by in a blur for Samantha. She and Alex picked out the rings together, but everything else was his idea. He was saving it as a surprise.

Again, they decided not to tell the kids anything. They would surprise everyone at the same time with their announcement. All she could think about was becoming Alex's wife.

When she left the wedding preparations up to Alex, she had no idea what he was up to. She was speechless when he booked flights for them to St. Louis. He wanted them to be married in his father's old church. He arranged for Nathan and Laura to keep the kids for the weekend. He said he and Samantha needed some time away together.

To her surprise, he arranged everything down to the flowers for the church. They spent the night before the wedding at his aunt and uncle's house in separate bedrooms.

"The next time I make love to you, you will be my wife," said Alex, kissing Samantha good night outside her bedroom door. "Sweet dreams."

Samantha slept like a log thanks to the sleepy-time tea

Aunt Martha gave her. She needed the rest and so did Alex. Tomorrow was their big day.

Samantha stared at her reflection in the floor-length mirror. The dress was incredible. It fit her like it was made especially for her.

The wedding gown was Alex's mother's. Aunt Martha had stored the dress in her attic and forgotten it until Alex called her. He asked her to arrange for him and Samantha to be married in his father's old church.

Aunt Martha took it upon herself to have the dress dry cleaned and pressed after learning Samantha was the same size as her sister had been when she and Alex's father married. Aunt Martha and a few of the other women from the church decorated it for the ceremony. This was not exactly the simple ceremony Samantha and Alex had planned, but everything looked beautiful.

Samantha's hair was pinned on top of her head. She fixed a veil of white lace and tiny pearls into her hair, and it flowed down her back. She held the bouquet of white roses in front of her. Looking down at the exquisite dress, she smiled. Alex was in for quite a surprise.

Aunt Martha assured Samantha that Alex had no idea about the dress. Though he'd planned everything else, the dress was her idea. He was in for quite a shock when his bride walked down the aisle.

"Samantha dear, it's time," said Aunt Martha, opening the door for her. "You look beautiful."

"Thank you for everything, Aunt Martha. You have been my fairy godmother. I'll never forget your generosity."

"You are more than welcome," said Aunt Martha, wiping the tears from her face. "Just make my boy happy. Come on. It's time." Taking a deep nervous breath, Samantha followed her.

* * *

Alex waited at the front of the church with the minister and his Uncle Frank. A photographer stood at the back of the church and also waited for the bride.

His heart was pounding and his palms were sweating. The tuxedo Uncle Frank had talked him into was black, with a white silk shirt and black cummerbund and matching bow tie. He shifted uncomfortably as he waited.

I love you, Samantha. I will do everything within my power to make you happy.

As the wedding march started, Alex turned toward the door. The vision floating towards him took his breath away. Samantha looked like a fairy princess all covered in white lace and pearls. His heart was full as he watched her walk down the white-rose-petal-covered runner. His heartbeat accelerated with each step she took.

As their eyes met, so did their hearts. A lump formed in his throat and his hand shook slightly as he held it out to her. The warmth of his smile brought tears to her eyes as she caught his outstretched hand.

The ceremony was short, but very memorable. Both their hands trembled as they exchanged vows and rings.

When time came to kiss the bride, Alex was more than happy to oblige, and not with just a soft peck on the lips. He pulled Samantha into his arms, and his mouth covered hers hungrily. Putting her arms around his neck, she returned his kiss. The waiting was over. They were now husband and wife.

After signing all the necessary paper work they went back to Alex's aunt and uncle's house for a quick celebration of wedding cake and punch. They didn't stay long because Alex had other plans for his new bride.

He drove them to his parents' old house. Alex took their bags inside, making Samantha wait in the car. Then he helped her out of the car, and swung her up in his arms.

"What are you doing?" she asked, looping her arms around his neck. Her tongue circled his ear. Alex trembled.

"Save it for later, Mrs. Carlisle. I'm carrying my bride over the threshold." Setting her on her feet, he kept his arms around her. "Have I told you how incredibly beautiful you look today?"

Smiling and pleased by his praise, she shook her head.

"You are enchanting. Where did you get the gown? It's gorgeous. It makes you look like a fairy princess."

"It was your mother's," she said softly. "Your Aunt Martha kept it." She watched the play of emotions on his handsome face. She noted the tears in his eyes and loved him even more. "I hope you don't mind me wearing it."

He shook his head, too choked up to speak, and hugged her to him. Closing his eyes, he just held her. The fact that she wore his mother's gown meant the world to him.

After helping her out of the dress, he changed into something more comfortable. Samantha sat on the bed in her slip and pantyhose, watching him. Samantha didn't know what to think when Alex didn't try to make love to her. Instead he told her to get dressed.

Speechless, she watched him take off the tuxedo and put on a pair of black jeans and a golf shirt. She watched him walk into the bathroom.

Stripping down to her white lace panties, she climbed between the cool sheets. He came up short when he saw her in the middle of the bed, with the sheet pulled up to cover her naked torso.

He walked over to the bed and stopped just inches short. Smiling, she removed the panties and tossed them to him. Alex caught them in midair smiling at her.

"Now I'm wedded. I want to be bedded." She smiled, crooking her finger at him. Alex tossed the panties over his shoulder and pulled his shirt over his head. He stripped slowly and watched her gray eyes turn sultry as she watched. When he was completely naked, she held out her arms to him. "Welcome to paradise, husband."

Several hours later, they showered and dressed. Following his lead, she put on a pair of jeans and a sweatshirt.

She found Alex in the living room staring at the pictures over the fireplace. She walked up behind him, sliding her arms around his waist.

All the old photographs were still sitting on the fireplace mantle. She picked up one of Alex when he was about five and smiled down at the picture. He was wearing a soccer uniform and kicking a ball. Placing the picture back, she picked up another one. This one was a family portrait. Alex took after his mother. He had her coloring, but his father's build. Reverend Carlisle was a handsome man with dark skin. He was tall with a medium build. Alex's mother had long black hair, and she was very petite. She was a beautiful woman. Her eyes mirrored her happiness.

He gave her a quick tour of the house. It was small, but cozy. She could almost feel the love that was put into decorating it. His mother was a wonderful seamstress. The wedding gown proved that.

Alex also gave her a tour of the town. Samantha loved the small-town atmosphere where everyone knew everyone else. She enjoyed seeing his old school and some of his old hangouts. They stopped to eat at one of the old hamburger joints that Alex had loved as a teenager. It was the place all the kids met after school.

Alex was sitting at the table reflecting on the past when he heard his name. As he turned around, a huge smile spread across his face as his eyes locked on his old running buddies. He was out of his seat and across the room in a flash.

"J.T., how the hell are you?" asked Alex, still smiling. They all shook hands and embraced warmly.

"Fine. How about you?" James Templeton, his best friend from grade school through high school, replied. The tall, lanky, dark-skinned man was editor for the local paper. After Alex's parent's death, he stopped coming home and had lost touch with most of his friends.

"I'm on my third wife," Curtis stated proudly. "They get younger every time." Curtis was a playboy who never grew up. He was the proverbial bodybuilder who spent more time in the gym than on an actual job.

"Guys, come have a seat," said Alex, walking back to their table and sitting down. "It's good to see you. It's been what, ten years?"

"At least." James smiled. "What are you doing in town? I was beginning to think we would never see your sorry hide again."

"I got married here this morning. Samantha and I are on our honeymoon. She went to the restroom. She'll be back in a few minutes."

"Samantha?" asked Curtis with raised brows. "Let me guess, blonde hair, blue eyes, and big breasts."

"One out of three isn't bad." Alex saw Samantha come out of the bathroom. Deciding to play a trick on the guys, he winked at Samantha who was approaching the table. "Hello beautiful." He watched J.T. and Curtis' eyes pop out of their heads as they stared at Samantha. "Where have you been all my life?" He winked at her, and she smiled, not saying anything. "Would you care to join us?" She held up her hand, showing him her wedding ring.

"I don't think my husband would approve," she replied, playing along with him.

He held up his hand showing off his shiny new ring. "My wife wouldn't either, but what they don't know won't hurt them." He held out the chair for Samantha and she sat down. The guys were still speechless as they watched Alex in action. "So how about dumping our spouses and meeting back here later, say around midnight?"

"I thought you'd never ask. I'll pack my toothbrush," said Samantha, getting up from the table and planting a long, steamy kiss on Alex. "I'll see you later. Don't be late, I don't like waiting." Smiling, Alex watched her leave the table and walk over to the bar.

"Uh, Alex, didn't you just get married earlier today?" asked Curtis, dumbfounded. "Damn. You da man. I want to be like you when I grow up. Can you teach me?"

"You're already like him," said James, disgusted by the whole scene, "and you're never going to grow up either—some woman will probably shoot you first. Alex Carlisle you are going to burn in hell one day. Obviously all those sermons went right over your head. So much for being a one-woman man. I feel sorry for your poor wife. What sin did she commit in a past life to be stuck with a player like you? She certainly has my sympathy."

"Samantha's very understanding. You'd like her. She's so serious—like you, J.T. I have to admit, she is beginning to develop a sense of humor. Maybe I'm starting to rub off on her. Would you like to meet her?" He waved Samantha over. Coming to his feet, he held out his hand to her and pulled her into the circle of his arms. Both guys choked on their beers when their eyes locked on her. It took only a minute for them to realize Alex and Samantha had played a joke on them. "J.T., Curtis, this incredibly beautiful lady is my wife Samantha."

After getting over the initial shock of meeting her, they

sat around and chatted for about an hour. They caught Alex up-to-date on everything in the old neighborhood.

After a long, leisurely shower, Alex gave Samantha a full-body massage. He told her not to move as he left the room. He returned a few minutes later with a bottle of champagne and a can of whipped cream.

"I've always been partial to whipped cream." She smiled back. "Do you have strawberries also?"

"I have anything and everything you could ever want," he promised, pressing her down into the mattress.

They spent a wonderful four kid-free days together. Most of their time was spent in bed. The rest they spent touring the city.

Their days and nights were spent with candlelit dinners and romantic lunches. A friend of Alex's owned a stable and arranged for them to go horseback riding. They shared a picnic lunch out on the trail.

Although they both missed the kids, they treasured their time alone. They made the most of every moment they were together.

Alex pulled Samantha into his arms for a quick kiss before ringing the doorbell. Her arms went around him and he dipped her.

"What was that for?" She asked, wiping her lipstick from his mouth. "Some of the things we did would make any bride blush," she laughed, smiling up at him. "I've never been tied to a bed before and had my whole body kissed. I liked the whipped cream thing too. We'll have to do that again, soon. I'm getting hot just thinking about it. I have an idea. Let's go back home to bed," she smiled, turning back towards the car.

He caught her hand and pulled her back in front of him. "No more stalling, Mrs. Carlisle. We have an announcement to make. Are you ready?" he asked, giving her one last kiss. At her nod, he rang the doorbell.

"Hi." Lauren, smiling and hugging both Samantha and Alex. "Come on in. Everyone's here per your request. What's going on, you two? Why the mystery?"

"Do tell," said Nathan looking from his daughter to his son-in-law. "Usually when we get called together for a family meeting, it's not good. What's he done this time?" Nathan asked nodding in Alex's direction.

"Plenty," Alex teased suggestively, winking his eye at his wife. "Where would you like me to start?"

"Alex!" Samantha was blushing as she elbowed her husband into silence. Sam looked up to see the expectant faces of all four children, along with Dana, Tomas, Jeremy, and Alicia. She looked to Alex to make the announcement.

Alex caught her hand and held it up for everyone to see. The matching wedding bands of gold and diamonds sparkled. "Samantha and I were married yesterday." Alex met Nathan's questioning gray eyes. The expression on his father-in-law's face was priceless. It went from disbelief to an almost-smile of relief.

First there was dead silence, followed by the piercing screams of two young girls. Lexi and Hope both ran to Samantha and Alex, excitedly talking and hugging them at once.

"You two got married! That's great! My wish came true," said Hope, smiling. "I have a father now." Alex kneeled down to her and held her at arm's length. Her words touched him deeply.

"Honey, you've always had a father, but yes, now it is

official." Smiling, he caressed her wet cheek. "I love you." She threw herself into his arms.

Samantha and Laura both wiped at their tears. They were all touched by Hope's words. She idolized Alex and they all knew it.

"We're going to live together!" Lexi cried, excitedly hugging Hope and her father. "Aunt Sam, can I call you Mom now?"

"Honey, you can call me whatever you're comfortable with."

Lexi went to Samantha and threw her arms around her.

"Yes! I knew it! I told you they were up to something. You owe me twenty bucks, Grandpa." Derek said, holding out his hand.

"Slow down." Samantha laughed, returning all their hugs and meeting her father's eyes over their heads. His expression was almost comical.

Amid hugs and congratulations, Samantha still watched her father. Without a word, he fixed himself a drink. He turned to face them and just stared.

A knot formed in her throat when Nathan actually walked over to Alex. Time stood still as the two men guarded each other.

"It's about damn time," said Nathan. Nathan stuck out his hand. Hesitantly Alex took the outstretched hand and shook it.

"Dad, if you attack my husband, you will have me to deal with." Samantha and Nathan stared at each and he smiled. Holding out his arms to her, she walked into them.

"Congratulations, honey. I love you and all I've ever wanted was for you to be happy," said the emotion filled voice. "Be happy sweetheart." He kissed her cheek.

"Congratulations!" Dana smiled. "It's about time you

two made it official." She wiped at her tears. "I'm so happy I could cry."

"She's so emotional these days," said Tomas, hugging Samantha. "I think she's pregnant," he whispered. Samantha shot him a questioning look. "Hey, the Good Book says be fruitful and multiply."

"Get away from me with that kind of talk," Sam laughed. Alex slipped up behind her and put his arms around her waist.

"What kind of talk?" he asked, kissing her neck. Samantha turned in his arms and kissed him.

"We'll talk about it later, much later." She silenced him with a kiss. They had yet to discuss the possibility of more children. From their passionate honeymoon night, and every day following, she knew there was a distinct possibility she might be carrying Alex's baby. The idea made her smile.

Samantha and Alex sat the kids down and told them they would be living at Alex's house until they found a bigger house. Alex already placed his home gym in storage and cleared out the bedroom he used for an office. They'd had Lexi's bedroom furniture moved into the bigger of the two rooms. The second room was set up for Matt. The two of them had rearranged Lexi's room and moved Hope's bed and chest of drawers into the room.

Derek was happy knowing his bedroom was just the way he had left it. Matt was also ecstatic when they told him they would all be living together.

With everyone still gathered in the room, Alex walked over to the baby grand piano and opened it. As he started to play, Samantha smiled. It was the song they had their first dance to at Dana and Tomas' house eight months ago.

As he began to sing, everyone gathered around the

piano. Samantha sat next to him on the bench, enthralled by the sound of his voice.

She'd heard Alex sing before, but never at this level. Tonight he was phenomenal. He had an incredible voice. Her heart was heavy with love and pride as she sat next to him on the piano bench. Tears filled her eyes and splashed down her cheeks.

"Children are a great inspiration. With them and because of them, I have done things I never thought I would do. Even more inspiring than my children, is my wife, Samantha. She keeps me sane, she keeps me honest, and she keeps me out of trouble and on my toes. I pledge my life and my love to you, Sam, and to our family."

She couldn't stop her tears as she saw the tears shimmering in his dark eyes.

"I am yours and you are mine, always. This is our second chance at love." He leaned over and pressed his lips to her softly.

Turning back to the piano, he began to sing again. When he finished the song, he stood up and pulled a crying Samantha into his arms. Their mouths touched and their tears mingled. Oblivious to the crowd around them, they didn't notice there wasn't a dry eye left in the house.

Epilogue

"Okay, this is going to be a little cold," said the nurse, squeezing the cold gel onto her slightly protruding abdomen. "Watch the screen. The blinking dot you see will be your baby's heartbeat."

Samantha and Alex both watched closely. Samantha let out a sigh of relief when she saw the heartbeat. She squeezed Alex's hand.

"And here is what we were looking for," said the technician, moving the wand slightly to the right. On the screen was a blinking dot. "Sorry, here's a better shot for you."

Samantha's mouth dropped open. There was not one, but two tiny heartbeats.

"Congratulations, it looks like twins. If I had to make a guess I'd say you are carrying a girl and a boy," the technician said.

"We're having twins," Sam laughed and cried at the same time. She stared at the screen in amazement. Her eyes moved to her husband, and she found him passed out cold on the floor. Her hand covered her stomach. "I think we shocked Dad. What do you guys think?"